FREEZING POINT

AFTER THE SHIFT BOOK ONE

GRACE HAMILTON

AFTER THE SHIFT

Freezing Point

Killing Frost

Black Ice

RELAY PUBLISHING EDITION, SEPTEMBER 2018
Copyright © 2018 Relay Publishing Ltd.

www.relaypub.com

AFTER THE SHIFT SERIES BOOK ONE

FREEZING POINT

GRACE HAMILTON

BLURB

In the dawn of a new Ice Age, families everywhere are taking to the road to escape the frigid landscape—but you can't outrun the cold.

No one could have predicted the terrifying impact of human interference in the Arctic. Shifts in the Earth's crust have led to catastrophe and now the North Pole is located in the mid-Atlantic, making much of the eastern United States an unlivable polar hellscape.

Nathan Tolley is a talented mechanic who has watched his business dry up due to gas shortages following the drastic tectonic shifts. His wife Cyndi has diligently prepped food and supplies, but it's not enough to get them through a never-ending winter. With an asthmatic young son and a new baby on the way, they'll have to find a safe place they can call home or risk freezing to death in this harsh new world.

When an old friend of Nathan's tells him that Detroit has become a paradise, with greenhouses full of food and plenty of solar energy for everyone, it sounds like the perfect place to escape. But with dangerous conditions and roving gangs, getting there seems like an impossible dream. It also seems like their only choice.

THANK YOU

Thank you for purchasing 'Freezing Point'
(After The Shift Book One)

**Get prepared and sign-up to Grace's mailing list
at www.GraceHamiltonBooks.com.**

1

"What's that?" Freeson asked, pointing beyond the wrecker's windshield.

Nathan squinted through the swirling snowflakes peppering the glass, but the wipers were struggling to give meaningful vision beyond the red expanse of his Dodge's hood. He thought they were on the spruce-lined Ridge Road running between Lake George and Glens Falls but he couldn't be sure. The cone of light thrown out by its headlights only illuminated the blizzard itself, making it look like a messed up TV channel.

Without any real visibility, the 1981 Dodge Power Wagon W300 4x4—with driver's cab, a four-person custom-sized crew cab behind that, a wrecker boom, and a spectacle lift—

grumbled deep in its engine as Nathan slowed the truck. To stop the tires fully, Nathan had to go down through the gears rather than by the application of the discs. There was a slight lateral slide before the tires bit into the fresh snow. The ice beneath was treacherous enough already without the added application of fresh flakes.

Who knows how thick the ice is over the blacktop, Nathan thought.

With the truck stopped, he tried to follow Freeson's finger out into the whirlpooling night.

For a few seconds, all he could see was the blizzard, the air filled with fat white flakes, which danced across his vision like God's dandruff. Nathan was about to ask Freeson what the hell he was playing at when he caught it. He saw taillights flicker on and the shadow of a figure move towards the truck's headlights.

Sundown for late April in Glens Falls, New York State, should have been around 7:50 p.m. The Dodge's dashboard clock said the time was 5:30 p.m. and it was already full dark out on Algonquin Ridge.

The world had changed so much in the last eight years since the stars had changed position in the sky and the North Atlantic had started to freeze over. The pole star was no longer the pole star. It was thirty degrees out of whack. Couple that with the earthquakes, volcanoes, and tsunamis wrecking countries around the Pacific Rim, and the world had certainly been transformed from the one Nathan had been born into twenty-eight years before. And this year, spring hadn't come at all. Winter had spread her white skirts out in early December and had left them there. It was nearly May now, and there was still no sign of her fixing to pick them up again.

A face loomed up in the headlights, red with the cold, hair salted with snow, the flakes building up on the shoulders of the figure's parka. It was Art Simmons.

Nathan zipped his own puffy North Face Nuptse winter jacket up to his chin, opened his door, and jumped down into the powder. The snow came up to his knees and he could feel the hard ice below the chunky soles of his black Columbia Bugaboots.

Even through the thermal vest, t-shirt, and two layers of New York Jets sweatshirts, the cold bit hard into Nathan. Without the meager, volcanic-ash-diluted sun in the sky, the early evening was already steel-cold and the blizzard wind made it near murderous. He rolled his hips and galumphed through the snow towards Art.

"Nathan! Is that you?"

Art had, until recently, been a Glens Falls sheriff. He'd been a warm-hearted gregarious man whose company Nathan enjoyed a lot. But since being laid off when the local police department had shut down, he'd become sullen and distant. Seeing Art so animated now offered the most emotion Nathan had seen coming from the chubby ex-cop since before Christmas.

"What's the trouble, Art?"

Art's words tumbled in a breathless rush. Sharp and short, it was clear that the cutting air had begun constricting his throat. "Skidded. Run off the road. I couldn't even *see* the road... I'm in the ditch... Been here an hour..."

"*Run* off the road?"

Art nodded. "Glens Falls has been overrun, Nate. Scavengers tracked me. If I wasn't trying so hard to outrun 'em, I wouldn't be here now. Hadn't driven so fast, when I lost them through Selling's Bridge..."

Nathan had heard the rumors of small packs of raiders using snowmobiles to hold up residents in their cars, stealing supplies and invading homes. But he hadn't seen evidence of them himself. He'd only been told by neighbors and friends they were operating in other parts of New York State, fifty miles further south than Albany, but not until now had he gotten any notion they might be as far up in the state as Glens Falls. But now that they were here, the lack of an operational police department in town might just make them bolder and more likely to try their luck with what they could get away with.

"Where did they go?" he asked.

Art shook his head. "Guess they lost me in the blizzard when I came off the road. Maybe gone off to track some other poor bastard. They won't be far."

Freeson joined them in front of the truck, banging his arms around his own parka to put feeling into his fingers. His limp didn't help him wade through the snow and his grizzled face was grim, but Nathan knew the determination in Freeson's bones wouldn't allow his physical deficiencies to stop him doing the job Nathan paid him for. The cold might freeze and ache him, but the fire in Freeson's belly would counter the subzero conditions for sure.

Freeson hadn't been right since the accident, maybe. Quiet at times, and quick to anger at others, but he was always one hundred percent reliable.

Together, they walked the ten yards down through the snow to the roadside ditch beneath the snow-heavy trees.

An hour in the blizzard had made Art's truck almost impossible to recognize. Nathan only knew it was a white 2005 Silverado 1500 because he'd worked on it a dozen times in the past ten years. The last time had been to replace a failed water pump that had fritzed the cooling system. Nathan smiled wryly. No one needed their cooling system fixed now—not since the Earth's poles had shifted. Since that unexplained catastrophe, the Big Winter's new Arctic Circle had been smothering Florida and the eastern seaboard, all the way up to Pennsylvania and beyond. It had frozen the Atlantic clear from the U.S. to North Africa.

Art told them he'd been turning the taillights on and off every ten minutes to signal to anyone who might be passing, trying to preserve battery life at the same time. He said Nathan's wrecker had been the first vehicle to show up since his slow-motion slide into the ditch.

Nathan scratched his head through his hood and looked up

the incline of Algonquin Ridge. The Silverado was trapped between two spruces on the edge of the ditch. The tail had kicked up as the front end had dropped, leaving the back wheels floating in space—or, would have done that if the snow hadn't already drifted beneath them and begun to pack in.

There was no leeway in the tree growth to get the wrecker onto the downslope of the road, either, though the easiest way out of this would have been to pull the Silverado down the thirty-degree incline. Instead, they were going to have to pull Art's truck up the slope and fight gravity all the way.

Nathan opened his mouth to tell Freeson to get back in the wrecker and start her up, but Art placed a hand on his shoulder and pointed into the trees. "Look."

Through the forest, three sets of Ski-Doo headlights were moving along two hundred yards up beyond the treeline. The blatter of two-stroke engines was dampened by the snow, but still unmistakable. This part of the ridge was well out of town and had once been a popular tourist trail. There were wide avenues between the spruce where summer people rode chunky-tired trail bikes, and winter people, Ski-Doos. They had room to maneuver.

"They're back," said Art.

Better get this show on the road.

In theory, it should have been a simple operation. Nate turned the wrecker around and reversed it towards the ditch while Freeson and Art cleared as much snow as they could.

As they worked, Freeson bitched about the way the town was dying and how you couldn't get much of anything from the last store in town, and that the hospital was going to be shutting down and you couldn't get fuel oil, and... and... and...

Nathan knew Freeson was just working his jaw to keep his mind off the cold, but the litany of unhappy changes on his lips, when run together like that, did nothing to spread warmth through the three men. In the past, Freeson would have been telling a stream of off-color jokes that would make Nathan groan at best and look for a stone to render his employee unconscious at worst. But since the Arctic Circle had shifted, leaving a trail of dying towns and cities in its wake, the resulting changes had been the only topic of Freeson's conversation. That was when he wasn't weeping because of the loss of his wife.

Nathan and Freeson latched the boom hook from the wrecker to the rear of the Silverado with a tow strap while Art got into his cab and started the engine. The blizzard maintained a steady build-up of snow on anyone who stood still for more than ten seconds, wind whipping at their faces like slaps from an angry girlfriend.

Through the trees, the scavengers' Ski-Doos circled like sharks. Not getting any nearer as yet, perhaps waiting for the right time to take advantage. They could have just dived down on the trio and trapped the truck where it was, but Nathan figured they were trying to raise the tension and get them more scared—scared enough to abandon the trucks without a fight, maybe.

At first the Silverado's wheels just spun fore and aft, throwing up a spray of snow and slush. Nathan stood on the back of the Dodge, operating the boom winch, and Freeson sat up in the cab, keeping the engine running steady in neutral with the brakes on.

It all looked like it was going to work fine—the stricken Silverado, wedged between spruce and the slimy mud bank, should have been popping out, cork-like, from the bottle of the ditch. However, as the Dodge took the strain, its winch whining and wheels spinning, their luck run out.

The Dodge hadn't been bedded in tight enough in the snow covering the icy road. With one sickening lurch, the Dodge slipped, failed to bite, yawed on the ice, and pitched Nathan six feet down into a snowdrift as it slid into the ditch next to the Silverado.

"Dammit!" Nathan cursed, picking himself up out of the snow. Freeson was already jumping out of the Dodge to see the damage.

"Don't get out!" Nathan shouted at Freeson, more frustrated at himself for not predicting this than at his employee for coming to check on him. "I'm fine! Start her back up!"

Meanwhile, Art had been distracted by the Ski-Doo lights, which were definitely getting nearer. The riders were still teasing. Still trying to instill fear in their prey, apparently.

It was working.

Nathan jumped as Art thumped the side of his truck, his breath steaming around him. "The shotgun's at Dot's place."

Dot Henderson—Dorothy in her professional capacity—was a forty-year-old librarian who had been Art's significant other for eight years, although they didn't live together for reasons that Nathan couldn't fathom. She was a woman of strong features and even stronger heart, and had been the rock Art needed when the police department had closed down. It was no surprise that Art had been going over there tonight with supplies. It made sense for them to pool their resources as this Big Winter rolled on.

Art stared at him. "You got your gun, Nate? I reckon their spines have caught up with their balls. Foreplay's gonna be over soon and they're gettin' ready for some action."

Nate shook his head. He only had the guns at his house for hunting; they didn't come with him to work. Glens Falls wasn't that kind of town.

Well, it *hadn't been.*

Art and Nathan set about unhooking the Silverado from the boom while Freeson tried to drag the Dodge out of the ditch under its own steam. But the wheels weren't in the mood to cooperate. Sixty seconds of spinning came and went, and it was clear the Dodge was going nowhere.

Art was getting antsy, and with good reason. The buzzing of the Ski-Doos was getting ever nearer. Nathan got the sense they were being emboldened by the three men's vulnerability, and it wouldn't be long before they forced the situation.

"We should get out of here. On foot. It's a mile to the Andersons' ranch. We can come back at first light."

Nathan knew Art was a man who felt naked without a gun, as fifteen years as a cop would do that to a fella, but it didn't matter. "No way am I leaving my livelihood to those assholes," Nathan said with a slow shake of his head.

They needed to get the Dodge out of the ditch, and they needed to get it out now.

The back tires had plowed away all the snow beneath and now rested on the slimy wet mud of the bank. Each turn of the wheels would only dig them in deeper. Although the blizzard was still silting up everything with snow, the fact that the Dodge was touching earth gave Nathan an idea.

"Free, unhook the towing strap."

As Freeson did as he was told, Nathan reached into the tool crate nestled behind the crew cab of the Dodge. Among the tools Nathan might need to help recover and make running repairs on any vehicles he might be called to, here was just what he needed. A sturdy fire ax.

He threw his knife to Freeson. "Cut the strap into four pieces."

Freeson looked at Nathan as if he were mad.

"We've got a spare back at the shop. Do it."

Nathan, one eye on the ever nearer Ski-Doos, went into the trees, picked a young spruce of just over fifteen feet with a trunk the circumference of his forearm, and felled it with four hard blows.

"What are you doing?" Art yelled. "Building a fire so you can toast some marshmallows?"

Nathan just glared at Art, breathing heavy, the cold ripping into his lungs and snowflakes stinging his eyes. Without a word, he chopped four, three-foot lengths of trunk and carried them to the Dodge.

Within two minutes, each section of spruce was strapped fast to a tire on the wrecker via the lengths of towing strap Freeson had cut for Nathan. The trunk sections stuck out horizontally from the bodywork, but were shallow enough to turn with the wheels without getting snagged on the wheel arches.

Freeson got the idea, but Art was angry. "We could have been halfway to the Andersons by now!"

"Shut up, get your gear into the Dodge, and then get in the cab. Give him a hand, Free."

While Nathan dug snow from beneath the front wheels of his wrecker, Art and Freeson lugged bags and boxes of supplies from the back of the Silverado to the storage cage next to the Dodge's tool box. Then, holding the door open, Nathan encouraged Freeson and Art up into the cab, sliding in beside them and slamming the door against the swirling snow.

Nathan started the engine, put the Dodge into its lowest gear, and feathered the clutch and gas pedal back and forth. When he felt the branches tied to the wheels bite into the mud, offering fresh traction, he rocked the truck forward and back until there was enough momentum to rise out of the ditch.

Freeson rebel-yelled as the Dodge started to climb out and

Nathan steered the wrecker back onto the road. The Dodge rolled fully out from the ditch and then onto the road, snowflakes splattering, wipers struggling, and Nathan thought about jumping out to remove the branches strapped to the tires, but then the first Ski-Doo burst from the forest and aimed itself straight at the Dodge.

2

While the spruce trunk sections remained strapped to the tires, they improved the Dodge's performance in the snow rather than hindered it, spreading the weight of the vehicle in the same way snowshoes do. Nathan didn't know how fast he'd be able to go before they tore away—hopefully not puncturing a tire—but he was going to have to risk accelerating from the advancing Ski-Doos anyway.

The three Ski-Doos spat snow and ground up mud in pursuit, headlights dazzling the mirrors as Nathan dared a glance backward.

Ahead of them, the snowy road rushed towards them, their wipers affording little view. Nathan stamped down on the gas, accelerating the Dodge with trees whipping by on either side.

It was five miles to the Glens Falls town limits. Five miles of snow-glutted roads and narrow bridges over frozen streams.

The blizzard was still raging, but the wind howled along with the Dodge now, coming from behind and thinning the flakes around it. They reached Unbroken Lane quicker than Nathan had dared hope. Deep in the forest still, but with a long stretch of snow-covered tarmac and no harsh corners to slow them down.

Nathan allowed himself more speed. This road, if followed, would take them all the way to the airport on the edge of town. But what made it easy for the wrecker to travel also did the same for the Ski-Doos, which were still biting at their tires.

"We're not gonna lose 'em," Freeson said. "It's two miles of straightaway from here to Barker's Rail."

Freeson was right, but maybe, Nathan thought, just maybe, he might be able to use that to his advantage. Below the boom and whine of the engine, he could still hear the slap of at least two of the four branches strapped to the tires battering the snow.

Nathan released his foot from the gas pedal, just a fraction.

Art felt the deceleration and screamed out, "What are you doing? They'll have guns! Stay ahead!"

But Nathan wasn't listening. If he'd calculated right, the lead Ski-Doo, a yellow, recent model Summit 800R, might take a second to respond to the Dodge slowing down.

Nathan's hunch rang true. The Ski-Doo slid alongside,

smooth as oiled ice. Nathan fed the steering wheel through his up-turned palms, letting forward momentum do most of the work.

"Ever see the chariot race in *Ben Hur*?" Nathan asked as two and a half feet of young spruce trunk smacked into the leg of the Ski-Doo rider, pitching him off and upending his snow-mobile so comprehensively that it spun away into the snowy night and broke its back against a pine.

Nathan hit the gas again, fishtailing and then correcting the skid as the power went down. Freeson was looking back in the mirrors.

"The other two have stopped for their buddy!"

Nathan thumped the steering wheel and hooted. The Dodge wrecker might be old and cranky sometimes, but like it had for his daddy before him, it had got them out of a succession of tight spots. He could have upgraded the truck many times over the years, but he hadn't been able to part with it. His daddy had left it to him in his will with the business, and now was absolutely one of those times when he was glad he hadn't changed it over for a newer model. It was a war horse and a chariot combined.

By the time they rolled past the long-closed airport into east Glens Falls, the blizzard had begun waning to just a heavy snowfall. The wind had dropped, too, taking a real slice of cold out of the ambient temperature.

Dropping Art at Dot Henderson's house on Ranger's Boulevard, Nathan and Freeson helped the ex-cop carry the supplies into the open garage as he thanked them for the rescue.

"I'm sorry, Nate," Art added lastly as they brought in the last box from the Dodge. "I shouldn't have been so sharp with you. I…"

"Man, forget it. It's tight for all of us right now."

Art looked down, and Nathan felt sure there were tears in the corners of his eyes. "You're a good man, Nate, but you saw those scavengers—it's every man for himself from now on."

Nathan shifted awkwardly in his boots in front of the crying ex-cop. Freeson hadn't stuck around to help the situation with a quip or a tart comment. He'd gone back to sit in the cab of the Dodge and left Nathan to it.

Thanks, buddy.

"Look, Art, it's gonna be okay. The government'll get this under control soon enough."

Art's eyes went suddenly clear of tears. "Nathan, grow a pair. We've been left to fend for ourselves. You heard Free. They're even shutting down the hospital. No police. No fire department worth its name. When did your boy last go to school?"

Nathan shrugged off the argument. "Nothing wrong with homeschooling. Cyndi knows what's she's doing."

"Of course. But for how long? The food is gonna run out. Gas is rationed, when you can get any."

Nathan held up his palms. "I gotta go, man."

Art seemed deflated, but nodded. He held out his hand for Nate to shake, and when he did, Art squeezed his fingers hard, gripping his hand for emphasis. "Nate, for your family's sake, find some people you trust and get the hell out of Glens Falls."

Before Cyndi even opened the door of their clapboard-clad, two-story ranch house out on Division Row, Nathan could hear his ten-year-old son Tony coughing.

Tony did everything he could to circumvent the effect his asthma had on his life, but the cold was prying apart the clamshell of his resolve and making significant gains. The sound bit Nathan's ears above and beyond the wind and the freezing temperatures. He could see the strain on Cyndi's face as her gaze flicked backward to look at the rangy ten-year-old sitting at the kitchen table. Her gray-green eyes were dark with worry, and her blonde hair, pulled back in a severe ponytail, seemed to sharpen her face in line with her mood.

Nathan and Freeson entered the house on a gust of flakes and a thick coil of cold. They were halfway out of their foul weather gear before Cyndi had confirmed what the kerosene lamps dotted around the family room were already telling Nathan.

The power was out again.

"Third time this week," Cyndi said to Freeson, leading them inside once she'd closed the door against the night.

"Get used to it," Freeson said gloomily as he limped after them.

Nathan tousled Tony's hair and looked down at the book his son was reading at the table. Most kids Tony's age would have been reading superhero comics or engrossed on an *iWhatever* screen. Tony, however, was flicking through the pages of a Dodge truck shop manual that he'd lifted from Nathan's bookshelf. The sight of it warmed Nathan a hundred times faster than the steaming cup of coffee Cyndi put into his hand.

Tony pointed a skinny finger to a page in the manual. "Hey, Dad, it says here you should change the engine oil every 7,500 miles. When I looked yesterday, it said you'd done 8,030."

"You keeping score, son?"

"Someone has to. You're too busy helping other people. Figured I'd keep an eye on the truck."

Nathan hugged his son's thin shoulders and they both laughed. "I'll change the oil this weekend. I guess you're angling to help, huh?"

"Kinda." Tony smiled, hugging his father back with appreciable strength. Although the brown-haired boy was tall for his age, the asthma that kept him in its grip had squeezed any of Nathan's muscular chunkiness out of his frame. It wasn't a sickly or wan thinness that he had, but it wasn't far off from it.

"Don't fuss, woman!"

Nathan's head spun at the harshness of Freeson's voice.

Freeson was sitting in an armchair near the blazing hearth and had taken off his boots. Cyndi—bustling, busy, and brilliant, as usual—was already knelt down in front of him, putting a hand on one of Freeson's naked feet and then the other.

"Get away from the fire," she said in a tone that would put up with no argument.

"Why?"

"Because that's frostbite, Free! Get up." Without another word, she pulled him to his feet and made him limp away from the fire. If one of Freeson's feet was biting, Nathan knew that putting it next to the burning logs would be the worst thing he could do. Cyndi had all the health smarts and more that were needed to diagnose and treat any number of ailments, and if she said Freeson's foot was frostbitten, then it was—however much Freeson might protest.

Cyndi sat Freeson down at the table with Tony and brought him a bowl of tepid water in which to thaw his bitten toes. Sudden heating could cause as much damage to a limb as the frost. It was always better to warm the affected area slowly. Cyndi got up from where she'd been softly massaging Freeson's foot in the water and dried her hands on a towel, fixing Nathan with a hard stare. "Didn't you see how hard he was limping, Nate?"

"Hey, you're the healer here. I just drive the truck," Nathan said with a flavor of mock indignation.

Cyndi smiled and thumped Nathan on the arm playfully,

but there was a seriousness to her tone. "It's a good job you brought him back for dinner, or otherwise he'd be at home ruining his good leg. This weather will creep up on the best of us, Nate. We can't give it a chance to get to us."

Nathan could only nod.

"I'm fine!" Freeson grumbled from the chair.

"Shut up, Freeson!" said Cyndi and Nathan together.

Freeson shut up.

Cyndi had already managed to make food for them despite the power-out, using camping equipment from her prepper storehouse in the garage. She came from a long line of woodsmen and outdoorsmen, and her father before her had been a great prepper in his day. She had learned everything she needed to survive from him, and even before the poles had shifted and the volcanoes erupted, she'd had her store of equipment ready against the back wall of the garage. The Tolley family was prepped for anything.

In the garage, there were racks of bulk dried goods: rice, beans, and pasta. Tubs of dried fruit. Cans of ham, chicken, and tuna, and seeds and piles of shelf-stable prepared meals. Alongside those, gravity-fall water purification equipment, stoves, kerosene, tents, and other equipment. Nathan sometimes felt his eyes watering at the expense of the growing stockpile over the last few years, but it had totally proved its worth now that the Big Winter had fallen across the eastern seaboard.

And there was no doubt that Cyndi was as innovative with

survival—the matters of health, light, food, and heat—as Nathan was with mechanical things. In that way, they complimented each other perfectly. His nimble hands fixing anything and everything; her sharply analytical brain essential for problem solving.

But Nathan still hated the strain the changed world was having on his wife and family. Cyndi should have been home-schooling their bright as a silver-button son and organizing the accountancy for Nathan's auto repair shop and recovery business. She shouldn't have been worrying where the next meal was coming from, using up her emergency stores, or hearing tales of scavengers attacking her husband up on Algonquin Ridge.

But with dinner served—thick pasta and meatballs in a rich sauce—conversation soon got around to what had happened when they'd stopped to help Art.

"They tried to run you off the road?" Cyndi was incredulous, but Nathan and Freeson nodded as they ate.

"If they'd stopped us, I reckon they'd have stolen the truck and Art's supplies, and left us out in the cold to die," Freeson said in the bleakest voice imaginable.

All Nathan could see were Tony's wide eyes as he listened to their tale of escape and danger.

"I don't think we need…" Nathan began, trying to mitigate the horror story so as not to give his boy nightmares, but Freeson, now that his foot was thawed and he had some food in his belly, was warming to his dire assessment of their situation.

"Man, they *would* have, no doubt," he cut Nathan off. "And if they'd followed us here, I wouldn't have held out much hope for our chances."

Nathan's eyes lit up and lasered into Freeson. "That's enough, Free! Let's just eat."

Freeson met Nathan's eyes with the mirror of his disapproval. "You can't just stick your head in the snow, Nate."

Nathan threw down his fork, but Cyndi put her hand on the back of his, sucking the anger from him immediately. "The situation is bad, sweetheart. You have to admit that," she acknowledged, but then she turned to their friend. "But, Free, save this for when Tony's in bed…"

"Mom!"

"Shush. Eat. Then bed."

Tony's eyes dropped, but he nodded and then tucked back into his pasta and meatballs.

Nathan knew following his wife's level head and survival instincts were the best and safest way forward, but Freeson, whether by accident or design, was rocking a boat Nathan thought he'd been sailing just fine. And now that Cyndi was determined to let Freeson stay until his foot was healed, he could see that the boat was going to get rocked even more.

The subject of leaving Glens Falls had been one that Nathan had managed to avoid discussing seriously with Cyndi, and she, because of all the prepper materials she'd amassed, hadn't pushed the subject. But now that Freeson was here, and his thoughts were clear, Nathan knew he wasn't going to be able to side-swerve the argument much longer.

When Tony had done the rounds of hugs and kisses and gone off to bed as directed by Cyndi, Nathan didn't even get a chance to speak before Freeson drained his coffee and said, "This town is a waste, man. We should get out. All of us."

Nathan felt his mercury rising, and it was only Cyndi's hand resting on his again that stilled his tongue.

"I know what the business means to you, honey. It means the world to me, too. But if your dad were here now, what do you think he'd be saying?"

Nathan knew exactly what his grizzled bear of a father would have said—he'd have said what he always had. "Family first."

It was the motto his father had lived his life by, and Nathan could feel the words tugging at him now. But the thought of taking his family away from their home, away from Glens Falls into the white unknown, screamed its own devilish danger at him. He felt damned if they stayed, and he might possibly damn them all if he agreed to leave.

"It's not just a case of putting our gear in the truck and driving away with smiles on our faces like we're going on vacation," Nathan said, trying to keep his voice as level as he could. "We have shelter here, two years of food, a good stock-pile of gas, and electricity most of the time, and winter *will* break. It can't go on like this forever."

Freeson snorted.

Cyndi squeezed.

Nathan boiled.

"Nate. We should at least consider it. I think things are going to get worse before they ever get better."

Nate looked at his wife, into her earnest eyes and down at her compassionate mouth. Cyndi would never even suggest this if it wasn't a pressing concern for her, and he knew it. Nathan could pop the hood on a truck and almost diagnose the problem with an engine before he touched it. He was good at the small, the particular, and the contained. Cyndi, with her survival knowledge and prepper concerns, was a big picture person. Nathan knew he should always defer to his wife in matters of survival. It seemed this mad idea had to be worth considering seriously for the first time, if for no other reason than the fact that his wife thought this might make sense. And, if he could have had anything in the world just then, it would have been eliminating the extra burdens the ice-bound world was putting on the love of his life.

There was silence for a while, and then Cyndi did that thing she did so brilliantly when it was needed.

She changed the subject, flawlessly.

It was like a balloon popped in the room and the tension dissipated immediately. She announced that, right now, no one was going anywhere. Not for a few days, at least.

"Freeson, you're staying here until I'm sure your foot is better. You're not working. Hell, you're not even walking."

Freeson held up his hand to protest, but Cyndi dismissed it with a wave of hers.

"But I need him, Cyn!" Nathan protested, immediately regretting the uncontrolled raise in pitch in his voice that made him sound like Mickey Mouse on helium. And, yes, he *did* need Freeson—but he also didn't want the grumpy asshat around Cyndi all day while he was out working, suggesting even more reasons to make them leave Glens Falls.

Cyndi dismissed Nathan with another wave, getting up to fetch Freeson fresh warm water for his bowl.

"Nate, you'll have to make do without Free. You don't want him losing his toes now, do you?"

Nathan had to admit that he didn't. But he also wished uncharitably that the frost had bitten Free's tongue off instead.

The next day was bright and bone cold.

The sky over Glens Falls would never be deep winter blue again, as the gray ash in the upper atmosphere had put an end to that, but at least it was clear enough to see the ghost of the full moon as Nathan drove to his auto shop on West Main Street.

He was in a foul mood, too.

Normally, the loss of Freeson would have been a PITA, but Main Street was pretty much deserted as he rolled into the parking lot in front of his building. The Dodge was the only truck he'd seen out in the snowbound city.

Today was going to be another glacially slow day, which was against everything Nathan would normally have expected for April. Townspeople's cars should have been emerging from a normal winter and needing all manner of attention. But without an appreciable move into spring this year, Nathan's business was taking as much of a hit as his sensibilities.

After an hour in the repair shop, mostly spent with him sat down and warming himself next to a burner running on recovered motor oil, Nathan realized that maybe he was wasting his time. No one was driving. If no one was driving, then no one was bending fenders, or breaking down or needing service. So many people had left the city in the last couple of months, in fact, he wondered if his mechanical skills would ever be called upon again, except to get someone out of a snowdrift...

It wasn't just the slow day and lack of business that was keeping Nathan in a foul mood, though. Before he'd left the house that morning, Freeson had talked openly again at the breakfast table about leaving Glens Falls, right in front of Cyndi and Tony.

Whereas last night Tony had been excited and thrilled by the tales of danger, that morning, after a night in the less than warm house, his breathing had been more vulnerable. Free's talk had started a mild asthma attack, which he'd treated with his Salbutamol inhaler.

Freeson had apologized for letting his mouth run away

with him but the damage had been done. Cyndi had taken Tony off to begin lessons in the family room, leaving Nathan and Freeson to move about the house as if the other was invisible.

Nathan knew they'd iron out this wrinkle in their relationship soon enough, but it had left Nathan feeling even more adrift and unsure of the future than he'd been feeling last night. Without Cyndi there to mediate between them, there'd been no chance of a fix that morning.

So Nathan had left the house and headed into town.

And it had been a complete waste of time.

At midday, Nathan got in the Dodge and drove out to the outskirts of town to see if anyone needed pulling out of snowdrifts—more to relieve the boredom and frustration than in nakedly public spirit.

Nathan didn't really enjoy touting for business like this, and made sure he told people he wasn't raising his prices any when he saw them—but it still made him a little uncomfortably opportunistic. After another hour of not coming across anyone to rescue, he found himself out near the airport and Dot Henderson's house.

When Nate rolled along Ranger's Boulevard, he saw Dot's garage was open, and she and Art were loading up her silver Ford F-350 with the supplies Nathan had helped bring over the night before.

Nathan pulled up onto Dot's drive, got out, exchanged a hug with the librarian, and shook Art's hand. His face must have telegraphed his disappointment because Art thumped the last box into the back of the F-350, pulled a tarp across the supplies, and said, "Sorry, Nate. We were going to wait another week… but after last night…"

"Where? Where is there to go?"

"Texas maybe. Mexico. Just away from here. See how far our savings get us. Start again."

The hard snow reflected in Art's aviators, his eyes set as hard as the resolve in his chin.

"Well, I'll keep an eye on both your properties," Nathan offered lamely.

"It's okay," Art answered quietly. "There's no need. We won't be back."

"Damn it!" Cyndi slammed the lid of the laptop shut and pushed the machine across the bed. The power had come back on while Nathan had been out talking to Art and Dot, but as the evening had worn on, other deficiencies thrown up by the breakdown of systems across the U.S. were beginning to show.

The internet was inaccessible tonight. Again.

Nathan had come back to a house still filled with tension. Tony remained quiet and subdued as he took apart and cleaned the family's Winchester Model 1876 lever-action rifle and their

M1903 Springfield. Both weapons had been left to Nathan, like the Dodge, by his father. Tony was usually diligent and thorough with this chore, but tonight his mind hadn't been on the task, and in the end Nathan had sent him to bed, finishing the job himself.

Freeson, feet up, drinking Nathan's beer, had kept his thoughts to himself for once, and for that Nathan had been grateful—he'd done enough damage already.

The tension got expressed most acutely through Cyndi. Her conversation came out clipped and tight, whereas it would normally have been warm and loving. Nathan had felt her spikiness from the moment he'd gotten back, and it extended now to the bedroom, where Nathan was coming back from the shower drying himself, seeing Cyndi getting annoyed with the laptop.

"No luck?"

"Nothing. Tony's medication isn't going to last forever. Just trying to get online to see what I can still order. You might even have to make a trip into Albany to pick it up."

Nathan nodded. "Sure. Not a problem, honey, but that's not what's eating you, is it?"

Cyndi's lips became bloodless lines as she clammed up, and Nathan knew his wife well enough to see that a fouled-up internet wasn't her only issue tonight.

"Look, I can take Freeson back to his place if you want... I know he's scared you and Tony with his crazy talk about leaving..."

Cyndi looked at him. "I don't think he's crazy. As I said. It's worth considering."

The comment took Nathan by surprise, and he sat down hard on the bed—he'd thought maybe Freeson scaring Tony into an asthma attack had put to bed any talk of the family leaving Glens Falls. But it clearly had not.

Dammit.

A chill equal to the cold outside the window ran through Nathan's guts. He sat on the edge of the bed and took Cyndi's hands in his. "Baby, we can't just leave. We can't give up the business for one thing, but you know better than I do how low our savings are. This winter has been a killer for the business. The government will…"

Cyndi threw her head back and laughed with derision. "I love you, Nate. You're a wonderful husband and father. More than I ever could have hoped or wished for. But you've got a hell of a lot to learn about rock and roll."

"I can't just run away from the business. I can't. It's tough right now, but me, you, and Tony will get by. The three of us *will* make it."

Cyndi's face fell. She reached behind her under the pillow and brought out two white plastic tubes and put them in Nathan's palm. "But what about the *four* of us?"

Nathan looked down at the two thick blue lines on the pregnancy tests and his world lurched sideways at an angle of forty-five degrees.

3

Nathan finally slammed the phone down. He'd been trying for an hour to get through to Doc Simpkins on Bay Street, but there was no answer.

At least with the power back on, the house was warm throughout and not just in front of the fireplace, and Tony's chest had been a lot better that day. But the news that Tony was about to have a brother or a sister had dropped several boulders into the gently rippling surface of Nathan's emotional lake.

Cyndi had been taking the pill, but Nathan wouldn't have blamed her for accidentally skipping a dose in error here or there, what with everything else going on. Hell, he'd fouled up enough things himself. But the fact was that there was a baby on the way, and like anything major that landed in their laps, it would just have to be dealt with. Both of them were of one mind on the subject of abortion, so the baby would be going full term, Big Winter or no Big Winter.

With that in mind, he'd decided there was no point in working that day and had stayed home to organize Cyndi's pregnancy for her. Well, that was how Cyndi had characterized it, anyway—making Freeson snort and lose the ability to make eye contact with Nathan, lest he giggle himself into a mirth-coma.

"I'm fine. Stop overreacting. I don't need to see Doc Simpkins. I'm not ill," she said again as she passed by him.

But Cyndi's previous pregnancy had been plagued with the high blood pressure associated with pre-eclampsia, and she'd suffered from killer migraines and impaired vision to a debilitating level. Cyndi had always been strong, healthy, and indomitable in Nathan's eyes, and that terrible confrontation with her mortality had shaken him in ways he hadn't been expecting.

Now he was clucking like a hen, and when Cyndi wasn't amused by his over-concern, she was more than a little ticked off by it. When Nathan gave up on Doc Simpkins and called the local hospital direct, Cyndi all but pulled the phone cord from the wall—possibly so that she could strangle him with it.

When he did make the call, he discovered she needn't have bothered. There was just a recorded message on the line telling them that the hospital was now closed permanently, offering contact details for the main hospital in Albany.

Albany was a fifty-mile journey from Glens Falls that would take an hour on a good day—but in the snow of the Big Winter? Even if the roads were passable, one harsh blizzard would make for plenty of places to be stranded.

"Nathan! Stop. Go to work. Chop some wood. Play some checkers with Freeson. Anything! Just stop panicking. The only thing raising my blood pressure right now is you!"

Nathan opened his mouth to argue, but Cyndi cut him off. "This is just displacement, Nate, and you know it. What you're really churning about is the fact that me being pregnant means we're one step closer to having to get the hell out of here. With the hospital gone, I for one am not interested in having a baby on the New North Pole. What happens when the power goes for good? Tony's asthma isn't getting any better, and if I get pre-eclampsia again, where does that leave us?"

Nathan felt like he'd been hit in the gut.

"Yes, while you were snoring away merrily last night, I was awake thinking."

"You've made up your mind then?"

Cyndi nodded, and then softened and hugged him. "You know I'm right."

Nathan just hugged her back, as gently as he could make himself. She was pregnant, after all.

At first, Nathan thought he was hallucinating.

But as he approached in the wrecker, the red wavering dot he'd noticed ahead in the gloomy afternoon light became a puffy anorak riding above blue jeans. There was a huge ball of fur worrying at the form's legs, which were walking purposefully along the side of the highway like the person was out on a Sunday afternoon power-walk.

The furball was a dog, and the form was a woman who was out, without a vehicle, in this iron-cold afternoon... *hitchhiking.*

She had her ungloved hand out beside her, and her thumb was raised as if there was a steady stream of traffic going past and she was just waiting for someone to bite.

The clouds above the landscape were gathering for another bout of blizzarding. The wind was getting up and the tops of the pines were twisting and swaying as the weather moved in. Nathan had left the house to get his thoughts together, and perhaps hope to help anyone who'd gotten stuck in the snow, but he hadn't figured on coming across a hitchhiker.

In the time before the Big Winter, Nathan wouldn't have thought twice about picking up a lone woman who traveled a lonely road with a storm threatening. But now, after the run-in with the Ski-Doo scavengers, Nathan felt himself hesitating as the Dodge trundled down the road towards her.

After all, it'd be an easy deception. Pretend to be hitching, stop, pull a gun on him, and wait for the Ski-Doos to show up.

Nathan hated that he was thinking like this, though. Damn

this new world, and this hard cold and the even harder feelings towards fellow travelers.

Nathan stopped the wrecker next to the girl, but checked that he knew exactly where his tire iron was. Just in case. Then he wound down the window.

"Hi."

"Hey, mister, thanks!"

"I didn't say I was taking you anywhere yet. You know there's a storm coming, yeah?"

"Do I look like a weather girl?"

Nathan had to admit to himself that she didn't. The girl, who could have been any age between twelve and twenty-five, was thin faced and olive skinned, and looked like she belonged in a band, not on cable news.

"And anyway, I haven't decided if I'm taking this ride yet. You're on probation, too."

Without waiting to be given permission, she opened the door wide and looked down at her dog. "Saber, what do you think?"

Nathan's hand twitched towards the tire iron as, without notice, the dog—huge, white, and gray faced, it had to be some sort of Malamute cross—leapt onto the passage seat. Instead of tearing into him with wild eyes and yellow fangs, it companionably licked Nathan's cheek before dipping its enormous head down and resting it in his lap.

"Congratulations, mister. You passed." The girl smiled, climbing up into the cab to squeeze in against her dog and slamming the door behind her before she held out her hand. "You can call me Syd."

Speechless, Nathan just shook her hand. Close up, she had bright nickel-gray eyes dancing beneath a short, spiky hairdo that was dyed blacker than a moonless night.

Syd made Saber leap over the seat into the crew cab and settled herself down into the seat. Blowing on her hands to warm them, she commented, "If my dog says you're okay, you're okay."

Blinking, Nathan put the truck in gear and pulled away from the curb. "Where are you heading?"

"What ya got?" Syd replied as if it was her standard answer to a question she'd been asked a lot already.

"I'm just out looking for people to help."

"Then you must be one of the good guys. Not many of those since I left New York."

"Hell, that's some journey in this."

"Yeah, it was."

Nathan could feel the weight of something or another behind Syd's answer, but it was clear she didn't want to go any further with explanations. What was strange was how immediately comfortable he felt with her in the cab - not in an attracted way, but in the way she was giving off such a trustworthy vibe. Nathan smiled. Perhaps he was a Malamute cross, too, and had the same ability to tell who was honest, like Saber.

None of Syd's behavior so far had given off any sense of a

threat, so Nathan was a little taken aback when she leaned forward to fiddle with the radio dial and he saw the stock of a pistol, probably a SIG Sauer M11 by the look of it, sticking out of a pocket in her jeans.

"Had to use that on your journey?" he asked.

Syd's face creased up, but after a second or so of following Nathan's eye-line, she realized what he was talking about. "Not since I ran out of ammo. You don't happen to have any nine-millimeter I can have? I can cook a mean curry in exchange."

Nathan smiled and relaxed a little. "No. No spare ammo, but my wife loves a good curry. Why don't you come back with me and you can at least feed us in exchange for warming you up? My boy will love Saber."

And that seemed to settle it. In just a few minutes of traveling, Nathan had invited an armed stranger back to his family home.

His dad's voice echoed in his mind. *Family first.*

It's okay, Dad, he thought. *I still know how far my hand is from the tire iron.*

"Shoot," Syd said suddenly.

She was looking into the side mirror through the condensation-stippled window.

Nathan also saw the yellow flash of a Ski-Doo in the reflection. There were two of them. An orange-black Renegade and a yellow-black MXZ that looked like a hornet. They both carried parka-clad riders, each sporting black beanies over full black ski-masks. And they both had what looked like AR-15s slung across their backs—they were gaining on the wrecker fast over the snowy surface of the road.

It was clear from her reaction that Syd knew who the Ski-Doo bandits were, or at least had had a run-in with them in the recent past. She pulled the SIG from her waistband.

"I thought you said you had no bullets?"

"Yeah, well, they don't know that, do they?"

Nathan dared not go much faster. The road was snow clogged, and the wrecker was the first vehicle that had rolled across its crisp top since the last blizzard. The Dodge was heavy enough to make good progress and the snow chains on the wheels were providing Nathan with the necessary confidence to push the Dodge up to forty-five, but that was it. The pines on either side of the road were close enough to repay any mistake he made with wreckage and injury. The Ski-Doos would have no trouble catching up in any case; they were designed for this terrain, and on a good day could zip along happily at eighty or more.

True enough, soon they'd grown large in the mirrors of the Dodge and followed it comfortably.

Yellow-black unhooked his AR-15, steering with one hand and leveling the rifle with his other. In the mirror, Nathan could see he was setting up to fire at the wrecker's tires.

If these were the same guys from two nights ago, and he had no reason to suspect otherwise, then they would be after a

38

touch of sweet revenge, and this time there would be no spruce trunks turning his Dodge into the *Ben Hur* chariot.

They had to get off the road and away from these scavengers before they shot out his tires.

The road they were on was on the outskirts of Glens Falls, and there was a big-box retail park and mall about a mile down the highway, where in happier times Nathan and his family had gone to shop and recreate. As well as stores, there had been restaurants and a cinema before it had all been abandoned as the town had died.

There was a turnoff for the retail park about three-quarters of a mile ahead now, if he could just make it there…

Watching the mirror as closely as he could, Nathan tried to judge when Yellow-black had the confidence in his aim to fire off a shot at the Dodge's tire.

The crack of a shot rang out and Nathan slew the Dodge to one side, sending up a wide arc of snowspray. Their backend fishtailed precariously and Syd was thrown sideways, banging her head on the glass. "Hey! A little bit of warning would have been welcome!"

Saber barked her agreement.

Orange had fallen back a little as he unhooked his own AR-15 to join the assault with his co-scavenger.

Nathan saw the sign for the Singing Meadows retail park up ahead, and gingerly toed the gas pedal to give them an extra chunk of speed. The pines on the side of the highway seemed to close in as they whizzed past with increasing velocity. In the mirror, Orange gunned the Ski-Doo. He was fixing to take his first shot and Yellow-black his second.

The Dodge was a good thirty or forty seconds from the off-ramp, and Nathan was going to have to try something else to distract these pursuers if they were going to make it in one piece.

He checked the mirror, the road ahead, and then the mirror again as the scavengers aimed. Nathan's hands tightened on the wheel.

Except, suddenly, he couldn't turn the wheel... it was locked. He looked down and saw that Syd's hand had snaked out and grabbed it. "Don't," she said, "let me handle it."

She was winding down her window with her other hand and the rush of cold air screamed into the cab. Syd let go of the wheel, knelt up in her seat, and stuck her head and gun arm out the window—aiming behind them.

She fired three shots.

"Hey!" Nathan protested. "You said you didn't have any ammo!"

"I lie!" she yelled, squeezing off two more. "You'll get used to it!"

In the mirror, Nathan saw the Ski-Doos slam on the anchors and scream to a halt in a welter of spray. Syd's shots hadn't injured them, but they were wary enough to break off their attack for the moment.

"They're not finished with us," she said, "and now I really am out of ammo."

"How do you know they're not finished with us?"

Syd looked away and hissed with irritation, "It doesn't matter right now how I know. I just do."

Nathan could see that he wasn't going to get any more out of her right now.

But later, he vowed to himself, he would make it his business to find out what she *did* know about the assholes who'd tried to kill him.

Twice.

They ran towards the mall's fire exit door, Syd looking back wildly and Saber running at her heels. Nathan smashed his tire iron down onto the door lock, ripping it from the wood so that the door swung open.

They just made it inside the vast abandoned space as three rounds from an AR-15 burst the door frame around their ears. Saber barked as Syd threw herself to the floor, skidding and then sprawling over the damp tiles.

Nathan pulled the door closed behind him and used the tire iron to wedge the bar mechanism closed. It wouldn't hold back anyone who was really determined to get into the mall, but it might give them time to find somewhere to hide. That done, Nathan reached down to help Syd up and they ran into the half-light.

The Ski-Doo bandits hadn't held back for long. They'd

seen that Syd had stopped firing and had gunned their mounts back up to full speed. They'd had no chance of hitting the wrecker's tires because they'd been too far behind, but Nathan had realized Syd's bullets had only bought them a few minutes' respite, so he'd hauled the wrecker down the off-ramp, spun around the cloverleaf, and floored the Dodge into the mall's parking lot, figuring that getting into the mall and going to ground might give them a chance to avoid a fight.

Yup. Got that one wrong.

They'd had just enough time to leap from the cab and head to the fire doors before the blatter of the Ski-Doos skimming across the parking lot had been punctuated by the harsh crack of AR-15 ammunition tearing into the tarmac. They'd gotten to the door just in time.

The mall had been abandoned since before Christmas. No one had been expecting it to open again, and so no power had been left on to run the heaters or keep the stores from succumbing to the damp and cold. There were drifts of snow in the central aisle of the three-story building and, as he ran, Nathan looked up to the glass roof, sixty feet above. Where the weight of snow and ice was being held back by some panes, some glass had cracked and other panes had broken through completely.

The building had the feel of an echoey old cathedral, like St Patrick's in New York, which he'd visited like a gawping tourist with his daddy—but this place was dark, freezer-chilled and crackling with underfoot ice.

A persistent showering of droplets pattered down from above like indoor rain, and their breath clouded torturously in the iron light as they ran. At least, where the glass was broken, what illumination was left in the rapidly darkening sky gave them some idea of their surroundings.

"We need to find somewhere to hide," Nathan grunted out as they ran.

"No good to just hide. They'll track us by our footprints across the floor. We need to find somewhere that we can not just defend, but hit back from. They don't give up."

Nathan looked at Syd with wide eyes. "You know these guys?"

Syd nodded, breathing hard. "You could say that."

But she didn't have time to elaborate as, thirty yards behind them, the fire exit door was unzipped down the middle by a volley of AR-15 rounds.

Syd broke away from Nathan and ran for a rain-slick stairway leading up to the next level. Saber barked and shot ahead of her, bounding up the stairs like a fur missile. Nathan followed, breath hot in his throat and his pounding feet at all times threatened by the floor skidding away under him.

The next level showed two rows of stores which, back when the mall had been open, had been small boutique businesses with a local flavor, plus a food court. It had been Cyndi's favorite section of the mall. You could buy anything from kids' toys to a celebration cake, get kitted out for a wedding, or buy a TV or fishing gear.

Now the once bright storefronts were dark and unwelcoming. Some had shutters pulled down while others were simply open spaces that spoke of hasty abandonment. Display cases overturned; smashed piles of frosted glass. Naked mannequins lay surrounded by spaghettis of electrical wires hanging from the ceiling. Cannibalized light fittings ripped down and shipped out.

The cold seemed bitterer here, too, even with the exertion from running. It pressed against his face, needling his eyes. He felt the shiver of it in his bones.

Maybe it was fear. *I don't want to die today.*

Syd and Saber ran past the wrecked stores and Nathan struggled to keep up, so lithe and speedy were the girl and her dog. At the end of the expanse of cream-colored tiled floor, at the head of the food court, there was a sorry looking McDonald's concession front. The 'M' sign was hanging down at an angle, pictures of food still above the counter going green with mold and, in the dark depths of the kitchen area, steel ranges and refrigerators gleaming dully.

Syd leapt the counter and Saber followed.

Nathan was about to vault the same counter when bullets spat out around him, smashing into the counter and chewing up the tiles. Yellow-black and Orange had already made up considerable ground and were on the same level, their murderous intentions clear.

Nathan lunged sideways, avoiding the counter and running on to the next store entrance. The area in front of it had been a dining court where he, Cyndi, and Tony had had many a burger or hefty cheese-covered jacketed spud, and the memories showing up against the sounds of bullets were surreal.

Is this my life flashing before my eyes? Nathan thought bitterly as he dived behind a desk that still held an electronic cash register beside an overturned chair. *Because if it is, I want a better last thought than a greasy burger!*

He could hear Yellow-black and Orange running down towards the McDonald's. Even behind the desk, hunkered down as tiny as he could make his taut-muscled frame, he felt exposed and vulnerable. Nathan kicked himself for not just running to the back of the concession area like Syd had done next door, but it seemed to be too late if he wanted to remain out of view. He'd blindly taken the first piece of cover that had presented itself—which would of course be the first place Orange and Yellow-black would look as soon as they came around the corner.

This concession spot had been a local chain's fast food pizza parlor. There were a few tables and booths left that Nathan could see around the corner of the cash desk, and beyond the restaurant proper there was an open-plan kitchen and prep area.

Nathan made up his mind to run for the kitchen. There would be more cover, and there might be a back entrance into the service corridors of the mall.

He stood up, but before he took even one step, three things happened in quick succession. Nathan heard the rustle of someone raising their arms, the spit of a bullet, and Saber's deep-throated growl.

Two bullets tore into the cash register, having been meant for Nathan's head, and he looked back as someone, a man, screamed a sickening yell of fear and pain.

One of the Ski-Doo bandits, who Nathan decided was Orange based on the blur of color, was on the floor writhing, trying to stop Saber from chewing through his wrist. His ski-masked face was stretched and screaming. Yellow-black appeared moments later, cycling his legs and throwing up his arms as he was pushed back by a six-foot-tall, steel catering refrigerator that sported bullet holes right across its door.

The refrigerator, on wheels for easy movement, was being barreled along by Syd from behind, and she was using it as perfect cover, moving too fast for Yellow-black to get his feet beneath him and get out of its way.

Syd gave another hard shove and Yellow-black fell backward and crashed to the floor, his AR-15 skittering out of his reach.

Nathan took his chance, picked up the cash register, and stalked towards the stricken scavenger. From two yards out, careful not to hit Saber, he threw the register with every ounce of strength at Orange's head.

The corner of the machine bounced into his skull, and Orange, who'd been trying to get the purchase to sit up and punch at the dog, went down like a fifty-pound sack of potatoes.

Yellow reached for the AR-15, but Syd was too fast for him; she reached down, put her hands under the steel casing of the refrigerator, and toppled it over so that it crashed onto Yellow-black, spread-eagling him like he was living in a cartoon.

"Get the other gun!" Syd yelled, picking up the AR-15 Yellow-black had dropped.

Nathan bent down by Orange, who was unconscious to the world. He picked up his AR-15 and yanked a Glock from the ski-masked asshole's belt.

"Score!" Syd yelled upon seeing the pistol. "Saber! Heel!"

"Let's get out of here," Nathan said.

"Yes. Let's!" Syd replied with the widest possible grin.

Damn. She's enjoying this.

They made it back to the wrecker with no incident other than Syd insisting that they should trawl the rest of the mall to acquire any ammo left behind for the guns—she'd been followed by Nathan, threatening to carry her out if she didn't calm down and stop riding her adrenaline like a surfboard.

Nathan had many questions for Syd, especially regarding what she'd known of Orange and Yellow-black before that day. She knew enough about these guys to say she thought they wouldn't give up. Had she been running with them and fallen foul of their sensibilities? Or had she some other reason to know so much…?

Either way, Nathan needed answers.

He just hoped to hell this wasn't leading up to him finding out she'd been one of the three bandits who'd attacked him, Freeson, and Art up on Algonquin Ridge.

Finally, they burst out from the mall, exiting through the same door they'd entered. Syd was still bitching about ammo, but Nathan's resolve was set.

He opened the Dodge cab door. "Get in. With the dog."

Syd hesitated, looking back at the mall with hungry eyes.

"What?" Nathan asked.

"I should have shot them. Both of them."

Society had plunged off a cliff in the Big Winter, but no way was Nathan ready to start becoming judge, jury, and executioner. Syd seemed way past that. Nathan pushed her up towards the passenger seat. "Under the driver's seat, there's a canvas roll. Pass it to me."

"What did your last slave die of?"

"Just do it."

There'd been times in the last hour or so where Syd had seemed wise beyond her years, someone who had lived far too much life in too short a time. Here she was, after saying she wished she'd executed the scavengers, going on to acting like a preteen full of belligerent attitude. She was a conundrum, for sure. Good to have in a fight, but bad to have in a kitchen if it was her turn to wash up. He still couldn't tell how old she really was, but Nathan was sure that whichever number he picked would be the wrong one. Best to roll with it. For now.

Syd rummaged under the seat and passed the package she pulled out to Nathan. He took it and jogged away from the wrecker.

"Hey! I thought we didn't have any time? You'd be a lot more fun if you were consistent, you know!"

"We've got enough time for this!" he yelled back at her.

Nathan had already reached the scavengers' Ski-Doos. He wasn't prepared to commit murder, but he was happy to kill their machines. He pulled off his gloves with his teeth, exposing his fingers to the bitter cold in the air. He immediately felt the burn in his knuckles, but his determination carried him on. Putting the gloves under his arms and unwrapping the roll, Nathan pulled out a jagged-bladed Bowie. With two quick movements, he cut the starter power cords on both machines and stuffed them into the pocket of his anorak.

Then he popped the back catch on both machines, lifted the black, wedge seats in turn, and dipped into each Ski-Doo's trunk. Both machines carried the standard-issue tool kit that came with purchase; six inches of vinyl roll containing a selection of flat wrenches, a screwdriver, a spark plug socket, and a starter tool. Nathan had fixed enough Ski-Doos in his auto shop to know that every snowmobile came with a line of flex and plastic hook that could be improvised to start the engine if the power cord broke out on the trail. He took both kits and put them inside his anorak, too.

That would occupy Orange and Yellow-black long enough for him to get the Dodge far enough away from the mall that they'd find it impossible to pick up the trail, especially if the oncoming storm dumped a ton more snow on the town.

He pulled his gloves back on and headed back towards the Dodge. For the first time in a while, Nathan felt on top of the situation.

It was a good feeling.

It lasted all but three steps, as the mood was immediately shattered. Syd called to Nathan from the cab, near panic stuffed into her voice. "Hey, mister, there's some woman on your CB! She's saying your home is under attack!"

4

"What did she say?" Nathan slammed the door of the cab, sliding into the driver's seat and firing up the engine. Bile washed its sickness up from his throat and across his tongue, panic tugging at his guts.

"She just said there were… I think she called them *scavengers*, surrounding the house with Ski-Doos. Then the channel went dead."

Nathan shoved the wrecker into gear and spun the tires around on their snow chains. The cab was still iron-cold even though the doors were closed, but Nathan was hot with fear and horror. While he'd been having a fight in the mall he hadn't needed to be having, Cyndi and Tony were in danger. He could have just stayed home.

Family first.

Nathan rounded the cloverleaf with fishtailing skids, his wrecker's engine growling and his heart near bursting. When he reached a straight section of snowy highway, he took the CB microphone from the dash, twirling the mic gain knob fully around. "Cyndi? You there, come back?"

All that greeted him was a mush of static and the sense that his whole world was sliding inexorably into the john. Who was attacking his house? He and Syd had dealt with the scavengers and their Ski-Doos at the mall. Could there be another group already in Glens Falls? Was there a tide of bandits heading north from New York City, about to overrun what remained of their community?

The consequences didn't bear thinking about.

He drove hard and tried to take stock as he went, clearing his mind. They had a Glock, two AR-15s, Syd's empty pistol, and a dog who knew how to fight. It wasn't much of an armory with which to go into battle when they didn't know the strength of the opposition, but it would have to do.

Syd sat silently, knees drawn up in the seat, arms crossed over her chest. The very image of clammed up and *I don't wanna talk about it*. Maybe she thought she'd said too much already in predicting the behavior of the scavengers. Perhaps she was steeling herself against the questions she knew would come. Whatever her reasons, Nathan figured he wasn't going to get far with her until she'd settled down. Maybe she was just getting ready for battle. Though, Nathan really didn't like the idea of *that*.

As he drove, the sky began darkening rapidly. The storm that had been threatening all day was moving in. The trees along the highway were whipping back and forth now, ice crust blowing off and hitting the windshield like thrown grit. Squalls in the road ahead shifted billows of snow, but Nathan didn't deviate or slow down.

He was busting through and he was getting home.

Nathan pushed all the possible potential horror from his head and looked down into the valley. Shots rang out across the distance. Someone in his isolated house was putting up a spirited defense of the property.

He'd rolled the wrecker down the last hundred yards of snowy road with the engine off, just to avoid alerting the attackers—whoever they might be—but might as well not have bothered. Cyndi and Freeson had two groups of Ski-Doo raiders seemingly pinned down behind their machines, loosely fifty yards from the house.

There were five machines and seven riders hunkered down, all of them armed, but waiting. They looked miserable and cold as the wind howled on, on their asses in the snow, guns across their thighs. Snow was building up in layers on their beanies and over their feet. They looked restless and mightily pissed, and they didn't look like people who would put up with this status quo for much longer. A shot came from the house, keeping the scavengers tied down. None of them were willing to risk their heads above their Ski-Doos to return fire. But as the storm raged, and their bodies got cooler, how long would they wait before attacking?

Syd's words were ripped away by the wind as she spoke.

"What?" Nathan bawled into her ear. The storm was huge and mighty, already scouring the land and surrounding trees with dredgers of wind. Snow blew across the valley, and Nathan's house looked tiny and vulnerable. Already, weak yellow lights were showing at the windows. At least the power had held out this long.

"I said they're just waiting for the dark and the storm! Once the snow gets up and the wind comes in, they'll be able to walk up to the front porch without a worry! No one will see them!"

Nathan knew she was right. The riders weren't pinned down and scared of being shot. They were just waiting for the elements to turn the situation in their favor.

There was no point trying for a conversation here where they were, as the sky roared and ice whipped in, so Nathan pulled Syd back to the Dodge. Once inside, he explained what he was about to do, and finished grimly by saying, "This isn't your fight, but I could sure do with someone riding shotgun right now."

Without hesitation, Syd reached over into the crew cab, past Saber, and picked up an AR-15. She flipped the safety and set her elfin chin forward. "Let's do it."

The scavengers weren't expecting an attack from behind. The wind and squalling ice kept the Dodge's approach from their ears until they were almost upon them.

Nathan knew his land well enough to be able to power the Dodge across the valley floor, off-road, sure in the knowledge that there were no ditches or walls to impede his progress. The wrecker got fifty-yards away before the scavengers, who had been hunkered down, looked around in comedic double-takes. Two got to their feet and pointed their AR-15s at the Dodge, but then had to dive for cover as they were shot at from the house.

Nathan put his foot down, the Dodge wheels throwing up huge sprays of snow past the vehicle's side windows. It was like being in a snowy powerboat screaming through the waves of ice.

"Hold on!" Nathan screamed as the Dodge smashed into the first Ski-Doo, scattering snow and machinery up to get barreled away by the wind. He put the Dodge into a skid then, turning around to bring Syd's window around to face the scavengers.

Syd was already winding down the window and pointing the AR-15 she held into the teeth of the wind. Such was the force of the storm now that she had no chance of being in any way accurate, but as her shots bit the air, the scavengers who were already crawling towards their Ski-Doos had to duck again and didn't get the chance to return fire.

Two lucky shots burst into the engine of the nearest Ski-

Doo, destroying the cowling and sending the scavenger who'd been desperately yanking on the power cord leaping away. He'd jumped away from the green Ski-Doo as if he was being stung by bees, Nathan noted.

"I told you to shoot above their heads! What are you doing?"

"I disagreed."

Seeing the beginnings of a retreat, Nathan pulled Syd back from the window, but she held tight to the gun and Saber growled with menace.

"Just fire overhead! Understand? They're going!"

There were only three Ski-Doos in working order, and now that the storm was blowing in fully, Nathan's vision was almost completely obscured, but he could still hear the engines starting. There were seven men to get on those three Ski-Doos, and without the storm, it would have been a turkey shoot for Syd, but somehow the Ski-Doos got their cargo of attackers away into the blizzard.

"Go after them! Go after them!" Syd shouted, firing into the swirling snow. Saber barked. He approved of the idea.

"No, let them go. I'm no murderer!" Nathan said. "I don't shoot people in the back. Roll up the window. Let's get inside."

Syd did as she was told, but Nathan could feel her burning disappointment in the cab as he rolled the Dodge across the fifty remaining yards to the house.

The boom of the storm and the razoring winds assailed

them as they ran across the snowbound lawn and made it to the porch. As Nathan opened the door, Syd turned and fired off three more shots defiantly into the storm.

Nathan ripped the gun from Syd's grasp and pushed her against the wall by the door. Snow and ice littered from her hair and shoulders, a look of shock on her face. It was the first time she'd looked less like a hard-nosed killer and more like a scared little girl. "What they hell are you doing?" he demanded. "I told you we're just going to scare them away!"

Syd tried to recover her composure. "They don't scare! They'll be back. We kill them or they kill us!"

Nathan's anger boiled. Saber barked and bared her teeth, and Syd pushed herself from the wall as the door swung open and Cyndi, wide-eyed, her cheeks streaked with tears, shouted, "Stop it, both of you!"

The knowledge that his wife had been crying dissipated the red mist of anger and Nathan's vision cleared a little.

What was I thinking?

Priorities.

Nathan hugged his wife and, when he'd squeezed all the love he had to spare into her frame, he let her lead him, Syd, and the dog inside the house.

"How about we get some introductions done before we all kill each other?" Cyndi asked, wiping the last of the tears from her cheeks.

"H-h-have they gone?"

Tony's voice made Nathan turn around. His boy was

clinging to Free on the other side of the room, his face creased with worry. Free didn't look much better, it had to be said. He had Nathan's Winchester in his hands and Nathan could see the trembling of Free's arms being transmitted through the barrel, even from this distance.

The sight of them took the wind completely from Nathan's sails. Anger with Syd and her desire to kill everything that moved could wait.

Nathan stomped across the room and took his son in his arms. He breathed into his hair and nodded, catching his breath. "Yes. They've gone. We're safe."

Nathan flashed a look at Syd as she snorted derisively but didn't rise to the bait.

Cyndi put her hands on her hips and put on her best apple-pie-mom face. "You both look wired and frozen. Let's get some food in everyone. Calm things down. The dangers are all outside, and we need to keep things civil."

Syd held her hand out to Cyndi. "I'm Syd and this is Saber."

It was the first thing Syd had said since they'd gotten to the house that didn't make Nathan want to throw her back out into the storm, so he took it as the start of an uneasy truce.

Cyndi introduced Tony and Freeson to the girl and her dog, and the evening quickly settled into a Xerox of normality, if not exactly the real thing—especially with the storm raging outside, the threat of scavengers, and a homicidal girl lounging by the fire with an enormous dog resting its head on her lap.

Out of her cold weather clothes, Syd looked a little too thin for comfort, like someone who hadn't had a square meal in a couple of months. Her hands never seemed to rest, full of nervous energy, playing with her own hair or the dog's fur, her fingers rarely still. Even as she warmed up and was fed, the girl looked cold. Like it was coming from within.

"That sure is a big dog," Tony said, approaching tentatively.

"She's a Malamute," Syd told him. "Sled dog. But I don't have a sled. You can pet her."

Tony reached out a hand to stroke the dog, and Nathan felt himself tensing, but didn't intervene. His fatherly instinct of wanting to make sure his son stayed safe in the presence of an unknown quantity like Saber was strong, but he also realized that perhaps there was a bridge to be built with Syd, and maybe Tony could be the foundation of that construction. Plus, the dog's first act upon meeting Nate had been to lick him in the face, so on some level, it was easier to trust the dog than the girl.

Saber moved her head towards Tony's hand, completing the circuit, and a big smile spread across the boy's face as he scratched behind her ears and the dog nuzzled against him.

With Tony distracted and apparently safe, Nate joined Cyndi in the kitchen where she was preparing dinner, looking to her for a recap of what had happened, and so Cyndi began explaining what they'd missed. "We saw the lights coming over the ridge, and as soon as we saw they were on Ski-Doos, we reckoned they might be a raiding party like the ones you ran into the other night."

"And today again," Nathan said grimly, though he'd decided against telling Cyndi, Free, and especially Tony about the details of the fight in the mall, and the murderous intent of Orange and Yellow-black. He didn't want to raise the tension and anxieties of his family any more than he had to.

"We already had the guns ready just in case. Free and I went out onto the porch. They got to within fifty yards and opened up. There was no pretense to try to talk to us. They were just bent on taking the house."

Nathan felt the anger rising in his gut as he listened. So much for keeping tension and anxieties under control.

"We got back inside and held them off as best we could, through the windows. Only had time to send the one message on the radio. Thank goodness the girl was there to take my call." Cyndi flicked her eyes to Syd, who was still talking enthusiastically to Tony about Saber. "If it wasn't for the storm rising and their hot-headed, shoot first and ask questions afterwards attitude, they'd have overrun us without any trouble. I guess they're just desperate for food and supplies— hunger makes people crazy. You came back at exactly the right time, honey."

Nathan only shook his head. This was a terrible situation. Although the storm was blowing hard, battering the house and keeping the human dangers at bay, there was going to be a time when there would be no storm as distraction, and if these scavengers were anything like Orange and Yellow-black, they'd be back for a reckoning.

Cyndi turned away from the food she'd been prepping and hugged Nathan hard. "Don't worry. We got this."

Nathan put his hand on her belly and squeezed a little, looking into the eyes of the woman he loved more than anything, except maybe Tony. "I hope so," he said.

Cyndi produced a dinner of chicken and mashed potatoes that tumbled into Nathan's stomach like Christmas, and afterwards a beer helped him feel a little more relaxed, but he still felt his eyes flickering towards any sound outside the house that could be interpreted as anything other than those created by the storm.

While Free cleared the dinner things and kept his own council, Cyndi sat with Syd and Tony; on the surface, she was fussing over the dog, but Nathan could see she was also into building a bridge with the girl.

"So you're not from Glens Falls," Cyndi commented after some more talk of Saber had passed.

"Nope."

"Albany?"

"We walked through Albany."

Tony stroked one of Saber's paws and the dog flinched a little. Not nastily, but enough to show she wasn't comfortable. "Foot sore," said Syd. "We've done a lot of miles."

Tony took off his own socks and put them gently over Saber's front paws. The dog licked his hand and rolled over, offering him her belly to rub. Syd grinned. It was the first time she'd shown such easy expression since she'd arrived. "Thanks, kid."

"How long have you been on the road?" Cyndi asked.

Syd's eyes flashed among them. "Look, why the questions? I'm just here. I was hitching. Nathan picked me and Saber up. It's no big deal."

"But you know those guys, right?" Nathan got up and wandered from the table to the fire. Hunching down and rubbing Saber's belly like Tony was.

"I don't think so…"

"Come on, Syd, we're all in the same situation," he told her quietly. "Any information you can give us to help would be welcome. We have to trust you, and you have to trust us."

Nathan could see Syd felt cornered and wasn't likely to roll over and show her own belly any time soon.

"Why don't you tell us something about you? That's the way people build trust—getting to know each other," Cyndi said, and Nathan swelled with love all over, glancing over with a nod for her wiser and more measured approach.

"My name is Syd B4…"

"Beefore?" Nathan asked, confused.

"No. The letter B, number 4."

He bristled, glaring back at her. "So, you're building trust by not even telling us your real name?"

"You can call yourself whatever you want," Cyndi smoothed out. "Everything's changed now. Why B4?"

"Number of our apartment. Where I lived *before* all this. Kinda my nickname. It stuck. The world isn't what it was before, except, with the name, I can keep some of it on me all the time."

Cyndi smiled. "I get that. Makes sense."

It didn't to Nathan, but he let Cyndi go on.

"You said 'our apartment'…"

Syd looked away, into the fire.

"So not just you and Saber?"

Syd shook her head. "My mom. She died."

Nathan's throat closed up a little as Cyndi answered, "I'm sorry."

There was silence for a while. The fire crackled, Tony stroked the dog, and they could hear Free moving around in the kitchen stacking plates.

"Mom… needed stuff. Stuff to stay well."

"She was ill?"

"Kinda. But addicted. You know?"

"And as everything changed, you couldn't get what she needed anymore?" Cyndi asked gently.

Syd looked at Nathan, her face flushing. "The guys in the mall, they were looking for me. I… After Mom died, I ripped them off… because they wanted… well, they wanted more for the food I needed than I could… or wanted to give."

Syd didn't need to elaborate; Nathan and Cyndi, exchanging a look, knew exactly what she was driving at.

"I was starving. Hadn't eaten in days. I went to their place in Queens and their top dog, Danny, started perving me bad. All slime and drool. You know how guys can get…"

Nathan looked down, feeling guilty just for being a guy. "Yeah. I know."

"The others had gone to wherever they stored their stuff. I knocked Danny unconscious with a pipe and got away with the gun, ammo, and a backpack of food. I stiffed them good. Hit the road with Saber. Jacked abandoned cars where I could, hitched a bit, walked, and traded. I guess they picked up my trail and sent those assholes out to track me down…"

"For a backpack of food and a bump on the head?"

"New York is dying, man. They'll have to all get out of there sooner or later."

"Still, sending guys all this way, just because of a small-time rip-off?"

"Danny… he's… not the kind of guy to let this go. He's got his ideas and his plans. A punk girl and a big dog traveling alone aren't going to be that difficult to find. I just hadn't figured he'd send so many. Seven guys isn't a huge chunk of his gang, but it's a lot. They caught up with me in Albany. I'd just scored a case of corned beef for me and Saber from a burned-out grocery store. I jacked a Buick and got out of town. Just. But… Danny's royally pissed. More because I hit him, I guess, than because of the food and ammo. He's big on face. Getting jumped by a girl…"

She finished with a shrug, but Nathan was going else-where. He stood up and paced. "So, these guys wouldn't be here in Glens Falls, shooting at *my* family, if it wasn't for you?" His voice was hard and accusatory.

Cyndi raised a placating hand. "Nate…"

Nate could see she was disappointed he'd let his anger get the better of him again. Syd got up, hugging herself tight. "Don't worry, I'll be out of your hair tomorrow. As soon as the storm passes, I'll get back on the road. They'll come after me and leave you alone."

Nathan clenched his fist. "There's no guarantee they'll leave us alone. Remember what happened in the mall?" To make his point, Nathan thumped his fist into his hand.

"I'm leaving tomorrow, too. You're welcome to come with me, Syd. All of you are."

Four heads turned towards the kitchen. Free was there in the doorway, drying his hands on a towel.

The mechanic had kept his own counsel all evening, listening by the fire, only speaking to insist that a frostbitten toe wouldn't stop him from helping out after dinner in the kitchen. Nate looked at him now like he'd started speaking Bulgarian. "Free? What? What do you mean?"

"We need to get out, man. Get somewhere warmer. Safer. If these guys will come killing for a bag of groceries and a box of bullets, how they gonna respond to us fighting them back like this?"

Nathan's fists clenched. Free's logic was sound, but to leave… to take his family on the road?

"Maybe he's right."

"He's not."

Cyndi sat up in the bed and turned on the bedside light. They'd both lain there in silence for an hour as the storm boomed on outside, rattling the windows, piling snow up the window panes, and whistling around the eaves.

They'd both known before they'd gotten into bed that their chances of sleeping were less than zero, but they'd silently agreed to try anyway. With the storm still blowing, they were safe from the scavengers for now, and so they needed to rest. But Free's intervention had thrown Nathan hard, and he could tell that it had resonated with Cyndi, too.

"Think about it, Nate. Come on. There are people outside willing to kill us for the little that we have. At least if we were on the road, we wouldn't be such sitting ducks."

Nathan sat up alongside her, running his fingers through his hair and then thumping his temples with the heels of his hands as he tried to come to terms with the situation. "Cyndi, where would we go? Tony's asthma means we need to be near somewhere we can get medication. You're pregnant, baby, and we need to be near a doctor. I know Albany's the nearest now, but at least we know where a doctor is. Tell me—where should we go that's not going to be overrun with scavengers, or where the infrastructure is there to support us and our family!"

She met his eyes. "Stryker."

The mention of Nathan's old school friend had him blinking. It was a name out of left field that he hadn't considered for an age.

"He was always going on about how Detroit was doing well in the cold winters. Even before the shifted poles. You know he did. You kept telling me how his emails were just so boring, going on about the subject. Well, maybe... maybe Detroit is an option."

Stryker had turned from being a solid buddy in high school to an itinerant trucker, drifter, actor, and stuntman—never settling anywhere for long until he'd wound up in Detroit ten years ago. It had always been one of Nathan's great regrets, that he'd never helped him with whatever mess had made him drop out of school and run as fast as he could from Glens Falls, so it had been a huge relief when the man had gotten back in touch with tales of a new life, a new relationship, and a sense that Detroit had streets that were, if not paved with gold, certainly filled with a golden hope for Stryker's future.

He'd gotten himself involved with some construction company that had been working with the city to future-proof the city against the worsening winters that were rolling across North America, even before the catastrophic changes in the Earth's rotation and axis had hit. There was still no sense from anyone what had caused the shift, but this was one city that had been preparing for anything, so that at least Detroit sounded now to be somewhere worth considering. And it was near enough to New York State that it be possible to get there, and might offer some refuge.

Nathan wasn't particularly surprised he hadn't considered the notion before, even as much as it made sense now that Cyndi brought it up. His ties to his daddy, and his daddy's business and the home in which he'd grown up, were as strong as ever. But sometimes there was a time when logic had to trump emotions…

And Nathan was about to relay that thought to Cyndi when there was a furious banging at the bedroom door, and Freeson shouting as he pounded his fist on the wood.

"Nate! Cyndi! It's Tony! Come now!"

5

On the floor of the family room, Tony gasped for breath in Cyndi's arms, his body shaking and his chest wracked with jagged gulps for air. A wheeze colder than the air blowing in through the open door from the white valley beyond iced Nathan's heart into a stilled chunk of frozen blood. Nathan kicked the door shut and paced.

This was the worst asthma attack Nathan had seen for ages in his son, and because he could do nothing to help as Cyndi tried to get Tony to stop panicking enough to accept the inhaler to his blue lips, he rounded on what he saw as the cause of the attack.

"Get that damn dog out of here!" Nathan all but screamed at Syd, who had been woken by the commotion and come down from the spare bedroom with Saber to see what all the fuss was about.

Saber stood her ground next to her mistress, her head cocked with concern for the wheezing boy, eyes glittering in the dying firelight. Syd ran her fingers through the fur over the dog's thick neck.

"How do you know it was Saber?"

"Because Tony was all over her all night!"

"In that case, don't you think it would have happened sooner?"

Nathan wasn't in the mood for logic. "Get that dog out of here." His eyes flicked to the Winchester propped up in the corner and he stalked towards it. Syd followed his gaze and the threat.

"You won't shoot the people who attacked your home, but you'll shoot my dog? Mister, you've got your priorities the wrong way around!"

The wheeze from his son burned in his ears like coals from the fire. Nathan's head was a rage of fear for his son and a wild cast to find something to pin the blame on. The dog was the obvious perpetrator of his son's condition. He took two steps towards the Winchester, but was surprised by two things before he made a third. One was Freeson putting his hand on his shirt, gripping it and stopping his momentum, saying, "Concentrate on your son, man, and we'll fix everything else when he's okay." The other was Tony's voice coming out from between wrenching breaths. "Dad… Dad…"

Tony's voice was cut off as Cyndi pushed the inhaler to his lips and got him to suck in a dose of Salbutamol.

. Nathan bored holes through Freeson's body, but the mechanic held his position.

"I'll deal with you later," Nathan spat at the mechanic, and with that he turned back to his son. Tony was taking another suck on the inhaler but at the same time was reaching out both his hands towards his father.

Nathan stepped across the room, eyeing Syd and the dog with full-on contempt as he knelt by his son, taking his hands in his own, swallowing them up in his palms. Tony's hands were frozen, the little fingers feeling as brittle as icicles. The boy's eyes were big and full of pleading.

"Dad... Dad... it wasn't Saber... please..."

Cyndi stroked her son's hair as his breathing started to become a little freer.

"Don't speak, son, just try to relax..."

"No... Dad... please..."

A fit of coughing broke the boy's face into a hollow, red-cheeked grimace of pain and bulging eyes, spittle flecking at the corners of his mouth.

Nathan all but got up again, ready to deck Freeson and throw the girl and the dog out into the night, but the boy shook his chill hands free of Nathan's palms and held on to his wrists. His eyes implored Nathan to stay while his chest expanded and deflated with internal agonies. Tony had no words, but he was shaking his head.

As Tony's breath drained of panic, he pulled Nathan closer and hissed up into his ear, "It... it... wasn't the dog... I went outside... without... without my coat or... scarf over my mouth... stupid... I shouldn't have... I'm sorry..."

The words hit Nathan like a felled tree. Since the Big Winter, Cyndi had impressed on the boy that breathing in the cold air without a scarf over his chin and lips would increase his chances of an attack. Winters had been worsening across the eastern seaboard for some time before the catastrophic and unexplained shift in polar locations had plunged America and Europe into a new Ice Age. To hear that his boy had gone outside without any protection was difficult to absorb, almost as difficult as the regret he was feeling now for blaming anyone and everyone without any evidence.

Freeson put a hand on Nathan's shoulder and squeezed. Syd's footsteps thumped up the stairs, calling Saber to follow her. The door slamming upstairs shook the house like the storm had.

"I'm... sorry... Dad..."

Tony pulled Nathan in so that he was caught in a hug between his mother and his father.

Nathan put his boy to bed when the attack had subsided and his own anger had dissipated. Conscious of not wanting to interrogate the boy too hard, he'd nevertheless been concerned that Tony had tried to leave the house. As the boy lay back on the bed, Nathan had stroked his hair and asked, "Tony, you know if you do stuff like that, you're going to drive me and your mom crazy, yes?"

"I'm sorry, Dad. I read in Grampa's 'stronomy book today how the stars used to look, before the Big Winter."

Nathan immediately thought to put his dad's library up into the attic space, and regretted it a moment later. You don't fix a problem by hiding it.

"There'll be a hundred chances to see the stars when the world comes to its senses and summer comes."

"What if there isn't a next summer, Dad?" the boy asked earnestly. "The world's on its side now—that's why the stars moved. You know we have hundreds more stars in the sky now—thousands more even—all up from the southern hemisphere. Before I was born, I'd have had to go to *Oz-stralia* to see them."

Nathan smiled. Tony was so bright and excitable, and his attitude infectious. He couldn't help joining in.

"Well, think of how much cheaper it is to see those *Oz-stralian* stars now, huh? The world falling over has saved me a fortune."

Tony giggled. "When I saw the storm was over and the sky was nearly clear, I wanted to go see what they looked like. The dust in the sky usually makes it impossible to see anything clearly. I was so excited, I forgot my coat and scarf."

Tony was old enough now to be reasoned out of a position

rather than have it addressed with punitive action. And besides that, Nathan found it very difficult to be angry with the boy for very long. He was a kid who could drive you crazy and melt your heart at the same time.

"Just… don't do it again, okay?"

Tony nodded. "But can we take Gramps' telescope out one night? Please?"

"Sure. But only if you go to sleep now."

With little boy energy, Tony immediately rolled over, closed his eyes, and, pulling the blanket up around his ears, began to pretend snore. Nathan smiled and kissed his son in response, heading back downstairs and wondering what he'd done right to be so blessed.

Tony had taken so much in stride, even with the changes in the world—kids were good at that—but Nathan knew the strain of not seeing his friends, most of whom had moved away, and not going to school, having the daily grind of the cold… well, it had all been transferred into an inquisitiveness to understand that might put his son in danger.

Might? Nathan had shaken his head at the thought as he'd rejoined the others. There was no might about it.

"It was the door slamming back in the breeze that woke me up," explained Freeson now that Syd had retreated to the guest room with Saber, but he, Cyndi, and now Nathan realized they were too wired to sleep.

They sat by the fire, rebuilt with fresh logs. Cyndi huddled on the sofa and Freeson rubbed at the toes of his healing foot.

Free's face wasn't difficult to read in the firelight. His hooded eyes and tight mouth were set like concrete in his grizzled features. "I thought maybe the Ski-Doo assholes had come back. I looked out the window and saw Tony stumbling back in. Guess he'd already started his attack."

"Thank you for calling us," Cyndi said.

Nathan was still smarting because he'd gotten it all so wrong with Syd, Saber, and Tony.

The room was warm, the storm over, and yet Nathan didn't feel like resting. There was no point in going into work tomorrow, not with the scavengers still in the vicinity and perhaps looking for a rematch. And then there was Syd—what should they do about Syd?

After she'd said she was going to leave with the dog in the morning, and Freeson's left-field bombshell about also wanting to leave had exploded.

Freeson was an odd fish at the best of times, but you didn't have to look at him long to know there was more below the surface than you might be comfortable asking about.

Freeson had been edgy and on a hair trigger since the crash that had killed his wife two years earlier. Marie, Freeson's wife, had been driving their renovated 1968 Dodge Charger on a trip they were taking up to Silver Bay on Lake George. Marie's sister, Grace, lived there with Tom, her oncologist husband, in a house that could have swallowed up five of Nathan's and still left room for Freeson's apartment. Marie had misjudged a bend in the icy conditions and T-boned the car into a knot of trees on Lake Shore Drive. Freeson had been thrown clear, snapping his hip in the process. Marie had been killed outright.

The tragedy had been compounded by Free's guilt over feeling like he should have been driving, given the weather, but had made Marie get behind the wheel instead.

He hadn't wanted to go and be made to feel *"inadequate"* by Grace and Tom's moneyed success and high-roller lifestyle. He hadn't seen why he should drive himself towards his own misery. Marie, a patient and uncomplicated perfume counter worker, had just agreed, knowing full well that Freeson would be calm enough by the time they got to Silver Bay. The irony that it had been Marie who had driven Freeson to his misery was not lost on him.

All he'd been left with was a limp, an insular aspect that bordered on the stand-offish, and an edgy, nervous, quick-to-anger temperament that made him sleep light and wear his regrets like a mask when he was awake. He was also prone to making snap decisions, flying off the handle, and generally being an ornery old goat thirty years before he should have been.

Nathan knew he had to tread carefully with Free. So he'd tried gently persuading the mechanic to change his mind, but Freeson was set. Everything was conspiring to make Freeson want to leave, and possibly having Syd tag along "in a totally non-creepy way, she's young enough to be my daughter"—and a big-ass dog to boot—seemed like a good enough reason to head for warmer climes. Syd, once she'd been satisfied by Cyndi of Free's honorable intentions, hadn't been against the idea. And the way Syd had dived into the cab of the Dodge with only a few sniffs from Saber told Nathan she made friends easily enough, as long as that dog approved.

Perhaps, now much later, with the scavengers repulsed and Tony's asthma attack over, Nathan would be able to talk Freeson into staying. He slid onto the sofa next to Cyndi and she snaked an arm behind him and snuggled into his chest. "You still set on going, Free?" he asked.

Freeson nodded. "No offense, Nate, but it's time. I'm not cut out for this. Those guys will be back."

Trying to keep the irritation out of his voice, Nate replied, "And you'd be okay about leaving us to it?"

Nathan immediately regretted playing the emotional black-mail card. Freeson had done right by him in staying this long when business had dwindled so much in the Big Winter.

"You could always come, too."

"We don't want to."

"We?" Cyndi lifted her head and fixed Nathan with a hard stare.

"Okay, I know I said it was worth thinking about… but… what with everything, and how Tony reacted to the cold tonight… I realize *I* don't want to go. I don't want to risk him, you, or give up on everything here. Our home. My business."

Freeson shook his head. "Man. What business? When was the last time we got a call to fix something? Pull somebody out of a snowdrift, sure, but to *fix* something? People don't fix their cars anymore; they just go and dig a new one out of the snow!"

Nathan lowered his gaze to the fire.

"You know the town is dying, man. We stick around, we're going to die, too."

Nathan could hear the lucidity in the argument, but he still fought against it. "We've got food enough for two more winters here. We've got guns, and if we don't use the truck much, we have gas."

"And in Detroit, we'd have safety in numbers, and friends," Cyndi reminded Nathan unhelpfully.

Freeson's eyes centered on Nathan's. "Detroit?"

Cyndi explained about Stryker and the work the Motor City's government had been doing to fortify the city against the worsening winters. Freeson's face lit up for the first time all night and he sprang up and across the room and lifted a bottle of whiskey from the dresser. With a sense of celebration, he poured himself a glass, drank from it, and swallowed it down before it occurred to him that it wasn't his whiskey he was drinking. "Sorry, man," he said sheepishly.

Nathan shook his head. "It's okay. Pour me one while you're at it."

Freeson got two more glasses down and began to unscrew the cap on the bottle once again.

Cyndi got up from the sofa, the sudden lack of weight and warmth against Nathan's chest making him feel momentarily sad. That tactile closeness he felt with his wife was one of his greatest pleasures. She was never one who shied away from public displays of affection, and he was all the more grateful for it.

"No thank you, Free," Cyndi said as a shiver of her absence passed across Nathan's chest. "I'm gonna hit the hay. I'll check on the kids before I turn in. You two talk."

"Kids?" Nathan and Freeson said almost together.

"Yeah, *kids*. You don't think Syd's as old as she makes herself out to be, do you?"

"I..." Nathan began.

"Ummmm..." Freeson finished.

"If she's older than fifteen, I'll eat both your hats, boys. She's a kid acting and dressing older. I did it myself when I was the same age. That's a teenage girl for you."

As Nathan thought about it, he couldn't believe he'd missed it. Cyndi was right. He'd been so taken in by the bold, hard-nosed survivor with the shoot first and ask questions later attitude, and the steely spine, that he had barely considered her age. She'd told him nineteen and he'd accepted it without question.

"I lie. Get used to it." She'd told him that in the cab of the Dodge. And yes, he really would have to.

Cyndi left them then with a giggle and a jovial, "Men!"

Freeson passed Nathan a glass. He enjoyed the liquor burning his lips and warming his throat.

"You think this Stryker dude will help us out?" Free asked.

"I've not said I'm going yet!"

"Way Cyndi was talking, I reckon you're going to be the only one left here in a couple of days if you don't. Good luck with that." Although there was a smile on Freeson's lips, Nathan could tell a serious point lay behind the jest. Nathan sat back with his glass, struck again by Freeson's situation and regrets over the death of his wife. The man would spend the rest of his life thinking that, if he hadn't been a pig-headed asshole, perhaps his Marie would still have been with him, still curling up on the sofa with him, leaning her weight and warmth into his chest like Cyndi had been sitting against Nate.

Am I making the same mistake?

Family First.

"Do it for Tony and Cyndi if you won't do it for yourself," Freeson offered, pouring himself another generously three-fingered measure.

"And *another*."

The bottle lip clinked and slid across the glass as Freeson looked up with sharp interest, whiskey dripping onto his pants. "You mean...?"

Nathan nodded. "Yeah. She is."

Freeson blinked, then passed the bottle to Nathan and drained his glass in one gulp. "Well, that settles it, I guess," he said as he came up for air.

Nathan poured himself another drink. "Yeah. I guess you're right," he said, surrendering, his mind full of a wrecked Charger mangled in trees on the side of Lake Shore Drive.

6

The scavengers didn't come back in the morning, and once Syd was told that Nathan and his family were leaving, too, she didn't head off first thing as she'd planned, even though she was clearly still angry with Nathan.

When she'd fed Saber from a can of corned beef Cyndi had given her, Nathan, just downstairs from his shower, made a point of taking her aside in the family room.

"Look, I'm sorry, okay?"

Syd didn't seem to be in the mood to be gracious or show gratitude. "Sorry for what exactly?"

Nathan held onto his irritation and packed it down with a couple of compliments. "I wouldn't have been able to run the scavengers off the land if it wasn't for you. I couldn't have done it without you. So I'm sorry for shouting at you…"

"And?"

Nathan chewed his lip hard, but didn't rise to the bait. "And I'm sorry for blaming the dog for my son's asthma attack, okay?"

Syd considered this for *just* enough time for it to be annoying, but for a short enough time for it not to boil Nathan over like an abandoned pot of milk on the stove. She actually seemed to be an expert at keeping him simmering without getting burned herself. Realizing it, Nathan filed the conclusion away for further use when the time came right.

Now, though, wasn't that time. "So, we don't have to be bosom buddies or anything, but how about a truce?"

Syd didn't argue, or work in a dig to wind Nathan up anymore, but neither did she agree to a truce. She just shrugged and took Saber outside for some exercise.

Once you crack the nut on the outside, Nathan thought, *there's a whole other nut inside*. Sighing, he went to see how Cyndi and Tony were getting on with breakfast.

Later that morning, Nathan called everyone into the family room for a meeting. Syd was still sullen and avoiding eye contact with Nate, Freeson had screwed on his *let's-get-this-done* head, and Cyndi was serene, switched on and determined. No change there.

Nathan felt happier about his son, too. Tony's color was so much better and he said that he was feeling fine just now. He was more excited to be getting off lessons with his Mom.

Nathan loved the basic *nothing-phases-me* attitude of the boy. He definitely had his mother's brains.

Nathan outlined the plan he'd drawn up with Cyndi that morning. When he'd explained to her that he'd come around on the idea of leaving Glens Falls, her sense of relief had driven her practical and pragmatic skills into overdrive. Within the hour, they'd had a strategy and some ideas about how they'd implement it, and now it was time to talk to Free and the others.

"I tried calling Stryker in Detroit, but the telephone is fritzed. We're still able to get onto the internet, so we've tried emailing him to check that it's okay to head there."

Syd seemed less than convinced that Detroit was a viable option and commented, "It'll still be cold there. Just as cold as here."

Cyndi nodded. "Yes, but there's floods and tornadoes in the Midwest, and there's earthquakes in California. Detroit may be cold, but looking at the rest of the states, it's at least stable. For now. So, considering that we've got a connection established there, it offers our best opportunity. It's also near enough to get to on the gas we have. Or, almost."

Tony was looking with wide-eyed wonder from Cyndi to Nathan, his face full of the promise of adventure. Nathan knew in his heart that the trip to Detroit would be anything but a fun escapade, but he wasn't going to say that out loud to his son. All he knew was that he would keep his son as close as humanly possible over the next few weeks.

While Freeson took the wrecker back to town to fetch clothes and essentials from his apartment, Cyndi and Nathan took Syd out back of the house. The snow out there hadn't been disturbed since the storm and offered wild drifts that came up past the women's thighs and Nathan's knees.

The backyard, if it hadn't been glutted with snow, would have been a concrete apron where Nathan stored auto spares that were too valuable or bulky to leave in his shop in town. There were also tubs of earth that now lay frozen and barren, into which, before the winter had come, Cyndi had planted fruit trees meant to augment her stores and make seeds for future cultivation. Beyond the tubs and the cases of spare parts, there was also the silver fuselage of a vintage 70's Airstream Trailer.

The Airstream looked like a Dakota with its wings sawed off. A rounded aluminum trailer, with door and windows, sat on six wheels, equipped with berths to sleep as many as six people with a small dining area, galley kitchen, and bathroom facilities all included. One side had been almost entirely obscured by snow, and the windows were frosted over, but it was still a weirdly impressive sight.

"Wow!" Syd said, revealing—as Cyndi had predicted—the young girl within the woman. Nathan got snow shovels from the outhouse and handing one to Syd, and with that they began to dig the trailer out of its snowy tomb.

After some time spent shoveling, Cyndi went inside the vehicle with Tony to check the propane levels for the stoves and reconnect the batteries, which Nathan had stored in the garage. As the seasons had stopped dead in their tracks and the Big Winter had covered New York State with its blanket of ice, the Airstream had hibernated, ready to be awoken only when the need arose.

Saber had jumped up into the trailer to follow Tony, and Nathan thought he detected a slight look of irritation from Syd as her dog continued bonding with the boy, but she didn't call the dog back. The truce, at least for the moment, was holding.

By the time Freeson drove back to the valley, it was early afternoon and the Airstream trailer had been excavated from beneath the now. Nathan and Syd fitted snow chains to its tires, so Freeson set about connecting the snow plow to the front of the Dodge. Before the Big Winter, the plow had been used to clear the concrete outside Nathan's auto shop, or in normal winters to get to town in the first place. Now it took Freeson just a few minutes to reach the road outside Nathan's house so the Airstream could be brought out and hooked up.

Steam rose from the vents in the Airstream's roof. Cyndi had fired up the stove and boiler to get the inside of the trailer warm and dry. It would take a few hours yet, but it would certainly be ready for when they decided to leave the next morning.

Syd, who'd jumped up inside to have a look around, pulled over a sliding window and stuck her head out to speak to Nathan. "Jeez. This place is half the size of my apartment. It's like a house on wheels!"

Nathan smiled as Cyndi handed him a cup of coffee she'd made in the trailer. Although there was no wind to speak of outside, the day being still and in recovery from the storm, it was still uncomfortably cold. Even after the exertions of digging the trailer out of the snow, the chill would soon bite back. The coffee was as warming as the whiskey had been.

"Where did you get it?" Syd asked, jumping down with Tony and Saber in tow.

"I didn't. It was my daddy's trailer. He spent fifteen years renovating it, and I spent the next five finishing. It was a shell when he got it, beat up to hell on the outside, and it looked like a tornado had been through the inside."

"You fixed it yourselves?"

"Not everything is as disposable as a razor," said Nathan, noting to himself that he sounded fifty-eight rather than twenty-eight.

Some days, he felt like a man out of time who had been born too late. Truthfully, he longed for the times of his daddy, and his daddy before him. Before the silicon chip and the internet and the microwaved meal. Nathan liked the honesty of the wrench, the authenticity of the lathe, and the trust of a well-made hand drill. He could deal with technology, but he wished he didn't have to.

"Okay, Grandpa!" Syd said, nudging his ribs with a bony elbow. Cyndi and Freeson thought the retort hilarious, and Nathan had to admit it had at least turned up the corner of his mouth momentarily.

And that was the last time that would happen for a while.

"I said, *what's up, honey?*"

Nathan blinked, and it suddenly hit him that Cyndi had been talking to him and he hadn't heard a word she'd said. In fact, he hadn't even heard her come into the bedroom.

Nathan had been sitting on the side of the bed going through an old photograph album. It was full of pictures of fishing trips he and his daddy had gone on when he'd been Tony's age. They'd been the best of friends, hiking up around Lake George, catching walleye and cooking them on makeshift hearths, picking scales off their greasy fingers and listening to the huge silence of the woods.

It seemed a dozen lifetimes ago, and it had been back in those distant days when Nathan's daddy had passed on his love of engines and automobiles to his son. Explaining the intricacies of the internal combustion engine, the powerful engineering of the pushrod OHV 90° V-configured gasoline engine, and the precision craftsmanship of a rack-and-pinion steering system. Nathan had of course lapped it all up, and each piece of knowledge had stuck with him so that he'd eventually been ready to take on his father's business. All that was left of those times now were these photographs and the compressed silence of the outdoors hollowing out Nathan's heart.

He was supposed to be packing essentials into his back-packs and taking them down to the Airstream, but he'd gotten stuck in a reverie so deep that Cyndi had almost had to shake his shoulder to lift him out of it.

"Sorry," he said, slamming the album shut and then standing up abruptly. "I was just…"

"I can see what you were just doing, honey. It's okay, I feel the same."

After a second, he met her eyes. "I haven't known another home, baby. I've lived here all my life. I was made in the room next door and born there."

"It's going to be a wrench for all of us. But we're doing the right thing," she added, hugging Nathan so that her breasts pressed pleasingly into his chest. She'd just come in from outside, and the cold had made her nipples hard enough he could feel them through the material of her shirt.

Damn.

Eyes on the prize, Nathan. Keep your mind on the matter at hand.

Nathan loved the way Cyndi made him feel, even after nine years of marriage. The passion he felt for her burned just as bright as it ever had. Whatever his mood or distemper, she could turn him around with a look, a stroke, or a hug. She was all woman, and Nathan knew he'd fallen on his feet the day he'd met her.

Cyndi's father had brought her into the family auto shop in town to have something adjusted on his own 4x4. Nathan couldn't remember what the problem with the truck had been because, as had happened with the album just then, he'd been lost in the moment. Only having eyes for the young woman who'd eagerly followed her father in to speak to Nathan's daddy.

Nathan had made sure to be in the shop a few hours later when the two of them came back to pick up their vehicle, and he'd settled the bill with them while his daddy had had his head stuck in another engine, up to his elbows in oil.

Nathan had noted their address, memorizing it, and in as non-stalkery a way as possible, he'd then hung out after school in a coffee shop nearby, wasting dollar after dollar on over-priced coffee until the afternoon that Cyndi showed up—and he'd then, with maximum faltering and imperial-level shyness, asked her if she'd like to come to a movie with him on a Friday night.

"I thought you'd never ask," she'd said.

In response, Nathan's face had transmitted pure confusion, and Cyndi had laughed. She'd told him, "This is my aunt's coffee shop. I come here every day after school to do my homework. I've been sitting in a booth over there, and you've failed to notice me for the last four days because you've been looking out of the window like your life depended on it. Not for once noticing that I'd gotten here before you. Every. Single. Day."

Cyndi had had the drop on Nathan ever since, and he loved her all the more for it.

"I want to take everything," he told her quietly, thinking back to that moment and looking around their room.

"If you take everything, we won't be leaving, will we?"

Nathan couldn't compete with her logic, and so he put the album he'd been holding so tightly back onto the bed. Cyndi looked up at him with huge, beautiful eyes. Then she picked up the album and put it back into Nathan's hands. "I think we can find room for that, don't you?"

He swallowed. "Thank you."

"But you really need to make some serious decisions about the other stuff. We need to prioritize food, fuel, and survival supplies for the Airstream. We've got to travel light."

Cyndi had already caught Nathan trying to stuff extra socket sets and tool bags into the storage bins of the Airstream that she'd earmarked for food. "No, Nathan, come on. You're not being practical," she'd told him earlier.

"But they're Daddy's tools!"

"And you can keep them, of course…"

"I can feel a 'but' coming on…"

"But you'll have to store them in the toolbox on the back of the wrecker."

"You know that's already full!" Nathan had protested.

"Tony can't eat socket sets, Nathan. And I can't treat his asthma with hacksaws. Prioritize."

"I agree, so I see no need for you to bring any underwear," he'd responded with a salacious grin, tapping her backside with the flat of his hand and giving her buttock a squeeze.

Cyndi had batted his hand away, but with a smile in her voice had told him to behave himself.

Now in the bedroom, holding onto each other like drowning sailors, Nathan could feel the memories already lifting from his head to float away into the distance of experience. Cyndi was right. They had to prioritize or they wouldn't make it out of Glens Falls, let alone across the state.

Yet he felt more doubt than he had the night before. Stryker hadn't replied to the email Nathan had sent, and that was a worry. Not a terminal concern that would derail their choice of destination before they started... but one that added an extra layer of uncertainty to the trip before they'd even turned a wheel.

"We should stay another two nights at least before we set off," Nathan said to the others that evening as they rested by their fire, their bellies full from dinner. Out of earshot, Tony was playing with Saber in the kitchen.

Cyndi agreed easily enough, but Freeson commented, "We've been lucky so far. The weather's still calm enough to give us a good head start. The snow on the roads will be powder and good for travel. Another lowering in the temperature and it'll turn to hard ice, and that'll slow us down. We should go tomorrow."

Almost all of the supplies Cyndi had stockpiled in the garage—the food, both dried and canned, and the propane and water purifiers, the candles, the tents, and the survival gear—had been transferred to the Airstream during the day with herculean effort on the part of everyone. Even Tony had done the best he could, sorting through his toys, deciding on leaving the majority of them in favor of taking as many books from the family library as Cyndi would allow.

Pretty soon, the interior of the Airstream had been cramped and dark with gear. Everywhere that could be was now stuffed with stores in boxes and tied down with straps. Progress down its length was nearly impossible without a map. Freeson had compared it to trying to negotiate a Pac-Man maze. Syd had looked at him like he'd been speaking Swahili.

Another pointer to her real age, Nathan realized as he glanced her way now.

He hedged, "I dunno, Free. Setting out without a definite invitation might not be the smartest idea."

"What kind of friend is he, Nate? The kind that would turn away a fella in need? One with a sick boy and a baby on the way?"

Put like that, Nathan had to admit that Stryker was absolutely not that kind of a man. Well, he hadn't been anyway, and the contact they'd had since he'd made it to Detroit seemed to suggest a man who was still honorable and trustworthy.

"I think we should go tomorrow, too," Syd said, her knees drawn up in the armchair, chin resting on them, hugging herself like she was feeling anxiety but wasn't comfortable about showing it. Nathan wondered if she felt worried about the scavengers coming back or something else was bothering her. It had been a couple of days now, and conversely, the good, bright weather meant those men wouldn't have been able to approach in the daytime without being seen; even the nights were too exposed for them to attack without the cover of a storm.

In the expanse of the valley, echoes deadened by the snow would transmit the sound of Ski-Doo engines across many miles. Even if they'd just been in the vicinity, they'd have been heard, especially with how light someone like Freeson slept.

Yet darkness was pressing at the windows of the family room. Nathan could feel the hugeness of the night beyond them, making him and his home feel vulnerable and exposed.

Even as Tony played with Saber, Cyndi lay her head on Nathan's shoulder, and he realized that he only had two hands to hold onto everything that he held dear.

He squeezed Cyndi close and kissed the top of her head. Her hair smelled fresh, and the skin beneath was warm. "Okay," he agreed. "We'll go tomorrow. Response from Stryker or not."

From the kitchen, Saber barked. Nathan knew it was because she was enjoying playing with Tony, but that didn't stop it from sounding like the dog was happy to be getting on the road again.

7
―――――

The hailstorm hit when they were twenty miles outside Glens Falls. But those twenty miles had taken over two days already in a journey that was less arduous trek and more a war of attrition.

Any happiness about having a definite plan of action, goal to achieve, or mission to accomplish, had been short-lived at best. Firstly, even though the custom-sized crew cab on the Dodge was roomy enough for three people, with Tony, Syd, Free, and Saber, it became somewhat of a squeeze. The dog did her best to keep down in the space between the two back rows of seats, but with them all inside, plus bags of provisions, it had taken a bit of logistical application from Cyndi to sort things out.

They moved the rucksacks of day rations onto the back of

the wrecker under a tarp for protection and, occasionally, Tony would sit up front with Cyndi, perching his bottom on the seat between her legs. Asked by Nathan if he was comfortable, the boy typically made the best of it, saying, "It's great being up front," leaning on the dash with his eyes glittering with possibilities. "I can see everything much better!" Nathan had tousled Tony's hair with great affection when he'd added that, and pushed the Dodge on.

Secondly, although they had the fuel, and the wrecker had the grunt to traverse the snowy roads—with the plow on its nose scything arcs of snow into the air—many of the roads they moved along were glutted with obstacles. There were broken-down cars, old trees that had collapsed under the weight of the snow, and boulders from hillsides that had slid downwards to snag and snarl up any progress. All of it had raised their uncertainty to a constant state of apprehension.

Sometimes, it would be obvious where humped snowdrifts hid lurking vehicles that could be bypassed by driving around them, but more often than not, the snow had drifted so high that Nathan couldn't be sure what was hiding beneath the piles of snow without jumping down from the cab and thrusting a ski pole into a bank of whiteness just to see what its point came up against.

In some places, Nathan and the others had no idea where the road was at all, and on three occasions on the slow flight from Glens Falls on the first day, there had been a grinding protest from the edge of the plow and a sickening bump from the front tires, the cab shaking its occupants around like dice in a craps cup.

The Dodge had run off the road on those occasions, and Nathan and Free had had to disengage the plow, pull it off the front assembly, and dig behind the tires on the Dodge and the Airstream. While reversing, they just had to hope they hadn't been railroaded too far off the highway by the pavement edge —so that they'd be able to get back on the highway without having to decouple the trailer, drive around behind it, and haul it onto the road backward.

"I guess we'll speed up when we learn better how to handle the conditions," Nathan said hopefully to the others as they took up coffee and snacks in the crew cab of the Dodge.

Driving in deep snow was one thing, but pulling a trailer like the Airstream added a whole extra layer of *'nope'*. Several times, on gradients or bends, it felt like the trailer tail was wagging the Dodge dog and furious corrections had to be made to the wheel to stop them running off the road.

They'd been travelling since mid-morning. In five hours, they'd gone only five miles by Freeson's reckoning as he consulted his maps.

On a good day, with the hammer down, Detroit was a nine- or ten-hour drive from Glens Falls. It was the kind of journey you could make in one lump if you wanted to, or you could stop for a leisurely lunch, and a slow late afternoon break, and still roll into the city before nightfall if you'd gotten an early start.

But Nathan and the others had been given a false impression of their ability to traverse the distance easily. Glens Falls had still had a population for the last few months. There hadn't been many people before the exodus had begun, so the town hadn't been so badly hit that people couldn't get around.

The roads they were attempting to travel on now didn't appear to have been plowed or journeyed along for months. That made sense to Nathan, though, now that he was forced to consider it. Why would people exiting the town stay within the new Arctic Circle? They'd instead travel south or southwest as quickly and hard as they could. Traveling straight west suddenly felt like the dumbest idea they could ever have come up with.

The first night in the Airstream—given that it was nearly impossible, and far too dangerous, to travel during the darkness—had lifted everyone's spirits.

They'd made camp at 5 p.m. Freeson, whose frostbitten toes were now almost healed to the point of his gait getting back to his familiar limp, had cooked up a storm, and in the Airstream, cramped though it was, the space was also cozy and warm, so the difficult day had turned into an easier night.

They'd been able to remain warm, the weather didn't feel any harsher than it would have at home, and although they'd left their home and the valley behind, and the day had been tough, Nathan had been warming to the task in hand. "Tomorrow will be better," he'd said, spooning chicken stew into his mouth.

"I think, tomorrow, one of us should walk ahead of the Dodge as we go, testing the drifts—say, fifty yards ahead? We could take turns and it'd certainly stop any nasty surprises." Ever the strategic thinker, Cyndi's suggestion had been a good one.

They weren't making more than a decent walking pace anyway, and all the stopping and starting was using their fuel up quicker than Nathan would have guessed. Sure, there were many gallons of it stored in jerry cans at the very back of the Airstream, and strapped around the boom and spectacle lift of the wrecker, but they didn't know what awaited them ahead. It made sense to conserve as much gas as they could, and Cyndi's idea helped that aim.

So, that day, Nathan had taken the first turn walking ahead of the Dodge and Airstream combo along the highway, probing ahead with the ski pole as he went. Cyndi had been right, as they'd definitely made better progress on the second day—it was still slow-going, and only thirteen miles had passed, but they'd left Glens Falls behind and Tony's infectious sense of adventure was getting to all of them.

"This feels like a vacation!" the boy said with a smile as wide as the road. Nathan was leaning against the cab now, taking a coffee from the flask Cyndi had prepared before they'd set out that morning. Tony, still in the Dodge but with the window cracked enough to speak to his father, had cheeks that were ruddy with good health, and eyes that drank in everything as if he were seeing it for the first time.

Surrounding them, the trees were hulking snow ghosts in the still air. The occasional bird would rattle a branch, causing a dusting of snow to fall, but otherwise the world rested silent and unmoving.

Syd kept trying to turn the cab radio to any station that might still be broadcasting so they could get a weather report, but nothing was showing up on either digital or on analog.

"Can I walk out with you, Dad?" Tony climbed half out of the crew cab window, his face ruddy in the chill air and his breath making clouds.

"Tony, the drifts are so deep I don't know that I'm tall enough to get through them! We might lose you completely," Nathan laughed.

"It's okay, Dad. Saber will find me!" And as if to agree, the dog barked.

Cyndi pulled Tony gently back inside. "Come on, sport, you don't need to be out in the cold air too long. You know what might happen."

"Aww, Mom, I feel fine."

"Everyone feels fine until they don't."

Freeson, who had been driving, had taken the opportunity of the coffee stop to consult his maps. "About another five miles to the I-87 and Saratoga Springs."

Two days just to get to Saratoga Springs. Put like that, the enormity of the task hit Nathan all over again. It was five hundred and fifty miles to Detroit. Even at ten miles a day, it would take a month and a half to get there—and that presupposed they'd have enough fuel, and that storms wouldn't hold them back, or that any of a hundred other things might not go wrong.

Nathan looked to the sky, which was beginning to fill with clouds. The change in them had prompted him to ask Syd to see if she could get some sort of report from the radio, as none of their cell phones were working. Although they were all fully charged, there was no signal to pick up, which meant no internet, and no idea of whether Stryker had sent a reply to the email.

Nathan wondered again if he really was a man born out of his time who yearned for the traditional, uncomplicated life, questioning whether he really could have lived back then without the means to communicate instantly across vast distances. Without the medical technology needed to create medicine for his son, or the ability of satellites to tell him what the damned weather was going to be doing next.

Above the trees, the sky had become fat with threat, as if to emphasize the worries running through his mind.

Nathan checked his watch, seeing it was three in the afternoon; they had two hours before dark, and there was another storm coming in. Those five hundred and fifty miles seemed an awful lot longer all of a sudden.

Hail crashed into the roof of the Airstream like all the buckshot ever made was being shot at the aluminum fuselage. Even though they all were in the Dodge now, they could hear the hissing rattle and ting of ice on metal as the trailer behind them rang out and pinged in response.

They'd made it another mile and a half before the sky had opened up its turkey shoot free-for-all and flung its volleys at Nathan's friends and family.

Nathan had been driving, and Cyndi, who had insisted she should take a turn, had been outside testing the snowdrifts, walking ahead of the plow as the first pea-sized lumps of ice had started to pepper the surface of the snow.

The wind had been picking up steadily as their torturous progress had continued, and as Cyndi covered her head and Freeson helped haul her back up into the crew cab, the hail hit with a ferocity that shocked Nathan.

The surface of the snowbanks boiled with it, the tops of the trees along this stretch of highway shivering themselves free of their icy blankets and shaking like panicked creatures with lives of their own. Meanwhile, the quickening twilight rushed overhead towards darkness with the speed of a door being closed on welcoming light.

"This is crazy!" Nathan hollered above the din as Tony clung to him in the driver's seat, hiding his face in his father's chest but occasionally peering out with wide-eyed shock at the onslaught. Saber did not appreciate the din at all as she moved between whimpering and trying to hide under Tony.

There was no space in the noise for small-talk, so only shouting would do. "Too dark to travel on!" Nathan yelled.

Cyndi peered into the gloom beyond the cut of the Dodge's headlamps. "Should we try to get the truck under the trees? That might give us some protection!?"

Nathan couldn't help being wary about driving off the road, even in smooth conditions. To get off the highway now would mean one of them going out into the hail, to test the drop to the treeline. He shook his head. "No! We'll wait it out!"

And so they did. Flinching as the roof boomed and the cab shook with the sound of gravel being dumped onto the vehicles, with Tony hugging onto his father and Saber barking at the noise.

They were just two days out of Glens Falls, Nathan thought. Just twenty miles into their five hundred and fifty-mile journey to Detroit.

Two days.

Jeez.

They didn't go out to check for damage to the Airstream and wrecker until morning. The hailstorm had lasted less than an hour, but it had been night when it had ended. And it had been followed by a fresh fall of snow.

Not a heavy blizzard, but a steady drop which had soon

enough silted up one side of the Dodge and actually had the effect of insulating the crew cab in its own igloo.

Another reason to stay the night in the crew cab was that everyone was dog-tired anyway. So they scrunched up, huddled together like an extended Inuit family for convenience and warmth. Nate and Cyndi up front, Syd, Tony, and Freeson, with Saber at their feet, behind.

Around 4 a.m., Nathan twisted in his seat under his blanket and caught sight of Saber snuggled up to Freeson's legs and across his legs. The mechanic, snoring, had his arms around the dog, in a half-hug. Nathan couldn't help smiling. Freeson was so rarely calm and relaxed these days, it was good to see.

The morning dawned as bright as it could with the high-atmosphere ash across its face, and Nathan jumped down into the fresh snow to check the vehicles.

Although the hailstorm had been the most vicious he had ever experienced, the damage to the vehicles was slight, thanks in part to their construction and the small size of the hail stones. There were pockmarked dents all over the surface of the trailer, and one window had been cracked—which Nathan quickly taped up—but otherwise it was perfectly intact.

After digging the Dodge and trailer wheels free of the new snow, they headed off with Nathan driving and Freeson going on ahead to make sure they didn't hit anything unexpectedly. It was slow, laborious, and boring, but by mid-afternoon they came off the cloverleaf at the turn for Ballston Spa, a few miles south of Saratoga Springs.

The roads here were just as glutted with snow, but at least they had a view across open lands, unobscured by trees. "Sure feels good to be out in the clear air," Cyndi said, rolling down the window and breathing in the coolness.

Freeson came up to the side of the Dodge and indicated that Nathan should wind the window down. "There's a motel here," he said, pointing to a snow-covered set of buildings half a mile away. "Stayed there with Marie once when we were too wasted to drive home. We could stay there for the night?"

Nathan looked up at the sky. Another day over, and only five miles covered because of the time taken to dig the truck and trailer out of the snow. "You think it'll be open for business?" he asked.

Freeson winked and smirked. "It will be."

Half an hour of hopeful travel later, they pulled the Airstream into the front parking lot of the Fillmore Inn. It had long since been abandoned to the elements. Modern in design, it had a central, two-story main continent of a building with five surrounding single-story ranch-style islands of rooms. Having parked, they approached the main building on foot.

Cyndi had passed Freeson a rifle before jumping down with her own. Nathan just kept his lips tight shut about it. He hated the idea that they had to approach something as innocuous as a motel armed to the teeth. The cold he could deal with, but the sense that his fellow man would do him more harm than the horrific conditions hurt his heart.

Nathan wasn't against guns per se, but neither was he someone who worshipped at the altar of the second amendment. Cyndi, on the other hand... well, that was another story.

The doors and windows in the building were boarded up with plywood that had been screwed into the frames. Ordinarily, this would have put off most people, but along with his rifle, Freeson had brought a pry bar and an ax.

As Freeson attacked the door's covering and Cyndi scanned the surrounding area, Nathan felt his discomfort rising. It wasn't like alarms were about to go off and cops would come skidding into the parking lot with lights flashing, but he liked to feel that his moral compass was still intact. Breaking and entering wasn't exactly his usual hobby.

Everyone else seemed unconcerned, though. Tony was throwing snowballs for Saber to chase, and Syd was using his pry bar to lift up other corners of the plywood coverings as if doing so was the most natural thing in the world.

"Maybe I didn't want to leave because I knew we'd have to start living a different kind of life," Nathan commented to Cyndi when she glanced his way for reaction.

Cyndi smiled and blew him a kiss. "Our lives are going to change in ways not even I can imagine, honey, but they surely have to if we're gonna make it all the way to Detroit."

Nathan knew she was right.

Perhaps he should carry a weapon after all.

Inside, the reception area was dark and stank of dampness, but hadn't yet succumbed in any meaningful way to the changes in the weather conditions.

A desk calendar was set to a date before Christmas, and that indicated when the place seemed to have been abandoned. Anything that hadn't been tied down had been taken. Nathan could see ghost rings of dirt on the tiled floors where the legs of tables and chairs had been lifted and removed.

Corridors extended in three directions into the gloom and the reception desk looked like someone with a bad case of resentment had kicked a bunch of holes in it.

"I guess someone didn't like losing their job," Nathan said as they passed it.

"Nice place, nice people. From what my hangover can remember," Freeson said.

"Let's go check on some rooms. I want the bridal suite," Cyndi commented, putting her rifle over her shoulder. Turning on her flashlight, she marched into the first corridor and called back with a laugh, "I don't know where you're sleeping, Nate!"

Tony, Saber, and Syd stayed in the reception area while the others scoped for rooms. All the doors had electronic locks, which were—of course—inoperative, but with judicious pry-barring they came open soon enough. The rooms hadn't been emptied in the same way as the reception area. Dead flat-screen TVs hung silent on mounts, and beds were made as if the maids had just left—someone had wanted to do a good job on their last day, at least in this corridor.

"You guys seen *The Shining*?" Freeson asked, prying open another door.

Cyndi thumped Freeson's arm and Nathan rolled his eyes.

"What'll it be, Mr. Torrence?" Freeson stood stock-still and mimed cleaning a glass like a bartender in a swanky ballroom bar.

Nathan knew *The Shining* was a film that Cyndi had refused to even stay in the same room with when Freeson had come over in the past for a beer and movie night. It was a movie that had terrified her as a child, and Freeson invoking its memory in the cold, silent, dark motel wasn't going down well with Nathan's wife. She pushed past Free and into the room, swinging her flashlight as she ignored him.

"It's good to see you in a better mood, man," he said as Freeson grinned, "but you know what she…"

Nathan was cut off by Cyndi's yell of horror. It echoed down the corridor and almost stopped his heart. Nathan, guts bunching, ran into the room behind her.

Cyndi's hand was over her mouth and she was staring at the bed with wide, terrified eyes.

Without processing what lay ahead, Nathan instinctively moved in front of her to get between her and whatever it was that had caused her to yell.

"Jeez," Freeson said simply, coming in behind him.

On the bed were two dead bodies.

The room had never got above near freezing, and they hadn't rotted much, but they showed sucked down eyes and hollow cheeks, and they were laying side by side like sleeping zombies about to wake. The bodies were holding hands, too. Dry, chicken leg fingers intertwined. They had, in life, been in their late fifties. A man and a woman, hair graying, clothes not cheap and not expensive. With a flicker of compassion, Nathan noted that there were wedding bands on both their left hands.

The room wasn't filled with the stench of rot or decay, either, but due to the cold, one of dead meat.

On the bedside cabinet were a half empty bottle of whiskey and some empty pill bottles.

Whoever they were, they obviously hadn't thought that leaving the hotel, and heading wherever into the cold, was the best option for them, and they'd taken their pills with liquor and settled down to die.

Nathan held Cyndi in his arms as she sobbed out her surprise while Freeson went back towards reception to make sure Saber, Tony, and Syd, who'd come running at the sound of Cyndi's yell, didn't come in and see the bodies.

The next day dawned bright, the sky bluer than it had been for many weeks. Perhaps the currents of ash in the air were clearing, Nathan considered, or had the vagaries of the weather

given this part of the state a window that wouldn't last? Whatever the reason, the sun put a warmth in Nathan's heart that
felt welcome after the last few days.

And the night had passed without incident.

Because of the dead couple, they'd gone to a different
wing of the motel, breaking into a large suite that offered
enough beds and sofas for everyone to sleep comfortably.
After the discovery in the first corridor, and Freeson's gags
about *The Shining* on top of them, everyone had thought
staying in the same room was the best idea.

They'd thus gotten food, lamps, and an oil heater from the
Airstream, and made quite a cozy den for themselves in
the suite.

After breakfast, Tony wanted to take Saber out to play
"snowballs" again, so Nathan went with him while the others
enjoyed the warmth of the room and the comfort of their beds.

Syd had turned out to be a heavy sleeper, and hadn't
stirred for breakfast or to see Tony go off with Saber. Asleep,
Nathan thought she looked even younger than Cyndi's esti-
mate of fifteen years, and he was surprised to feel a pang of
paternal concern for the girl. She'd obviously had things hard.
Perhaps he should have been cutting her a break from the start.

While Tony played with the dog, Nathan gave the Dodge's
engine the once-over, checking and adjusting the timing chain
out of habit rather than necessity. It felt good to get his hands
dirty again in an engine. His natural habitat and all that.

"What's up, Saber?"

Nathan looked around from the raised hood.

Tony was thirty yards away, across the expanse of white, snowball in his hand in mid-throw. Saber wasn't anywhere to be seen.

Wiping his hands on a rag and putting his gloves back on, Nathan walked to where his son stood in a circle of disturbed snow and fresh paw prints. The boy was shielding his eyes against the sun and looking around the side of the building.

As Nathan approached, he could see Saber standing frozen, her ears pricked, nose pointed away from the motel towards the treeline. "What's she seen, Tony?"

"Dunno, Dad. She was catching and chasing the snowballs great, and then she just stopped. Come on, girl! Saber! Play!"

Tony threw the snowball he'd held and it landed to the right of the dog, but she didn't move or take her gaze from the trees.

Nathan couldn't miss the sense of anxiety in the dog. It only began transmitting ever more sharply to him as the dog whimpered and lowered her tail. He didn't need another signal.

"Tony, go inside. Get Mom and the others to load up quickly."

"What's going on?"

"Just do it, son," he muttered, and then he turned the boy away by the top of his head, nudging him back towards the motel's entrance. Tony didn't need a second bidding, and walked as quickly as his asthma would allow, kicking up snow as he went.

Nathan struck out towards the treeline and Saber dutifully followed, still occasionally whimpering.

Nothing moved in the trees, but the black branches intertwining ahead of them reminded Nathan uncomfortably of the dead hands on the bed.

Ten yards from the trees, Nathan noticed two things that concerned him. Footprints in the fresh snow, and tracks that might have been made by pushing a heavy piece of machinery into the trees.

He followed the tracks to the edge of the forest, but it was as dark and silent as the motel had been when they'd broken into it. Saber whined, spun twice, and put her tail between her legs.

The area of snow here was messed up, as if there had been a lot of activity, as if someone had stopped here and worked on the machinery again before pushing it into the trees. Something sparkling in the snow caught Nathan's eye. He bent down to pick up a flat piece of metal and brushed off the snow with his glove.

It was a flat wrench, like the kind that came with the tool kit on a Ski-Doo.

Nathan began to back away.

8

They didn't sleep anywhere other than the Airstream for the next ten days. They'd covered nearly a hundred and twenty miles in the ten days following their motel stay, and Nathan had changed from being the reluctant leaver to the motivated driver. He'd so far vetoed any suggestion to repeat their time at a motel or venture into a house along the way.

"There's no evidence that those tracks could have been one of the assholes who attacked us at your place," Freeson had said on the fifth or sixth time passing a motel or farmstead that might have afforded a welcome break from being crammed into the Airstream.

Nathan didn't look around at his friend as he gripped the wheel and feathered the gas pedal, not wanting to speed up out of anger and roll the snowplow over his wife. "It doesn't matter. The trailer is easier to defend if we're attacked. In a motel or a farm, especially one that's been boarded up, we might not hear a Ski-Doo approaching. We didn't back there, did we? We just slept like babies while they watched us from the trees."

"You don't know that."

"I don't, it's true, but I'm not taking any chances with the lives of my family."

There was a tautness to his voice that Nathan didn't enjoy. He knew Freeson was just craving a stretch for his legs and sleep in a real bed—and, twelve days into their journey, it might be a fine luxury, but allowing it might also lead to their downfall. Especially if the scavengers *were* on their trail.

"I don't want you to take any risks with your family, Nate, but we're all going a little bit stir-crazy. I know I am. And Cyndi told me last night she was thinking of murdering you in your sleep," Freeson joshed.

"It's true," Cyndi laughed, joining in.

"Just think about it, yeah?" Freeson asked. "That's all I'm asking."

Finally, it was Cyndi throwing up into the snow—as she jumped down from the truck to take her turn walking ahead, testing snowdrifts—that suggested to Nathan that he might be pushing everyone too hard. It happened an hour after they'd set off on their twelfth morning of travel, when Cyndi opened the door of the Dodge to go out and take over for Syd with the ski pole but disappeared from sight as if she'd fallen into a hole.

Nathan leaned across the cab and looked down to where his wife was uncontrollably throwing up against the tire of the Dodge. The vomit steamed in the cold air like a witch's stew, and the mess looked like she'd thrown up not just that morning's breakfast, but everything she'd eaten over the last three days, too.

Nathan jumped down beside her, rubbing her back as she wretched again. "You okay, honey?"

Cyndi's head came up. Her cheeks were covered in red blotches and her eyes brimmed with tears. "Of course I'm not fine, you doofus; I'm throwing up."

A snigger from the cab told Nathan that Freeson had at least found the exchange entertaining. "You know what I meant. Are you ill… or…"

Cyndi nodded, struggling to catch her breath. "It's morning sickness, yes. It's not what Freeson cooked for breakfast."

"Hey!" came Freeson's indignation from the cab.

Cyndi wiped her mouth and then firmly took the ski pole from Syd's hands. "I'll be okay, Nate. But if the wind changes, your face might set like that."

True enough. Nathan could feel emotions and concern leaking through his expression. He'd been so intent on getting them as far away from the Dead Body Motel (as everyone seemed to be unhelpfully calling it now), that he suddenly felt like he'd lost sight of some specifics while dealing with only the big picture. Before the Big Winter, his life had been uncomplicated and pretty settled. Everything had changed now, and he didn't like being wracked with doubts that were causing him to screw up and lose his grasp on the important stuff. "I'm just worried, baby," he told her. "You know how tough things were for you last time, and now you're ten years older…"

Cyndi sighed, squeezing Nathan's hand. "Nathan, when you're in a hole, stop digging, yeah? Pre-eclampsia is an illness, sure, but pregnancy isn't. My blood pressure is fine."

"How do you know?"

"Because I use this every morning." She reached into the crew cab and ferreted about under the seat. When she bobbed up, she held a battery-operated wrist cuff blood pressure machine. She plonked it down in Nathan's palm. "You've been too wired to notice. I was sick yesterday, too."

"And the day before," Syd said, climbing up into the truck. "I heard you in the trailer."

The comment made Nathan feel even lamer—why hadn't he noticed if Syd had?

He nodded after another moment passed, catching Cyndi's eyes. "We'll find somewhere to stop tonight, maybe stay a coupl'a days. Freeson, take a look at the maps; see what we can get to before nightfall."

The railroad station was boarded up in the same way as the Dead Body Motel had been. Before the Big Winter, it had served Rome, NY, and they'd had to travel north instead of west to get there, but Freeson had assured them they could get there before dark.

On the road, before Nathan had made the decision to find a place where they could shelter, they hadn't seen any traffic for days, and he was beginning to think they were the last people left in the state. The railroad station was just as deserted, and did nothing to shift him from that notion.

Cyndi had suggested the railroad station because it had a frozen river nearby where they should be able to crack through the ice to replenish their water supplies. It was also easily defensible since there were no nearby buildings to hide approaching scavengers. On none of the stops over the last week had there been evidence of Ski-Doos or bandits, but Nathan was taking nothing for granted.

Once they settled on a space inside the railroad station, they brought in lamps, oil heaters, and supplies, setting up temporary camp in a room behind the booking office that had been a staff/sleep-in area for night crews. A couple of windows up above the main concourse had been broken by the weather and a chilly breeze blew through the center of the building, but the crew room was secure and soon warmed up.

There was a bed, two armchairs, a sofa, and a pool table, and once the room was warming, Freeson wasted no time in setting up the pool table and playing with Tony. Saber looked on, her bright eyes darting with the moving balls and her head cocking at the snicks and clicks as they cannoned off of each other.

Nathan grinned to see Freeson letting Tony win.

While Cyndi prepared food, Nathan took Syd outside across the deep snow covering the tracks, through some dense, white blanketed brush and down to the water's edge. They broke the icy crust near the bank and began filling as many water carriers as they could before their hands turned blue and the breath burned in their throats.

As they started to maneuver the latest barrels back towards the railroad station, Nathan thought he'd try again with Syd, asking, "You've still not told us everything, have you?"

"Don't start."

"I'm not. I just… look, I trust you, okay? There's no doubt about that, but you're still not leveling with us about every-thing, and if we're going to travel together, we really need to be on the level, right?"

Syd blew into her hands and then thumped them against her sides to keep the circulation moving. "I just don't like being interrogated is all."

"I get that."

"Then stop interrogating me." In a different mouth, the

demand could have sounded harsh, but Nathan caught the curl of a smile on the corner of her lips, and he felt that he'd moved things along between them—if not to their end point, certainly in the right direction.

"Okay, I won't. You tell me what you've got to tell me when the time is right for you. Deal?"

Syd clearly appreciated having the pressure to talk about her past lifted as the start of a curled lip turned into a full-blown grin and her face became the second sheet of ice Nathan had broken in the last half an hour.

The wind was picking up and the sky roiled with heavy clouds as they got the last barrel back to the station. As the clouds opened with first a flurry and then a full-blown blizzard, Nathan felt relieved they'd made it back just in time.

The blizzard lasted two straight nights and days. If Nathan and Syd hadn't gone straight away for the water when they had, the party would have run out on the first morning.

Cyndi had become proficient at using the gravity filter to purify the water of any pollutants before boiling and got them up and running with a clear and clean store of water pretty soon. The stock would last them the best part of a week before they'd have to get another load.

Stuck in the crew room, with the storm blowing outside constantly, the pool table was a godsend to keep bored minds in order. Syd drew up a league table on a whiteboard attached to one wall that had previously been used for crew rosters. She'd found dry erase pens in a steel stationery cupboard she'd pried open.

Nathan thought the place had less of an abandoned look now, and more of a moth-balled feel to it. As if railroad workers had been told that the present emergency wouldn't last forever and that they could expect to be back at work sometime in the future.

While the others played games at the pool table, Nathan found time to talk to Cyndi about the normal stuff of life—how Tony was doing, how she was feeling about the baby. "I feel fine Nate, truly. I've got more than enough to worry about with getting us to Detroit, rather than worrying about my passenger."

Nathan smiled, "We'll have to stop calling him or her the passenger someday, maybe start thinking about some names."

Cyndi waved a hand dismissively. "Oh, I don't have time and energy to put into that." But Nathan could see the twinkle in her eye that told him she had probably gotten the name thing sorted in her head already and had just been waiting for the right time to tell him what it would be.

Man, I love you, he thought. And then, because it was worth saying out loud, he said, "Man, I *love* you."

And he did. From top to bottom and all routes out.

Being snowed in at the railroad station allowed them all to rest, but it didn't make the wider issues they were facing relax any. Cyndi was still having her morning sickness, but it was usually just the one bout. It came like clockwork every morning around nine, and Nathan found himself, if not exactly getting used to it, at least appreciating that it was part of a normal pregnancy, so that nothing could be said to be going wrong. Cyndi found that if she had a lighter breakfast and saved a bigger meal for lunchtime, then she wouldn't suffer again.

Syd had also seemed more comfortable in the group since her trip down to the river to get water. The longer they had stayed camped at the station, forced into living in the same room, the more she'd taken it upon herself to become a social secretary. She'd not only organized the pool league but had found a deck of cards for poker and blackjack in the evenings, and told half-remembered fantasy stories to Saber and Tony before bed. The three of them were turning into quite a team.

For his part, Freeson was getting back to something like his normal self, too, and had been cracking a few jokes that, although Nathan had heard them on occasion in the past, made it feel like they had him back in the zone he'd once occupied in their lives.

The journey was tempering them in many ways. It may have brought out the best in them, Nathan considered, as the vehicles were made ready to move out. But that said, the stop in Rome had fixed a new dynamic in the group, one that meant that, for the first time, Nathan felt they were all moving in the same direction. Syd's willing integration with the others over the past few days had cemented that for him, and he was glad of it.

It took most of the third day for them to dig the wrecker and the Airstream from the snowdrifts that had almost covered them outside the station. One entire end of the trailer had been smothered all the way up to the roof.

As they worked, Saber came out of the building with Tony, took one look around, and started growling and barking. Nathan's heart jumped with wondering whether it could be the Ski-Doo raiders again.

But no, it was Freeson who pointed out the tracks in the fresh snow on the far side of the station wall. They weren't the tracks of Ski-Doos, either; these had been made by the paws of wolves. Saber had been making sure any wolves in the vicinity were aware whose territory this was.

Thankfully, they didn't see or hear any wolves as they finished packing up the Airstream and Cyndi got it warmed up for the journey. Saber was still wary and seemed more than happy to jump up into the Dodge and stop worrying about wolves as they rolled out of Rome.

Once they were back on the road, the fresh snow gave them a good grip on the surface, and the tire chains bit in securely. Freeson had taken the first shift feeling ahead in the snow drifts, even as the snow plow carved its way relentlessly behind him.

On the second hour, it was time for Nathan to take his turn, and he swapped places with the ruddy-faced Freeson, who seemed to be in the highest of spirits. So much so, Nathan asked him with a smile, "You haven't been at the whiskey again, have you, bro?"

"Only when you're not looking," Freeson replied with a wink, and with that he climbed up into the cab to take the wheel.

They made good progress that morning—the best they had for a while. There was a long stretch of the NY-365 where recent snow had spared the already icy surface, and this offered enough visibility for Nathan to get back up inside the cab and for the wrecker to continue without the chaperone.

It felt satisfying to get the wrecker and trailer moving up until the needle was just edging over 15 mph. After the last week, this was akin to Indy car racing at the Brickyard, now they weren't moving at whatever pace one of them could have walked ahead at.

Nathan saw the taillights of the black Armbruster Stageway six-door limo before anyone else did. At first, he rubbed his eyes, wondering if he was seeing things as Freeson drove the Dodge.

"See that?" he asked after another moment.

Freeson peered through the windshield, three-quarters of a mile up the road. The lights were white and red, and the right indicator was blinking on and off. Nathan could almost hear the ticking of it in his head.

The wrecker rolled on.

Cyndi and the others hung over the front seats from the crew cab, looking forward with some amazement. It was the first vehicle they'd seen for days, and for it to just be stopped there in the fast lane, covered in a dusting of snow, was unusual to say the least.

"Should we stop? See if they're okay?" Freeson asked.

Nathan's general demeanor of wanting to help anyone who needed help, especially in a stranded vehicle, was about to say an immediate "Yes." But Syd beat him to it.

"No. Never stop," she said. "They're there in the middle of the road for a reason. To make you think they're in trouble."

Her voice was filled with the sound of bitter experience.

The back end of the limo approached with accusatory speed. Nathan tried screwing his natural instincts down under the lid of practicality, but the dissonance between what was being suggested and what he had spent his life doing won out as the limo began to slide past them.

"Stop!" he demanded.

Such was the command in Nathan's voice that, without thinking, Freeson stamped on the anchors. The wrecker slewed to a halt at an angle and they heard the Airstream thumping into its linkage, shaking the Dodge.

"This is a mistake!" Syd hissed, but Nathan jumped out of the cab and onto the road, walking defiantly towards the limo.

There was a light dusting of snow, which suggested the

vehicle had been moving at least somewhat in the last few hours since the storm had abated.

The headlamps were on, but inside the car was dark, and as the windshield was dusted and a little crazed with recent frost, he couldn't see inside.

There were footprints alongside the limo, but Nathan was stopped in his own tracks by the shape of them. They weren't the huge, rounded impressions of boots in the snow. Instead, they had a triangular toe end, and there was a deep dot in the snow behind, as if someone had drilled a pool cue into the snow. They were the footprints made by stiletto heels.

Unexpected as seeing the limo had been, the vehicle's appearance paled into nothing next to the footprints.

"Hello?" Nathan ventured as he approached the passenger door where the line of footprints emanated from. "Is there anyone in there?"

Nathan bent to peer through the window, and that was his mistake.

The door burst open savagely, smashing him in the face and temple with biting force. Such was the explosion of movement and the power of impact that Nathan was dropped on his ass in the snow with a throbbing head and a numb cheek. He didn't have time to say a word before a flurry of fur exploded from the back of the limo and bore down on him.

A wolf? The image of the paw prints outside the railroad station flashed into his mind like the start of his life flashing before his eyes. Nathan had only a moment to raise his hands before the furred fury raised a tire iron above its head and prepared to smash out his brains.

Two shots rang out from behind Nathan. They smashed into the car, holing the hood and blowing a hole in the windshield.

"Next one's for you, lady."

Syd's voice. Harsh and brittle on the cold air.

Nathan lowered his hands then and saw that the fur he'd thought was a snarling animal was actually part of an expensive coat.

He'd never seen a tire iron wielded in hands that had fingers covered in glittering diamonds the size of pebbles, or nails so red and pointy they could be Dracula's fangs after a good meal, but that was what he saw now. The face above the fur coat and below the tire iron was full and framed by slender arms, showing less than shock at being fired upon, Nathan noted immediately, and more an expression of *affront*. As if the first words out of her mouth would not be "Don't shoot me!" but "How *dare* you!"

The woman's face was immaculately made up, too, though her straight blonde hair was awry from the stiffening breeze and her explosion from the limo. Nathan got the idea that her hair wasn't used to being a millimeter out of place. Now, the woman's mouth was twisted into a snarl, and he could see perfect teeth sitting behind lips that looked like they'd cost a million dollars.

"Put. It. Down!" Syd commanded.

The woman threw the tire iron to the road's verge as if she'd suddenly realized there was something dirty in her hands. Comically, she then looked like she wanted to wipe her palms clean, but wasn't going to do that on her fur coat, so her hands remained in mid-air as if she didn't really know what to do with them.

Nathan got up, dusting the snow from his ass, but he could still feel the wetness seeping through his jeans. "Hey, lady, we only stopped to see if we could help."

"Told you it was a bad idea," said Syd, lowering the Glock she held.

"I thought you were... I thought you..." The woman's voice was cultured and precise, but it seemed as if the whole incident had suddenly overwhelmed her. She slumped back to sit half inside the limo, her stilettoed feet still heel down in the snow, toes pointed to the sky. Her legs and ankles were rich-lady thin, and the skin below the hem of her skirt, even in the cold, appeared tanned and healthy.

This was a woman who obviously had decided the Big Winter was just something that happened to poor people.

"Henderson is dead," she said simply, indicating her driver's seat with a nod of her head. Nathan peeked in over her shoulder. There sat a thick-set black man in a natty chauffeur's uniform, slumped over the steering wheel. For a moment, Nathan could only hope he wasn't dead because of Syd's shooting, but quickly noted that the bullet had passed through the interior of the limo without hitting him when he saw a hole in the back seat instead. Nathan breathed out his relief and turned his eyes back to the woman.

"You were lucky I'm out of bullets," the woman said, lifting a gold-plated Desert Eagle from the footwell beside her with one slender finger. "I've never touched a tire iron in my life. That was a tire iron, wasn't it? I'm assuming it was a tire iron, but one can never be sure with the tools of artisans. They have such quaint names."

The woman was babbling, and Nathan guessed that the cold had done for the driver during the night, and that the woman's fur coat had been the only thing that had saved her. It was a substantial garment, but even so, she wouldn't have lasted another night out on the road in the limo, fur coat or not.

Nathan extended his hand. "Come on. Let's get you in the trailer. Get you something warm to drink."

The woman said her name was Lucy Arneston, and Nathan was surprised when Cyndi replied, "I know."

Lucy looked up with narrow eyes at Nathan's wife, the look of contempt transmitted without any attempt at politeness to the people who had saved her life. "That story in the *National Enquirer* was a farrago of lies. My lawyers were in the process of preparing a rebuttal…"

"I don't read the *National Enquirer*, lady," Cyndi cut her off succinctly. "Just because I don't dress like you, there's no need to jump to conclusions. The wrong ones, I might add. You're the Lucy Arneston who was married to Randal McQuarry, the senator, a couple of actors, and the model guy. The one you said had a shoe size bigger than his IQ."

Lucy arched an eyebrow. "Yes. I was quite proud of that line."

"What are you doing out here? In that interview in *The Atlantic*, you said you got a nosebleed leaving New York."

"Did I say that, too?"

"Yes, you did. Just asked if you would be moving to Washington to be closer to Senator McQuarry."

Lucy smiled at the memory. "I must have been in exceptional form that day."

Cyndi passed Lucy a steaming mug of coffee as Freeson leaned in and poured a generous nip of whiskey into the mug before dumping a slug into his own.

"To answer your question about why I left, then that's simple. New York is dead," Lucy sighed as she sipped the coffee. "Or good as. I was trying to get to an airport, but nothing was flying. My driver said we should keep going west, until we found an airport that was still operational. Then last night we were set upon by thugs. Thugs on those... ski motorbike things..."

Nathan and Cyndi exchanged glances.

"Ski-Doos?" Nathan asked.

Lucy drank down some of her coffee and then nodded. "Henderson outran them as I shot through the window—

thank goodness they didn't know it was my last clip and I was out. I hit two of them... I was a pistol shooting champion in my teens. Daddy always said I had a natural eye for it and he was right. They also didn't know they'd shot out one of my tires. Henderson was a very good driver, and he took the limousine as far as he could. I wrapped myself in the fur and tried to sleep after that. I didn't even realize he was dead until this morning. I think the cold did it. My *God*!"

The sudden change in tack in Lucy's babbling took Nathan by surprise as Lucy grimaced and wiped the back of her hand across her lips, commenting, "That is the most disgusting coffee I have ever tasted in my life!"

Without another word, Lucy put the cup on the floor of the trailer and snatched the bottle from Freeson's hands, thirstily taking a slug of whiskey from the neck. "Passable. Not Johnny Walker, but it will do. Now. Which one of you is in charge here?"

Glances pinballed around the trailer. It wasn't a question that anyone had thought needed an answer before.

"Well, it's my coffee you're hating on, and it's Nate's Airstream, so take your pick," Cyndi said.

Lucy looked from Nathan to his wife and back again. "Ten thousand dollars."

Cyndi stared at her. "I don't understand."

"Alright. Fifteen thousand dollars. For you, lady who reads *The Atlantic*, and you, man who owns a trailer, to take me to the nearest airport with a flight out of this godforsaken, frozen hellhole."

The figure hung in the air for ten seconds before Lucy's demeanor jackknifed again. Without warning, her face crumpled, tears welled in her eyes, and her lips started trembling. "Please… please, I'll give you anything, but please don't leave me here to die."

9

"What the *hell* do you think you're doing?" Nathan bellowed as he jumped down from the trailer to see where Tony and Syd were.

He'd left Lucy's tears behind as she'd turned into a full-on wailing fit of weeping and misery. The whiskey had pierced the dam on her real feelings, a barrier that had allowed only superficial babble to dribble through before. Now, Cyndi and Freeson sat with her and comforted her inside. Nathan had been left feeling like a fifth wheel, so he'd come outside to check on Tony. But when Nathan opened the trailer door, what he saw sent his own emotional barometer shooting up the tube.

The hood, trunk, and all six doors of the limo were open. All he could see of Syd was her backside sticking out one of the back doors as she rummaged inside. Tony stood beside Syd, flicking through a purse, digging into it and pulling out credit cards, pens, and notepads. Beside him in the snow was a small pile of items already liberated from the limo: Bottles of spirits, an attaché case, a chauffeur's cap, and an open carry-on suitcase full of expensive underwear.

Lucy's gold-plated Desert Eagle rested in the dusting of snow on the limo's roof.

Tony spun around at Nathan's voice and his fingers involuntarily snapped open, dropping the purse into the carry-on case.

"I… I…" he began.

Syd pushed herself out of the limo. "Hey, Nathan, don't have a cow. We're just seeing what there is to salvage. No biggie."

Nathan had reached them now and pulled them both by their wrists away from the car. Tony's eyes dropped. "Sorry, Dad, we just…"

Nathan cut him off. "Be quiet. Syd, you do not teach my son to steal!"

"*Salvage*," Syd said with maximum snot.

"It's stealing. And show some respect!"

Syd twisted out of Nathan's grip and took a step back, pointing at the trailer to illustrate her point. "That damn woman was going to brain you with a tire iron!"

"Not to her! There's a dead man still in the driver's seat.

For Pete's sake, how far have you fallen, girl? Is this how your mom would have wanted you to behave?"

Syd's back straightened and she looked Nathan directly in the eye. "My mom would have wanted me to do whatever it took to survive. There might have been food, ammo, anything we could use here. You wanna die just because you'd prefer to have a conscience?"

The words bit deep into Nathan, but he didn't back down.

He'd had to make so many adjustments already, but teaching Tony to steal was not one he was prepared for, even if Syd's logic was sound. Nathan turned his attention to Tony. "You are not to do this again, understood?"

Tony couldn't lift his eyes, but nodded shamefully. "I'm sorry, Dad."

All Syd said was, "You're not my dad."

There was no way they could dig a grave for Cal Henderson, the chauffeur they'd only met in death—the earth was too hard, and the snow turned to ice close to the ground.

"We can't just leave him," Nathan said to the others. "Doesn't feel right." Nathan really didn't feel great about leaving the chauffeur's body to the elements and the animals who would come calling in the days and weeks that followed.

It took some time to persuade Lucy to give them the go-ahead, after they'd removed all her things, to burn the car. "Do you have any idea how much that car cost?" she had whined.

"Well, it cost your driver his life," said Cyndi, and Lucy had shut up at that. The crying had subsided then. Her make-up had run, giving her the panda-look of the wet mascara victim. Syd, at Nathan's insistence, had brought Lucy's make-up bag back to the Airstream. When Lucy had seen the mess her face was in, she'd insisted on being left to fix her make-up, telling them they could "do what the hell they wanted with the damn car."

Nathan covered Henderson with a blanket, tucking it around his stiff body in the driver's seat. He'd wished he could make the dead man look more comfortable, perhaps laying him on the back seat, but his body had become fixed in his driving position by rigor and the cold. So Nathan had simply covered him where he sat after putting his cap onto his lap.

Nathan and Freeson unhooked the Airstream from the Dodge and used the boom to drag the limo to the road's verge. The afternoon was falling to twilight as they splashed fuel over the limo and Nathan set a match to it.

Lucy stayed in the trailer as the limo burned, two hundred yards away down the road. The others and Saber watched from nearer one hundred yards out as the flames lit up the encroaching dark, sending a pall of black smoke high into the air.

Tony squeezed his dad's hand as they looked on. "Vikings," he said quietly.

And Nathan agreed. The limo was as big as a boat, and the way the flames shimmered on the ice and snow gave the impression of a long ship, alight, slipping its mooring and sliding out into the fjord to take Cal Henderson to his final Valhalla.

Nathan picked up Tony and hugged him close.

Because the highway was relatively easy to travel now, Nathan decided they should move on from the burning limo for at least a couple of hours and get some distance between them and the flames which might draw anyone, especially scavengers, to the vicinity.

"You want me to get in there?" Lucy peered into the open door of the crew cab. "But there's… a dog."

Saber stuck her head out and licked Lucy's pointed finger. "Dear God," she said before hiking her leg up and climbing into the cab in the most undignified way possible.

Nathan drove, with Cyndi alongside him, Tony sharing the seat between her legs. Freeson, Syd, and Lucy squeezed into the crew cab, Saber lying obediently in the foot space.

"What a delightful smell," Lucy said as Saber settled down beside her, rubbing her head against the fur coat. "Perhaps she thinks they're related."

Although it was meant as sarcasm, Nathan and the others chuckled companionably. Lucy might not be their idea of a fellow traveler, but her inadvertent comic timing changed the dour atmosphere in the crew cab as they struck on into the darkening night.

They encountered no other traffic for nearly two hours and managed to average between fifteen and twenty miles per hour over that time. Nathen felt nearer to Detroit now than he did to Glens Falls, which was saying something. He knew it wasn't true in terms of miles, but it certainly felt that way in terms of trajectory.

As 7 p.m. came and went, Nathan began looking for a place to pull off the road to park the Airstream for the night. He didn't think it was a good idea to simply settle on the highway so he looked for an off-ramp that might lead into a small town or a retail area. Somewhere out of the way, but with options for a quick getaway if they needed it.

Nothing came up for another few miles, and Nathan was coming around to the idea that they would need to stay on the highway when Free leaned over from the crew cab, pointing off into the distance. They were at the top of a rise in the road, and a wide expanse of landscape filled with snowy forest stretched out below them.

"Look; lights."

There was a dot of yellow below them. Off the highway and too distant to make out any detail. The Dodge continued rumbling towards it.

They leveled out on the road, the landscape swallowed up by the reduced perspective, and the lights disappeared.

"Any ideas?" Nathan asked the others.

"We'll know when we're nearer, I guess," Freeson said, and Nathan heard him checking the Winchester over on his lap. Ever since the attack on Nathan's house, Freeson had tried never to be more than two arm lengths from the weapon, and it was always next to him in the crew cab.

There was a bend in the highway a mile or so ahead, and the encroaching trees, with their cargoes of snow and icicles, had conspired to keep the view consistently unchanged. But Freeson was pointing away from the roadside trees and seemingly into the forest.

Nathan slowed so that he could take his eyes off the road and stop worrying about hitting something unexpected. And yes, there, in the trees, dim lights.

"Is it a fire?" asked Cyndi.

"No," Nathan answered, squinting. "That's electric light."

Nathan picked up speed and, fifteen minutes later, they took an off-ramp and curled around into the forest, to a wide area of tarmac in front of *'Marty's Trucker Love.'*

It was a snow-covered, one-story building with an attached gas station, a forecourt that had been cleared of the latest snow, and windows that burned with all the light of welcome —as if the Big Winter had forgotten to fall here.

The wrecker and Airstream combo hissed onto the wet, almost clear concrete. There were three rigs already parked across one corner of the lot. Their cabs dark, their trailers unlit. Two were designed for transporting goods, the third being a fuel tanker that looked like Christmas to Nathan's eyes.

Cyndi had indicated the day before that they were still doing okay on the fuel reserves packed into the back of the Airstream, but that they'd need to start thinking soon about getting more gas. *Marty's Trucker Love*, intact and burning with warming light, looked like just the kind of place where they might at least find fresh supplies of fuel.

As a group, they hurried across the chill concrete and Nathan pushed the diner's door open. A blast of warmth hit him like he'd opened an over door.

Days on the road had gotten Nathan used to being damn cold almost all the time. The heaters in the crew cab were old and used up a lot of fuel, so they'd kept them to a minimum use. When they were in the Airstream, snuggled in their sleeping bags, they were used to their breath condensing in the air. But *Marty's Trucker Love* apparently made no such attempts to save fuel or power.

The floor was of blue and white checkerboard tiles, the diner booths and seats being red plush vinyl. Pictures of Elvis, Buddy Holly, the Big Bopper, and Little Richard smothered the walls in all their rock 'n' roll glory. A counter at the far end of the diner glittered with chrome and plastic.

A portly woman in an apron, with an ice cream sundae of white hair balanced on her ruddy face, waved them inside from behind the counter. An equally fat septuagenarian in a red checked shirt and 11th Airborne Division cap—a white eleven on a red circle, abutted by white feathery wings—was already appearing from a door next to the counter. Nathan noted that the man had a carving knife in his hand, but held it blade down, and his other hand was extended in welcome.

"Well, hello!" he said, as if the situation was the most normal in the world. "Welcome to Marty's, folks. I'm Marty. Take a seat and Betty will be along in just a shake of a lamb's tail to take your order."

Nathan's party exchanged incredulous glances. All except for Lucy, that was, who took one look at the place and said, loudly, not caring who heard, "Tell me, did we all crash and die on the road without knowing it to wake up in a 1950s hell?" Her tone had been loud, uncaring about who heard, which Nathan had come to recognize as Lucy's default position when it came to conversing with the 'lower orders.'

Nathan didn't know where to look, and he wished the ground would just open up and swallow him whole, but Marty was made of stronger stuff, it seemed. "Ma'am, I don't know about hell, but you look like you've just fallen straight down here from heaven."

Lucy's mouth dropped a little, and she slid into a booth seat next to Freeson, who, Nathan noticed, didn't seem to mind her closeness one damn bit.

Betty arrived from around the counter and flipped an order pad over, licking the end of her pencil. Up close, Nathan could see her face was lined like a road map. She was easily the same age as Marty, if not a little older. Her apron wasn't as clean as it had appeared from afar, and Nathan got the sense that their bonhomie was a little more forced than it might have been in better circumstances.

"How's business?" Cyndi asked, saying out loud what Nathan had been thinking in checking out the lay of the land. No one wanted to look a gift horse in the mouth, but some things really were too good to be true.

"Oh, business isn't as brisk as we'd like, but we get by."

"Must use up a ton of fuel to keep it this warm and lit."

Marty had stood nearby throughout the exchange, and inclined his head to answer. "We got a generator, and enough fuel to see me and the missus out."

Betty put her arm through Marty's and gently turned him around. "Why don't you go out back and get us some steaks from the freezer? These folks look like they haven't had a square meal in days."

Marty pushed the peak of his cap back and kissed Betty on the cheek. "Why don't I just go and do that?" And with that, the man trotted back towards the kitchen door.

"Don't you take no notice of him. We're just as badly off as everyone else since the spring didn't come. My husband likes to tell tall tales."

Nathan detected a little desperation in her voice, maybe from knowing that Marty might have said too much for safety's sake. These were dangerous times to be sitting on a good supply of fuel oil or gas.

Nathan reached out and squeezed Betty's hand. "It's okay, Betty. We'll pay for whatever we need now that you can spare. What's yours is yours."

Betty smiled in relief. "Tell you what, why don't I just go get you folks some coffee, and you can decide among yourselves how you'll be wanting your steaks? I'll also mash up some potatoes and fix you a pepper gravy the likes of which you will never have tasted!"

She was glossing and sidestepping, but Nathan decided not to press her on it—she was doing the best she could.

"Hey, honey." Marty appeared behind the counter, lifting up his cap and scratching his bald head beneath it. "I know you wanted me to get something, but I can't for the life of me remember what it was."

Betty's shoulders drooped as she walked towards him, and Nathan saw—in both her frame and in Marty's confused face —the layer of distress that underlined their situation just below the surface. They were both old and trying to make the best of it in the Big Winter. But here it was obvious the threats to Betty and Marty were not just the weather. Betty's husband seemed to be losing his faculties.

Nathan had been through the same process with his own father, who'd faded away with encroaching senility until he'd not been the man he'd once been; instead, he'd become forgetful, frustrated, quick to anger. In the end, the cancer that finally took him had almost been a blessing in the face of his dementia.

And as the evening progressed and the steaks were delivered and consumed, it became clear that Marty's senility was more advanced than Nathan had initially assumed. He would ask Betty or Nathan the same question three or four times and would call Nathan *Billy*. His opening gambits had been just that, gambits. He'd probably said that same stuff a million times, and it was just brain and muscle memory that got him through. Now, when a conversation was freestyle, he found it difficult to keep up.

When Marty collected the plates up to take them out back for washing, Nathan took Betty aside and commented, "I guess it can't be easy for you, with Marty going like he is."

Betty smiled. "Oh, he's just fine; don't you worry yourself."

Nathan touched her shoulder, shaking his head. "My dad went the same. I guess he's the reason you've not left, yeah? He needs the familiar around him. He can cope with that. Out on the road... different matter."

Betty nodded, deflating a little and sinking into the booth seat across from Nathan and Cyndi. Syd and Tony were on the other side of the diner now, playing salt cellar chess. Freeson sat in another booth drinking from Betty's store of bourbon with Lucy, hanging on her every word as she spoke about her four marriages, her money, and her houses.

Nathan hadn't seen Freeson so willing to just sit and listen for an age, but he'd been one of those guys, before his accident, who'd fill any space he could with a line or a joke. Now, his big cow eyes were fixed on Lucy in a way Nathan figured he'd need a crow bar to pry him away from.

So Nathan and Cyndi sat with Betty while the others talked and Marty washed up. He came back three times to ask if Betty still wanted the steaks, and three times more she sent him back to do the washing up. Over the conversation, it just became clearer that the warmth and light of *Marty's Trucker Love* was a real-world representation of the love Betty obviously felt for Marty.

"If I changed anything, left the lights off at night or didn't run the heaters the way he liked them, then all hell would break loose. If we *left*, all hell would break loose. Best I can do is wait here until it all runs out and hope that the cold takes us quick."

There really wasn't anything to say to that. Betty had it all worked out, and she added, "I have to do the best by Marty. He's always done the best by me."

"Hey, you folks! Welcome to *Marty's Trucker Love*. Who wants my wife to rustle them up some dinner?"

Nathan and Cyndi smiled towards Marty, and a tear wound a lonely path down Betty's cheek.

When it came to settling up, Lucy, a little the worse for bourbon, reached into her purse and brought out her credit cards.

At the cash register, Betty smiled, but shook her head. "That's a mighty fine set of credit cards you've got there, my dear, but we're not able to process cards at this time."

"But I don't use cash. No one uses cash anymore! Well, not anyone who *matters*, that is…"

Nathan came up to the register, reaching into his back pocket and pulling out his wallet. He pulled out a number of twenties.

"Again, Nathan, that's a nice lot of cash you have there, but it's no good to us. Our supplier, when he comes to deliver food supplies, will only deal in gold or jewelry." Betty's eyes alighted on Lucy's wrist hopefully, acknowledging the white-gold, diamond-encrusted bracelet that hung there. "Now, that —*that* I can take in exchange for tonight's food, and all the fuel you may need to get you on the road again. But credit and cash, they're no longer any good to us now…"

Nathan didn't know if it was genuine indignation or a bourbon fueled meltdown, but, in a second, Lucy exploded towards Betty and he and Freeson had to grab at Lucy's arms and drag her away from the counter. "You thieving bitch! How dare you! How *dare* you!"

Lucy was kicking out, her teeth bared, eyes burning. "Let go of me! Let go!"

Marty's face crumpled. The old man was retreating, suddenly scared by the noise, tears welling in his eyes so that the precariousness of his psychological health was revealed in all its rawness by Lucy's anger.

Freeson bent to Lucy's ear and whispered something Nathan couldn't hear. In response, she went limp and stopped struggling almost immediately. She shook herself free of Nathan's hand and hugged Freeson close.

Whatever Freeson and Lucy had been talking about over the bourbon had definitely had some impact, because Lucy put an arm around his waist, her head on his shoulder, and let Freeson walk her slowly back to the booth where they'd been sitting.

Freeson put his forehead against Lucy's and they continued whispering while Nathan turned to Betty, who was now comforting her sobbing husband.

"I'm sorry," was the best Nathan had. Betty nodded, her face one of resignation. It was the face of someone who was tired of being strong for both she and her spouse.

"It's the supplier. Gold or jewels. Nothing else. I wasn't trying to cheat you. I promise."

Nathan wished the counter wasn't between them so that he could at least reach out and touch the woman, offering the solace of human comfort if nothing else.

Betty took Marty back into the kitchen, where she sat him on a chair near an ancient cassette player and hit the *play* button. Elvis' "Jailhouse Rock" came on and, within a moment, Marty's face was cleared, his tears stopped and his toe tapping along to the music.

By the time Betty reached the counter, Freeson had returned from the booth with Lucy's bracelet and was ready to hand it over. Lucy had her head in her hands back in the booth, but as Freeson passed the bracelet to Betty, Lucy raised her head to them and mouthed, "I'm sorry."

10

Betty let them stay the night in the diner.

She kept it warm and cozy for the party, bringing blankets and pillows from their apartment above the diner. The booths' benches were wide enough for them to lay down comfortably. Cyndi and Nathan shared one booth, and Syd, Tony, and Saber another. Freeson and Lucy shared not only the same booth, but the same bench. It seemed her head hadn't moved from his shoulder the entire night. At about 3 a.m., when Nathan came out of his booth for a call of nature, he saw that Lucy was asleep with her head in Freeson's lap, covered in a blanket, and the mechanic's hand was on her shoulder, his chin on his chest, snoring gently. They looked like they'd known each other for a thousand years.

Morning came with them being awakened by Betty

moving around in the kitchen, making eggs and bacon for everyone human, and sausages for Saber—which, if the dog's reaction was anything to go by, made Betty her friend for life.

But it wasn't the cooking that caught Nathan's attention with a shocking intensity. It was a TV to the side of the range that Betty had turned on. It was playing reruns of *I Love Lucy*, and Nathan watched incredulously as the episode ended and a "News Flash" came up, warning of another ice storm moving in from the north in the next few hours.

Nathan leapt towards the counter. "Betty, that's live? Not your VCR?"

Betty looked at him as if he was a child who'd never seen the Magic Moving Pictures before. "Yes. We got cable."

"You got Wi-Fi?" he demanded next.

"Yes. Of course. We might be old, but we're not ancient. I'm quite the silver surfer, doncha know? Why?"

But Nathan had already begun heading towards the Airstream.

He returned in under two minutes with Cyndi's laptop. They fired it up, asked Betty for the password to the Wi-Fi— which she told them with a definite twinkle was "LoveTruck-27"—and they logged in.

Stryker had replied to Nathan's email, and his message was chatty and warm, offering Stryker's Skype handle along with his note.

Cyndi fired up the program, rang Stryker, and turned the laptop screen with its built-in webcam towards Nathan. There was an ecstasy of finger drumming while they waited, and then Stryker appeared.

He hadn't changed that much since Nathan had last seen him in the flesh. Thinner perhaps, a little older and with a little less hair at the temples, but still blond, and Nordic with the kind of face both women and men would say was on the pretty side of manly if they buttered their bread on that side. In the laptop's screen, Stryker was bare-chested and looked like he'd just gotten out of a shower. Behind him, in bright sunlight streaming through a high window, were massive towers of hydroponic trays, fat green leaves trailing healthily over the sides.

"Hey, man! Good to see you! Although, you look terrible."

"Thanks," Nathan said, grinning. "You look like someone I still want to punch."

They laughed like friends who'd only seen each other in a bar the night before, the way the kinds of friends could when they slipped back into each other's worlds. As if time had stood still. And when the laughs passed, Nathan quickly caught Stryker up with the situation.

"I knew things were bad outside the city, but I didn't realize it was that bad."

"It's taken us nearly two weeks to travel a hundred and fifty miles. If the weather reports are accurate, there's another ice storm coming in, too. Who knows what that's gonna do to our progress."

"Dude, you get your ass here and your worries will be *over*."

Cyndi's hand squeezed Nathan's shoulder. "You make it sound perfect, Stry. Nothing is perfect. Not anymore."

"No, I admit it's not perfect."

Ah, now, here it comes.

"Man, It's *better* than perfect."

Typical Stryker, Nathan thought as his high school friend reached out of the shot, picked up a towel, and started to dry his hair vigorously.

"You're what, four hundred miles away? Say you can get here in another month or so. Maybe quicker if the weather turns. I'll have you a house sorted by then, a patch of land to grow your own food under glass, school for Tony…"

Cyndi reached over, catching his attention with her wave. "How are the hospitals, Stry?"

Without hesitation, Stryker answered, "Perfect, honey. The hospitals are probably the best in the country. Why? Is somebody ill… or does Nathan need his balls re-attached again?"

Cyndi shook her head and looked down at her belly. "Quite the opposite, Stryker; quite the opposite."

Stryker spent the next few minutes extolling the virtues of Detroit, its public services, its thriving economy based on barter and donated work hours. How food was growing in hydroponic centers like new-hanging gardens of Babylon. And how, magnificently, it was the only place in the north of the country that had been prepared for worsening winters.

Because of the work folks had done over the last decade to combat the effects of global warming, it was better placed than any other city in the U.S. to ride out the Big Winter and the crazy change in the sky. "It's the jewel in the crown of America, dude. The *jewel* in the *crown*."

"You don't work for the Detroit Tourist Authority, by any chance, do you?" Nathan asked with joshing sarcasm.

Stryker pulled on a hideous Hawaiian shirt. "Dude, if they didn't already have one, I'd be the first to set it up!" Stryker finished with a smile so wide it threatened to meet around the back of his head.

"You're really going to head northwest?"

Betty was collecting up the blankets and pillows from the booths and had overheard some of the conversation with Stryker before the cable internet went into one of its intermittent phases and they lost the connection.

"I think so, yes." Nathan couldn't help feeling a niggle of anxiety about Stryker's full-on hard sell for Detroit, but Cyndi's mind had been made up already, even before she'd heard about the schools and hospitals.

"Everyone who's stopped here in the last month has been heading south," Betty continued, picking up the folded blankets in her plump arms.

Marty was cleaning surfaces in the kitchen that he'd

already cleaned three times before. Betty followed Nathan's gaze. "He's happy enough."

"You don't want to head south?" he asked gently.

Betty shook her head. "How would I cope with Marty? He knows this place. It's... what do they call it... imprinted? Maybe if the Big Winter had come two years ago, before... well, before Marty's difficulties begun. Maybe then..."

Betty looked into Nathan's eyes, and he could tell she was near enough reading his mind. "I guess you were imprinted, too, on your place."

He nodded.

"Thing is, Nathan, you've got the chance to get out and make a difference to the lives of your family. You should take it. I just don't know if northwest is the *right* direction. If Detroit is so damn amazing, why have we been getting so many people going south?"

That hadn't occurred to Nathan at all. Could it simply be put down to most people not knowing Detroit was doing well? Or could it be that only getting his facts from one source wasn't the best way of going about things?

The shifting sands of his resolve moved a little beneath him, her question coupled with the *too good to be trueness* of Stryker's hard-sell on Detroit setting off alarms in his head. But could he risk not taking Cyndi, in her state, to Detroit? It was certainly the nearest settlement to them that would afford, on Stryker's word, real medical care for his wife.

Again, Nathan felt pulled in two directions that he didn't

like. He went outside to the parking lot to get some air and saw Freeson lifting the hood of a turquoise 1990 80-Series Turbo Diesel Toyota Land Cruiser that was parked between the trucks. It hadn't been visible when they'd rolled in. Freeson was looking it over and Nathan could already see that Lucy sat inside the vehicle, looking at her reflection in the rearview mirror and straightening her hair with her fingers. While Nathan had been on the computer talking to Stryker, they'd been busy looking for other transport.

"Cutting out on us?" Nathan asked as he approached.

Freeson uncurled from where he'd been staring into the engine. "Of course not! This is Marty's old truck. He doesn't need it anymore, according to Betty. Figured we could do with a back-up in case anything happened to the Dodge. More storage for supplies and diesel. Makes sense."

"And I could buy six of these new for what I gave them with the bracelet." Lucy had wound down the window and stuck her oar into the conversation. "I believe I can take what-ever I want."

Nathan thought Lucy might be the kind of person who'd believe that in any situation, but bit back the retort.

Free closed the hood of the Toyota with a tinny thump that echoed across the parking lot. "But if you think it's a bad idea, compadre, just say the word."

"Oh, so this *isn't* a democracy," Lucy said tartly as she began re-applying her lipstick around her perfect mouth.

Freeson looked a little uncomfortably in Lucy's direction,

but like Nathan, he didn't rebuke her rudeness. Nathan could see that, in a short time, because of this crisis throwing them together, he and Lucy were already stuck to each other. Whether it was mutual respect, love at first sight, or one using the other to fill a physical or emotional hole, the jury was still out. But Nathan could see he was dealing with a single unit now, not a pair of individuals.

Nathan also knew that anything he did to send this unit away from his family would lessen his family's own chances of survival. Freeson and Lucy would probably be a better prospect for Syd and Saber, too. Maybe he needed to think about the needs of the whole group equally. Both Lucy and Syd had contributed much to the overall progress of the company. *Family First* might mean putting Nathan's own concerns on hold.

Freeson asked, "So, is that an okay, boss?"

Lucy's lips turned down at Freeson's use of the word 'boss'—but she'd obviously decided not to stir the pot anymore.

"Yes." Nathan held up his palms, offering "It's a sound idea to have a back-up truck as long as there's enough diesel for our needs."

"Only four hundred miles to Detroit," Freeson said, kicking the tires on the Toyota.

And that was that.

The cable didn't come back on before the ice storm hit.

And with the weather, the diner shook as if was made of cardboard, but the shuttered windows held, and the generator giving all the power and heat kept the worst of the storm at bay.

They'd managed to fill all their diesel cans from the tanker, though, and gotten them back to the Airstream before the storm came. Betty had found them a bunch of other cans out back to put in the back of the Toyota, too, even if Lucy had complained bitterly about having to travel to within just a few feet of that "terrible smell of hydrocarbons." Freeson had ended up covering the jerry cans with plastic sheeting and hanging up a hundred air freshener strips he'd found in the gas station store to alleviate the stench of fuel.

They finished getting their supplies organized just an hour before the storm hit. This meant that, as soon as it passed, Nathan figured they'd be able to hit the road quickly enough. He hadn't figured on the storm lasting for two whole days.

For those two days, the diner was blown, battered, and shaken. Having the shutters down at the front of the diner during the onslaught affected Marty the most. On and off, he'd become morose or agitated. When that happened, Betty would take him in back and sit him next to the cassette player—and as time went on, they all became experts in the lyrics of Elvis songs. Even Syd, who had never heard of Elvis before.

"Kinda cool," she said of him as the first evening wore on

and Marty's tape cycled through for the third time, "but he still sounds like history."

Nathan slid in beside her in the booth. "You ready to talk?"

"Rather listen to Elvis."

Tony was on the other side of the diner now, cuddled up with Saber. Cyndi had gone out back to help out Betty, and Freeson was sitting quietly with Lucy, attending to Betty's bourbon—happily, with less gusto than the night before. Lucy's hair was tied back and she wore one of Freeson's sweatshirts. Nathan hadn't seen the fur coat all day, apparent security blanket that it was. Their unit. Growing stronger.

They were smiling at each other, too. Freeson said something, and Lucy threw her head back in a full and throaty laugh. There was an edge of salaciousness to it that Nathan recognized as a reaction to one of Freeson's more risqué stories. The sort of stories Freeson hadn't told Nathan since before the accident. Lucy might be a piece of work, but she was already showing that, in whatever capacity their relationship was developing, she was good for Freeson.

Syd broke into his thoughts. "I said, 'I'd rather listen to Elvis.' Do you usually glaze over when someone answers your questions? It doesn't make me trust you more, ya know. In fact, it has the opposite effect."

Nathan snapped his head back in Syd's attention. "Sorry."

"She's trouble, ya know," the girl added.

"Lucy being any more trouble than you?"

Syd grinned at the joke, but answered, "I've seen her kind

before. She's a user. You want to make sure she doesn't break your friend's heart. Because as soon as something better for her comes along, she's going to grab what's new and shiny with both hands."

Impressed by the measure of Syd's maturity, Nathan thought it sounded again like she was speaking from bitter experience. "Who did that to you?" he pressed.

Syd's eyes flashed. Her lips set, and Nathan thought he was in for another example of her clamming up, but eventually her eyes and mouth softened. "Maybe I wasn't entirely on the level with you."

Nathan didn't say what was in his head—*Ya think?* But Syd caught the gist of it.

"Every time I've let someone in since my dad left, I've been damaged. Yeah, I know, that sounds dramatic, but, Nate —seriously, *every* time. My mom'd get a new man, I'd give him the benefit of the doubt, and he'd either be a waster, using us for a place to crash, or beat on Mom or me or both, or… well, hell, I don't need to tell you the other things he did with me. And then there was Danny," she went on before Nathan could process or react to what she'd said. "I thought Danny would help me and Mom—she had a habit, and he had a gang, and access to pills, and he *liked* me. Said he *loved* me… and, again, he was just another user. *User loser.* So, no, I don't open up easy. Not anymore."

Nathan met her eyes evenly, holding them. "Well, you just did."

Syd blinked, and blinked again. "Guess I did."

"Should I be flattered?"

"Maybe. But just make sure my trust isn't beaten up and used like usual. I've gotten good with a gun," she added pointedly.

Nathan snorted. "Yes, you have."

It was the most words he'd heard coming out of Syd's mouth in one conversation, outside of with Tony and Saber, and he couldn't help being surprised by the level of detail she'd given him. Here was a child forced into becoming a woman far too early. The shrapnel from that process, an explosion of emotions that were still spinning up from ground zero. The paternalistic bloom grew in him again, and he wanted nothing more than to take her in his arms, like he would have Tony, and squeeze the hurt away. But he was sure she wasn't ready for that kind of response. Her face alone told him that maybe she thought she'd gone too far.

"It's okay," he told her. "I won't tell anyone. Not until you're ready."

Syd smiled, leaned across the narrow table, and kissed Nathan's cheek. "No funny ideas, okay? That's just for being a stand-up guy. They're a premium commodity these days."

And so the storm blew itself out on the second night, and the day blossomed cold and gray. The ice storm had left the vehicles in the lot bearded with snow and icicles, which Tony had a great time going around breaking off and throwing like sticks for Saber to retrieve.

Cyndi had negotiated for some more food supplies with Betty—getting a good selection of frozen meats, which she worked with Syd to stow in a large plastic freezer box, which she'd also acquired from *Marty's Trucker Love*—on the premise that keeping the meat on the exposed back of the wrecker would keep the meat fresh and frozen. The air temperature was very rarely rising above freezing, after all, even in direct sunlight.

Once the Dodge, Airstream, and Toyota were ready to head off, Betty and Marty came out, wrapped in parkas with their hoods up and scarves across their faces. "Goodbye and good luck," Betty said as she began a round of hugs that even included Lucy. Betty squeezed Nathan so hard he thought his eyes would pop, and told him, "You're a good man, Nathan. It's been a pleasure to have you here."

"You sure you won't change your mind and come with us? There's plenty of room now we have the Land Cruiser."

"Leave?" Marty said with some disdain. "Leave my business and my people? Don't be a fool, boy. We're on course for our best winter ever, and as soon as summer comes, we'll be set up for life!"

Betty hooked her arm through Marty's. "That's right; we'll be set up for life."

She smiled at Nathan, and both of them waved the convoy off to load up.

Freeson led the wrecker and Airstream combo back onto the ramp and the highway.

Cyndi drove the Dodge and Nathan craned his neck back as much as he could. Betty and Marty stayed there waving until he could see them no longer—the trees lining the highway, heavy with their new layers of snow and ice, blocking the view.

"You liked them, didn't you?"

Nathan tuned his head back to face the road, watching the Land Cruiser skittering a little as Freeson got to grips with an unfamiliar car on the icy, snowbound road ahead of them.

"Yes. How could I not? Good people."

"Marty reminded you of your dad."

He paused, acknowledging the point. "Yeah. That forgetfulness and optimism. That was him all over. He would have stayed in their position, too. It would have been the best option."

Inside Nathan, all the anxieties of not knowing if he was doing the right thing swirled below his breastbone. Nathan knew he had to let those feeling go, though. The decision to go to Detroit had been made. He was in a minority of one in having any doubts at all, it seemed, and he really didn't need to be transmitting his worries to all of the others.

It would be okay.

Family First.

He glanced back through the window, trying to get one last look at the truck stop and its occupants.

Nathan felt he couldn't see the woods for the trees because

of the woods and the trees. Life imitating his concerns perfectly.

The warmth of the cab, and the smoothness of this section of the highway, soon caught up with Nathan, and he felt himself drifting on the cusp of sleep, the gentle rocking of the Dodge carrying him away on the lullaby of engine noise.

He only opened his eyes when Cyndi started screaming.

11

W here the Land Cruiser had been on the road ahead, was a rising billow of fresh snow, as if something had exploded beneath the tarmac and sent up gusts of ice crystals. Nathan woke in a panic as Cyndi hit the brakes hard, the wheels of the Dodge slithering so that the truck partially jackknifed, bringing Nathan's side window to face forward. His hands were dug into the dash and his eyes were blinking in the harsh light.

Syd and Tony's hands had thumped on the back of the driver and passenger seats in an effort to steady themselves, and Saber barked furiously until the Dodge slew to a halt.

The wrecker's hood and roof rattled as lumps of snow and ice fell from the plume of smoky white, landing on the Dodge like fat rain.

"What? What happened?" Syd leaned forward from the crew cab as Saber barked beside her.

Nathan shook his head. "I don't know. Where the hell is the Cruiser?"

As the falling icy debris abated, and the air in front of them began to clear, first the tail lights, and then the back wheels and the rear window of the Land Cruiser became visible.

A hole had opened up in the road ahead of it—perhaps it had been covered in snow, filled in by the ice storm. Or it had been set as a trap to catch vehicles in just this fashion.

"Get the guns," Cyndi said, her voice cracking. "I see one Ski-Doo and I'm going to end them. *Whoever* they are."

Nathan pulled a Glock from under his seat in the crew cab. It felt thick and unfamiliar in his hand, but he knew Cyndi was right. Until they knew this wasn't a trap, they'd need to be on guard.

Cyndi and Syd took AR-15s, and Nathan pushed Tony back into the cab as he tried to follow him outside. "No. Stay there with Saber. Keep your head down until I tell you it's clear, okay?"

Tony nodded and retreated into the shadow of the crew cab and the large dog followed him back, tail flat between her legs.

Outside, it was harshly cold again. The two days in Marty's truck stop had made Nathan soft, unaccustomed all over again to the cold. He'd even been sitting in the truck without his padded North Face jacket, and he instantly regretted it.

He walked towards the Toyota.

It was at an angle of forty-five degrees to the road, stuck partially into a hole that looked to be seven feet deep and fifteen feet wide. The Land Cruiser engine had stalled, the left-over heat from the pistons ticking through the metal. Nathan listened intently for any sounds that could possibly be those of an approaching Ski-Doo, but all around them was the dull, dampened sound of the Big Winter. Nothing more.

As Nathan reached the lip of the hole, it became clear how precarious Freeson and Lucy's predicament was.

They hadn't fallen into a hole in the road.

It's a hole in a bridge.

The bottom half of the road had fallen away entirely. Two hundred feet below, they could see a frozen creek surrounded by scrubby brush. Leaning forward, Nathan could see past the hull of the Toyota all the way down.

Nathan looked back the way they'd come. Since he'd been asleep, he hadn't noticed that the trees had run out and they'd begun crossing a wide, deeply cut ravine. The bridge was a good two hundred yards from end to end, and he guessed that if they could see the surface of the road, it would have cracked to blazes by the harshness of the Big Winter. This was another thing to add to the itinerary of risks to make them all wary. The U.S. road system had been a piece of work before the Big Winter, especially on the roads away from the highways. Now, concrete, tarmac, and ironwork was permafrosted to hell. Months and months of growing ice could tear concrete like this apart. There were no road gangs out fixing things, and so infrastructure was suffering big-time. Maybe within a year or so, most of the bridges would be out or too dangerous to cross.

Of course, the other even more chilling explanation was that the bridge had been sabotaged deliberately to catch travelers, like flies caught in a web of iron and concrete.

Jeez.

It suddenly occurred to Nathan that they needed to get the wrecker back from this hole—now. What if the entire bridge was unstable?

"Cyndi, get back in the Dodge; turn it around and take it off the bridge. Now. The whole lot could go any second."

Cyndi didn't need to be told twice. She backed off and jumped back into the cab, turning the wrecker to complete the circle the jackknife had started and running the Dodge and Airstream combo back the fifty or so yards up the road, to get it off the bridge.

The Land Cruiser's back tires were still on the surface of the road, but the front tires were balanced on a rusted drainage pipe and a square of concrete. That levitating chunk of sand, gravel, and cement was still partially attached to the far side of the hole by its internal grid of iron reinforcements. And below that, the huge empty space of air went all the way down to the frozen creek.

Then another problem arose—one that Nathan should have

predicted. From inside the Land Cruiser came a raised, shrieking voice and a thumping on glass. The passenger side door opened next, and Lucy all but launched herself into space, only stopping at the last moment as she saw the drop beneath her.

"Get back in the car, Lucy," Nathan called down to her.

"Don't just stand there, you fool! Help us!"

"We're going to try, but you really need to stop rocking the truck. Seriously. I don't know how long whatever's holding it up will last, and you moving around and panicking isn't going to help. Okay?"

There was silence, and Nathan waited to hear Free's voice reasoning with her, but it didn't come. He pushed down worry for his friend, and asked instead, "Okay?"

"Yes. Yes. Okay. I'll sit still. Should I shut the door?"

"Gently, and wind the window down so I can talk to you."

"I've hurt my legs on the dash," she added belatedly.

Nathan ran his hand through his hair. "Let's concentrate on one thing at a time, yes? Close the door."

Lucy took a few seconds to build up the courage to reach back out for the door handle and pull the door closed with a gentle snick of the lock. In that time, Cyndi had walked back from the Dodge.

"The signs were down in the snow and wind. That's why I didn't realize we were approaching the bridge. Dammit. Road blind. Only thinking of the miles covered and not the present danger. Stupid. Sorry, Nate. I drove on without thinking and, *wham*, Free was in the hole. We'll have to go back to being ultra-careful, I guess. Check bridges out first next time."

If there is a next time, Nathan thought.

The window on the passenger door of the Land Cruiser rolled down.

"Okay, Lucy, how's Free?"

"How should I know?"

"Just take a look at him." Nathan tried to keep the frustration out of his voice. Maybe Syd was on the money about Lucy. Just a user, only concerned for herself. But to save Freeson, he was going to have to save Lucy at the same time. Nathan wasn't going to be able to bring the Dodge any nearer to pull it out with the winch, not safely, and there was nowhere near enough cable on the wrecker to reach the Land Cruiser from where the bridge started seventy yards back.

"He's hit his head, I think. On the windshield. He's unconscious."

"Is he breathing?"

"I'll check."

What a great person to have in an emergency.

"Yes, he is. Like he's asleep."

"Okay, Lucy, we're going to get you both out. I just need you to stay calm and relaxed."

"I'm two hundred feet above a ravine. That's not a position that's easy to relax in."

"I know. But try. You said you'd hit your legs—are they okay?"

"I hit my knees on the dash, bruised but not broken. I'll live."

"That's great."

"If I don't fall down this hole, that is."

"Okay, Lucy, just hang tight."

"Like I have a choice."

Nathan motioned Cyndi and Syd away from the hole, looking back up the road to where the Dodge and the Airstream were.

"We need cable, and we need it fast. How far are we from Marty's?"

"Three hours," Cyndi answered quietly.

Nathan stared at her for a moment. "You let me sleep that long?"

"You looked like you needed it. The road was fine. … Well, fine until now."

Syd pointed upward. "What about those?"

Nathan and Cyndi looked.

Syd was pointing at the utility poles running the length of the road.

The utility poles were made of some kind of treated pine and were topped by cross braces carrying a number of different

lines. Electrical power, coaxial for cable TV, and some telephone lines for those people who hadn't made the switch to
digital cable. Nathan felt a twinge of regret for what he was
about to do, knowing he might be taking away Marty and
Betty's TV and internet. Their power came from a generator,
but their links to the outside world were all transmitted
through distribution networks of lines and poles just like these.

Still, there wasn't any choice. Nathan kicked the Dodge
engine into life, pushed the shift into first gear, and rumbled
forward.

The pole he'd linked to the winch on the back of the
Dodge with three lumber chains, normally carried for moving
fallen trees as needed, started to bend from its moorings in the
ground, and then it began to lean forward at a crazy angle.

Nathan jumped down from the truck. Then he, Cyndi, and
Syd ran to the stricken pole, pushing at it so that it would shift
and fall away from the Dodge.

The pole needed a hefty amount of force to be toppled, but
once it started to fall, nothing was going to stop it. It resisted
momentarily as the cables Nathan had been trying to free held
it against gravity, but then it crashed into the snow, throwing
up a spume of white crystals.

The pole had fallen without sparks or a sizzle of released
power, but Nathan was taking no chances. Using his voltmeter,
he made sure all the cables were dead and then drove the
Dodge on to the next pole and repeated the procedure.

While Cyndi turned the Dodge around and backed it as

near to the bridge as they dared, Nathan cut the cables free, tied two thirty-yard lengths together to form enough cable to reach the Toyota, and did the same with the six other lengths of cable. The reef knots would hold, and used as one, there should be enough breaking strain to pull the Land Cruiser up out of the hole.

If it didn't fall into the ravine first.

Nathan was so cold now, he was already having trouble thinking straight. "Let me," said Cyndi as she watched his blue fingers fumbling with the knots. "Go and get your coat. Now."

Nathan did as he was told and, when he got back from the Dodge, he saw that the cables were ready to have logging chains attached to both ends and then be fed towards the Land Cruiser.

Cyndi attached the line to the winch, and Syd and Nathan took the lines to the hole on the bridge. The Land Cruiser's window was still open and Lucy was looking backward at them, craning her neck to see them. "Where have you been? We're going to fall! The damn truck has already shifted twice!"

Nathan could immediately see what she meant. The warmth of the coat was helping his mind unfog, and even as he looked into the hole, the wet front tire of the Land Cruiser that had once been resting on the drainage pipe slipped to one side. The weight of the truck had pressed down on the pipe and started to bend it across the middle. There was an ancient joint in the pipes, just below the tire, and as Nathan watched, he could see it was separating—millimeter by millimeter.

"Hang on down there—we're going to pull you out now!"

The chain was threaded around the Land Cruiser's tow bar, five lines of cable ready to take the strain when Nathan raised his hands to signal to Cyndi.

Even at this distance, the whine of the winch was clear to hear. The cables stretched taut and began to apply backward force to the Toyota, which shifted just as the drainage pipe broke away and fell into the abyss. There was no going back now; if the cables failed, the Toyota would fall.

The base of the Land Cruiser scraped agonizingly over the ruined blacktop, but Nathan knew the exhaust and transmission should be tough enough to take it. The Land Cruiser was a resilient, cross-country 4x4 vehicle, with a pedigree for near indestructibility. However, he feared the edge of the hole might not be as strong as the bottom of the Land Cruiser, and that might be the undoing of them.

The friable surface of the road was chewed away as the Toyota ground its metal guts into the edge of the hole. The crack of breaking concrete suddenly sounded louder than the grinding of the underfloor of the truck.

For a heart-stopping second, Nathan thought the road beneath all of them would drop away and send them to their doom, and Syd's hurried steps backward suggested she feared the same.

But the Dodge and its winch were doing what they did

best. In less than a minute more, the Toyota had enough of its back end over the lip of the hole for Nathan and Syd to leap forward, grab the bumper, and help seesaw the Land Cruiser back onto the horizontal plane of the bridge.

"Yes!" Syd shouted as the Toyota scraped back from the edge of oblivion.

The front tires bit into the edge of the hole, caught, and rolled the vehicle back up onto the road.

Lucy opened the door and Nathan slammed it shut. "Wait. We gotta get you off the bridge!"

Lucy nodded and Nathan now moved to the front end of the Land Cruiser as Cyndi continued winching, and began pushing the car off the bridge.

As they reached the end of the bridge and the start of the road, Nathan was breathing hard, cold and trembling with adrenaline. He didn't care. He wanted to get to Free's side of the Land Cruiser.

But before he could open the truck door, three things happened at once.

Lucy threw herself from the car almost as quickly as she'd done so from the limo, desperate for the safety of terra firma, one of the strained utility cables closest to Syd finally frayed and snapped, lashing her against the cheek and sending her spinning and bloody into the snow, and five people in ski gear walked down from the treeline near the Dodge—their faces covered in balaclavas, AR-15s carried in their gloved hands.

Blood spewed through Syd's fingers and into the snow. The gash to her cheek was deep and ragged—an inch higher and the cable would have taken her eye. An inch lower, she'd have had her very own razorblade of a smile.

Lucy took one look at the advancing skiers and raised her hands. "Don't shoot me! I'm rich!"

Which, in any other circumstances, would have sounded funny, but Nathan wasn't in the mood for laughing. Instead, he was moving around to the driver's side door of the Cruiser.

The lead skier, a man with a gruff, commanding voice, shouted in their direction, "Stay where you are!"

"Damn you!" Nathan yelled back, spitting the words out like hot nails. "My buddy is unconscious in the car. He may have swallowed his tongue, so I want to check on him. Shoot me if you like, but I'm not stopping."

Nathan's crunching footsteps were the only sound being made. Even Syd, bleeding through her fingers as she was, wasn't making a sound.

Nathan tore the Toyota door open and reached inside to check on Freeson. The mechanic had the mother of all bruises darkening his forehead, and he'd bitten through his bottom lip so that blood smeared his chin from the wound. But he was breathing, his color was good, and as a hand raised and waved, he managed to whisper, "Shut the door, man. It's freezing."

Nathan reached in, reclined Freeson's seat, and checked that his airway was fully clear, and that there was no bruising to his throat that could swell up and take them by surprise.

When Nathan turned around again, Syd had gotten up and was pressing a scarf to her cheek; it had been handed to her by one of the skiers. The lead guy, as he took off his ski mask, was revealed to be an African American in a camouflage army surplus jacket, and carrying a few more pounds than he needed to. He rested his AR-15 against the Toyota and held out his hand for Nathan to shake.

"Steven Reynolds."

Nathan eyed the hand, and then took it. "Nathan Tolley."

Reynolds' grip was firm and meaty. Nathan wouldn't have wanted to meet him in a dark alley, even though the other man probably had twenty years on him. "Sorry I yelled," Reynolds told him. "Couldn't be too sure you weren't going to the truck for a gun. Can't be too careful these days."

"Ten-four on that," Nathan replied. The skiers were all taking off their balaclavas now. And they were of similar linage to Reynolds, he saw, if not all related. There were three women and two men among them, all in winter camouflage of various hues. But their faces and haircuts didn't suggest a military bearing. The women appeared to be of similar age to Steven, and the men were more Nathan's age or younger, though it was hard to tell with how wrapped up in their winter clothing they were. They all carried packs and had thumped through the snow on ski-boots.

If they hadn't been in the middle of the winter apocalypse, it could have a been a scene from Aspen, with skiers making their way back to their chalets before changing into more suitable clothes for a spot of après-ski.

"Can I put my hands down?" Lucy asked plaintively.

"Yes," said Reynolds and Nathan together.

As it turned out, the Reynolds were a family, but made up of sisters, uncles, cousins, nephews, and nieces rather than your typical nuclear family. One of the women, Beryl, said she was a nurse, and with a medikit from her pack, she cleaned and steri-stripped Syd's cheek professionally. Beryl's sister, Mary, who'd said she'd been a surgical nurse in an emergency department, gave Freeson the once-over, declaring all he needed was "a rest, some observation, and some painkillers."

"I'm fine, everyone; no need to check on me," Lucy said with maximum sarcasm to a bunch of ears that weren't at all fussed with her condition.

Mary took pity on Lucy and gave her shins the once-over, bending over and feeling them like she was palpating a horse's leg. "Just bruised, honey. Try not to fall down anymore holes and you'll be fine."

Cyndi had joined them at the Toyota, coming armed, but Nathan had signaled to her before she'd walked twenty yards that the Reynolds were okay and that she could retreat down from DEFCON 5.

The Reynolds helped them push the Toyota back to the Airstream and transfer Freeson to a bed inside. While Cyndi made coffee, Lucy looked unsure of where to sit, what to say, or how to make amends for her lack of concern for Freeson, finally perching on the side of his bed and making soothing noises towards his sleeping face.

"We're skiing cross-country," Steven told them as they sat with coffee in the Airstream, the windows steaming and the air warm enough for everyone to have gotten out of their coats. The young men, Randal and David, were cousins, and Steven's nephews. They were both, they said, PhD students who'd been studying the polar shift and axis tilt which had caused the increased cataclysmic change in volcanic, earthquake, and tectonic activity on America's west coast.

"So, what caused it? Do we know yet?" Cyndi asked. "We all know the government just fed us a load of crap about cores, magma, deep drilling in the Arctic, and even North Korean nuclear tests setting off chain reactions. The *stars* have moved. It's like the world fell over on its back. What do you know?"

David looked to Randal, and Randal sighed before speaking. "It's still not clear—it could be all those things, or none of them. Best guess is the crust of the Earth has shifted."

Nathan and Cyndi looked at each other in shock.

Tony said, "Wow!" which made Beryl and Mary, who had crammed themselves into the back of the Airstream, smile and coo with delight at the boy's brilliantly lit up face.

"The crust shifted? Is that even possible?" Nathan asked once he'd torn his eyes away from Cyndi's.

Randal shook his head. "We thought not. But we just don't

know. Crazy guy back in the 50s, Hapgood, wrote a book about his *Crustal Displacement Theory...*"

David interrupted, "Well, really, the theory was from the 1850s, when another crazy guy called Adhemar..."

Randal rolled his eyes. "Anyway, however you slice it, they were *both* crazy. Their theories stated that too much ice building up at the poles could cause the crust to shift—to literally slide around the mantle, the layer beneath the crust—and cause the Polar Regions to shift. It's garbage because, a) The ice is reducing, not increasing because of global warming, and b) plate tectonics just don't work like that."

Tony's face was a picture of incredulity; all it would take now would be for a dinosaur to stick its head through the window and he'd be in kid heaven. Nathan picked up and cuddled his son, who wriggled in his lap to make sure both ears were on the pair of scientists.

David took up the explanations. "But here's the thing. Few years back, NASA discovered that the tilt of the Earth is affected by how much water there is in the deep aquifers along the 44th parallel. They found there was less water there than they expected—maybe due to global warming, they're not sure—but maybe, and this is pure speculation, there's been another huge loss of water. That destabilized the crust and caused it to slip and slide to a new position. Took about eight years, but here we are. It would explain the earthquakes, volcanoes, and the Atlantic freezing as far down as Florida."

"It sounds utterly insane," Nathan said, shaking his head.

"Tell us about it," said Randal. "We're the poor suckers who are going to have to write about it one day. In a hundred years, there will be two scientists sitting in a trailer telling everyone that *our* theories are just as crazy as Hapgood's."

"Can it go back? Back to how it was?" Lucy's face was full of genuine concern. She leaned forward on the edge of the bed where Freeson lay. Her eyes seemingly pleading with Randal and David to tell her everything was going to be okay.

"We really can't say. Now we're out of the loop, we don't know what the current theories are. We were in Anchorage arranging tests, but the earthquakes and new volcanoes made it impossible to stay. Everyone headed south. Last we heard, they were evacuating everyone from Alaska into Canada, or across the sea to Russia and China."

The Airstream fell silent, except for Lucy's gentle crying. "This isn't going to get back to normality any time soon, is it?" she asked, her eyes sparkling with tears.

"Tell them," Steven commanded quietly.

David and Randal exchanged glances again, as if neither of them wanted to say it. So, sighing, the older man began. "Okay," said Steven, "before the government had to give up on research up in Alaska, and the northern Canadian wilderness, they had enough modeling to suggest this is the big one."

"The Big Winter?" Nathan asked after a moment, concerned that he'd missed something important.

"No. Not the Big Winter," Steven corrected him tiredly. "That's just a symptom, not the disease. The illness… well… the feeling is that it's terminal. This might lead towards the end of everything. This might be *the* extinction event."

12

———————

"Who left you guys in charge of optimism?"

Everyone looked at Freeson, who had lifted his head off the bed and was comforting the gently sobbing Lucy, their roles reversed. The irony of the behavior wasn't lost on Nathan, who clamped his mouth shut.

Steven gave a bitter smile. "We're only telling you what the government isn't, guys. We're telling as many people as we meet. We're heading south. Once we get out of the U.S., and across Mexico, we're thinking Brazil might give us a few years' grace. But we just don't know."

"We're heading to Detroit, on the word of a friend who's there," Nathan said, hoping for some affirmation from Steven.

"We don't know anything about Detroit. We've been avoiding cities since leaving Toronto. Most of them are burning and empty now. We're staying away from the obvious routes, too. Especially after our run-in with the Seven-Ones."

Out of the corner of his eye, Nathan saw Syd stiffen and her eyes bulge.

She'd be a terrible poker player.

"The *who*?" asked Cyndi.

"A gang," Beryl said. "We only just made it through Niagara. They ride fast and hard on Ski-Doos. They catch you, they..."

She broke off, eyeing Tony, who was still on Nathan's lap. Nathan caught the idea that she was about to say some stuff that might not be good for him. Nathan lifted the boy back onto his feet, and said, "Hey, why don't you and Mom go take Saber out to do her business, and I can fill Mom in on all this boring adult stuff when you get back?"

Tony nodded vigorously. "Okay, Dad."

Cyndi started putting on her jacket and passed Tony his coat and scarf to wrap around his throat and mouth. "Good plan, Nate," she said, and smiled. "I'll give you fifteen minutes for the adult stuff, and then we'll be back, okay?"

Beryl nodded and gave a half-smile.

Cyndi, Tony, and Saber jumped down from the Airstream's open door and Beryl continued as it was pushed closed. "The Seven-Ones. They catch you, they... kill you, take your stuff, and..." the words died in her throat again. Now it seemed they'd trailed off because of the distressing thoughts Nathan saw backing up behind her eyes. It wasn't just Tony's sensitive ears that had obstructed her recounting the things they'd been through.

"They carve Seven-One in the foreheads of those they've killed; it's a kind of sick calling card," Mary said, disgust running through her words like infected veins of sickness. "We've found three burned out settlements already, and a road train like yours attacked, looted, with everyone murdered. That's why we're staying off the roads, traveling light on skis cross-country. It's why we didn't come out on you straight away from the woods. Wanted to make sure you weren't a honey trap."

Nathan took this in and it opened up a well of fear in him. The news they were more vulnerable to attack on the road was a hard notion to fit into his head. "We've had three run-ins with Ski-Doo gangs already. Managed to get away." He reached for a positive, but it came out unconvincingly weak. "I don't think they've been tracking us."

"There hasn't been a pattern to what we've seen," Steven said, draining his coffee, "and other than Niagara, when we tried to stop them ransacking homes and killing folks, we haven't run into them again. We lost them in the forest. Best to stay in places where the Ski-Doos can't travel easily, and they don't like to travel without them. I guess they're not really country folk. City kids who've learned to ride Ski-Doos but don't know much else, I reckon. But they're out there. If you're already on the lookout for them, you can defend your-self; at least forewarned is forearmed."

The Reynolds slept the night in the Airstream with Lucy and Freeson while Nathan and the others got snug in the crew cab of the Dodge.

Nathan checked the Toyota over before the night settled in, thinking hard about what Steven had said. The vehicle was beat up underneath, but it was serviceable, and started the first time Nathan tried it. The tire pressures were good and the supplies of fuel under the plastic sheeting in the back had been well strapped down by Freeson, so that they hadn't shifted.

The Reynolds' news—both about the global situation and the particular news about the Seven-One gang—was difficult to process. How could Nathan be expected to save his family from the gangs on their Ski-Doos while at the same time just keeping them alive long enough to experience whatever this was, even if it was the end of the world?

What was the point of anything? This dark dose of ennui and nihilism dropped away into his internal abyss like the Land Cruiser had tried heading into the hole in the bridge.

What pipes and broken concrete in his soul were holding up Nathan, though? Who would winch him out of this hole?

While the others slept, Nathan spent much of the night awake as his family, Syd, and Saber snuggled around him. Sleep finally caught up with him in the small hours of the morning, but he dreamed of avalanches, falling trees, and cherry-red erupting volcanoes.

He woke up mostly unrested. Cyndi had already let herself out of the crew cab to go to the Airstream for ablutions. Syd and Tony were stirring, but not yet fully awake.

Nathan hauled himself out of the truck, the cold air cutting through him but freshening him fully awake. The Reynolds were already lining up outside the Airstream, zipping up their camouflage jackets, putting their guns over their shoulders, and pulling on their balaclavas.

"Thank you for your hospitality, Nate. Sorry we couldn't bring you better news," Steven said, holding out his hand. Nathan shook it, for a moment not knowing how to respond.

In the end, he just shrugged and said, "It's better that we know instead of not knowing. And you're welcome. I guess you guys are heading south now?"

Steven nodded his head. "We have to go collect our skis and other equipment from up there where we left them in the woods, but yes, we'll be on our way. If I might offer you some advice?"

"Shoot."

"We think the Seven-Ones are going for the low-hanging fruit: settlements that are staying put but poorly defended and the like. We think they're patrolling the highways where they can, figuring that's where people are mostly likely to travel."

That made sense—it's where they'd attacked Lucy and her limo.

"We suggest you stay off the highway as best you can if

you're still intent on traveling to Detroit. Take the road least traveled. It might keep you off their radar."

"Thanks," he answered. "Sounds like good advice."

The Reynolds made their goodbyes with hugs and handshakes, and then Nathan watched as they trudged back into the trees to get their equipment.

Cyndi turned to Nathan immediately. "We've got more of a chance getting to Detroit more quickly than we have getting to Mexico."

"I'm not thinking of going to Mexico. Or Brazil or anywhere else but Detroit. It's okay."

Cyndi put her hands on Nathan's shoulders and looked hard into his eyes. "You forget I know you, Nathan. I know that look on your face. They've rattled you. And me, I admit. But I want that hospital, and I want that school. Beryl gave me an exam this morning when I told her I was pregnant, and she said everything's fine. But the longer we're on the road with the stress that can cause, the more chance I have of the pre-eclampsia returning. I want to be in Detroit if that happens. In a few weeks, Nate, I'm gonna be four months pregnant. I want to be in a warm house, knowing Tony's being educated and you're learning to grow vegetables."

"Okay..." Nathan shuffled his feet and tried to articulate the fear he was feeling, his worries about their future. But there were no good words for him to use. Cyndi was the articulate and pragmatic one, so he just boiled it down to as few words as he could. "It's just... the gang..."

"Hold on; you're wavering on Detroit again?" There was a mixture of irritation and frustration in her voice.

"No. No, it's… now we know more about the gang, and we know they're working out here… I'm just…"

"The gang hasn't been on our trail; you know that. We were two days at Marty's and we saw no one. Everyone is going south. We're going west. I figure the Seven-Ones are trying to catch up with those folks, moving on commonly traveled lines. They won't be bothered with outliers like us."

Nathan knew her logic was sound. He hated himself for vacillating and wavering. *If Dad were here, he'd have given me a good shake, and I deserve it.*

Cyndi rubbed at his cheek with her hand, softening. "Look at you. No coat again. Your cheeks are blue, you've got frost in your eyebrows, and your nipples are sticking out like rivets!" As if to underline the statement, Cyndi reached up and twisted Nathan's left nipple hard.

"Owww!"

"Get back to the wrecker and get your coat! That's an order, soldier."

Rubbing the sore nub of flesh on his chest and scowling back over his shoulder at Cyndi, Nathan crunched back towards the Dodge.

As he approached, he saw that the passenger side door was slightly ajar and heated voices were coming from within. Syd and Tony were having a low-voiced argument.

"But I don't want you to go!" Tony was saying, the whine

in his voice familiar—it was Tony's emotional blackmail tone. "You're my only friend!"

Nathan could tell his son was on the verge of tears, and he had to check the paternal instinct to throw open the cab door and barrel in to protect his son. Nevertheless, Syd's reply stilled his hand. He threw a look back to Cyndi to see if she was watching his progress on getting his coat. She'd already gone back into the trailer. Nathan pretended to be looking into one of the day provision rucksacks, but bent his ear closer to the door. Syd was trying to placate Tony now. "I'm not going unless I have to. But if the Seven-Ones turn up, I'm going to have to go, and I'm not going to be able to take Saber with me. I need you to promise that you'll look after her. Tony, I'm depending on you."

"I'm gonna tell my dad on you!"

"Please, Tony, don't. I don't want your parents to know this. You've got to help me, Tony! Dude, I'm giving you my dog, and it's only if I have to get out of here in an instant. If I stay here, and the Seven-Ones come, you and your family are in much more danger than you would be if I wasn't here. Believe me!"

Saber barked like she was trying to persuade Tony, too. "You think I wanna leave my dog behind?" Syd added.

"No."

"There ya go then. It's because I trust you to look after her that I will."

"Okay," Tony answered quietly.

"So, you'll do it?"

There was a silent pause, and Nathan could almost hear the cogs whirring in his son's mind. And then the boy said, "Yes."

"And you won't tell your dad or your mom that the Seven-Ones are after me? Because if you do, I'll have to go right now. Right this second. Okay?"

"Okay."

"Spit."

Nathan heard them both spitting into their palms, and the wet slap as their palms met.

He waited another thirty seconds before he opened the door to ensure that they didn't think he'd overheard them. If he just blundered in, then Syd would be gone in a flash and his son would be bereft, losing the bond that he'd made with the wayward wild child.

With that thought, Nathan had to admit to himself that he didn't want to lose her, either.

The Toyota slowed, and Nathan did the same as he followed behind in the wrecker, gently applying the brakes. Cyndi was driving the Land Cruiser and Nathan wished there was a CB in it, too, so that he could see what had caused her to roll to a stop.

They'd just passed a track going off at right angles to the one-lane rural road they'd been traveling on. For the last three hours, since turning around and heading away from the broken bridge, they'd taken Steven's advice to ride non-highways. At least until they were near enough to Detroit, that's how it would be until they could make a break for it and roll in as fast as they could over the snow.

They were in a region of Pennsylvania, south of Lake Erie, that was deeply wooded. The towns like Olean and Salamanca, as well as many farmsteads they passed, had been dark, burned out, and dead. The only evidence of another vehicle they'd seen all day had been the high contrail of a jet flying through the ash gray sky. It must have been a military jet, as commercial jets that flew that high had all been grounded since the plumes of volcanic ash had been pumped into the sky from the west of the country. The ash would clog any engines that hadn't been properly converted and shielded. Small prop planes could still fly if they stayed low, but the ice storms moving with savage regularity across the sky had put an end to any regular services.

Cyndi got out of the Land Cruiser and pointed down the spur that they were just about to pass.

From behind Nathan in the crew cab, Freeson lifted his horrifically bruised forehead and asked, "Everything okay?"

Lucy, in whose lap that purple, yellow, overripe head had been resting until the Dodge had jounced to a halt, soothed Freeson's hair and told him to rest. Syd followed Nathan out of the truck, jumping down into the crisp, undisturbed snow and taking the safety off her Glock as she did so.

Nathan looked to where Cyndi pointed; maybe a hundred yards down the spur road, which was dark from tree branches meeting overhead, was the unmistakable, chunky blue and gold form of the latest model Ford Police Utility Interceptor. It was parked diagonally across the road, its back end pointing towards them, with the nose, and more importantly, driver's seats too far around to see into.

Nathan hadn't seen a police car in a long while. "What do you think?" he asked Cyndi.

"Leave them," answered Syd.

Nathan and Cyndi both narrowed their eyes at Syd and she shrugged. "Just offering an opinion, guys. If it walks like a trap, barks like a trap, and craps like a trap... it's a trap."

"She might have a point," Nathan conceded.

"And they might have news about Seven-One activity in the area. They might be able to tell us the best routes through here to Detroit. They might have set up a roadblock because of the Seven-Ones, Nathan. Or they might be in trouble. Any of the above tells me we should go take a look."

"Okay," Nathan said, "I'll go and check the lay of the land."

"Oh no you won't," Cyndi said, handing him an AR-15 from the Land Cruiser. "You shoot like a bitch, honey. I'm coming with you."

Cyndi was right, and Nathan knew it. Shooting was not his forte at the best of times, and she was a great shot. His AR-15 would just be for show, while hers would be the one that made a difference.

"Me, too," Syd said.

Nathan shook his head. "Syd, no. Stay back with the others. You're backup if this goes pear-shaped."

Syd had drawn breath to protest when Lucy, who had been listening out of the crew cab window, said, "Please, Syd. I'm looking after Freeson and Tony. We need you as lookout."

"Can I use your Desert Eagle?" Syd asked with a twinkle, immediately taking advantage of the situation.

"Yes, you can use the Desert Eagle," Lucy said with the resigned voice of someone telling a child that they could stay up and watch the late movie on TV.

"Cool," Syd answered, and with that she climbed back into the cab.

Nathan and Cyndi began to walk down the spur.

There were tracks in the snow that led directly to the Interceptor, which seemed freshly made, not having time to have been frozen hard by the overnight frost.

"Not been here long," Cyndi confirmed what Nathan had been thinking. Cyndi was a naturally gifted tracker as well as an all-around prepper, teacher, accountant, super-mom, and hard-nosed negotiator. She made Nathan proud to be in her orbit, let alone be her husband. She could be annoying as hell, too—and she proved that by reaching over to the AR-15 in Nathan's hands and clicking off the safety.

"You might want to do that before we meet any resistance," she said with a smile.

"You're not too old for a spanking, you know."

"Promises, promises." She winked back.

The Interceptor stood fast. The doors didn't open, and the engine didn't start. When they were within thirty yards of the rear of the vehicle, Nathan tapped Cyndi's arm and they stopped. He pointed. Across the rear panel of the liftgate could be seen a line of bullet holes, like silver-edged daisies in the blue of the metal. Six of them. The frequency and tight line of the holes suggested they were spray from an automatic weapon. Even more reason for maximum caution. Nathan wondered as they started moving forward again, what they might find inside.

They reached the Interceptor, and nothing changed; nothing moved. The overhanging trees with the domes of snow made it feel as if they were entering a dank, arctic cave, and the gloom deepened as they approached, to a fairy-tale light in an enchanted forest. Were Nathan and his wife just following bread crumbs to the Wicked Witch's Gingerbread house, like Hansel and Gretel...?

A chill that had nothing to do with the ambient temperature rushed through him. Maybe they should have listened to Syd and moved on.

Cyndi and Nathan split from each other. Nathan went to the passenger side, Cyndi to the other, the two of them raising their weapons to their shoulders—ready, hopefully, for anything that might occur. Nathan kept side-eyeing the trees in case there were Seven-Ones waiting to yank the starters on their Ski-Doos, burst out of the woods, run them down, and carve up their foreheads.

He mentally slapped himself when the image of all that followed. Those kinds of thoughts weren't helping.

He edged forward; one more step and he would be able to see inside the front of the Interceptor. He craned his neck, opening his eyes wider, willing them to see around corners when he heard Cyndi exclaim, "Well, damn it all to hell!"

Nathan looked across the roof of the Interceptor to see that Cyndi was already straightening up and putting the AR-15 to her shoulder. He took that last step and looked inside the police utility vehicle.

There were two youngsters inside, each no more than twenty. The male was black, shaven-headed, strong boned, and a little on the thin side. The girl with him was pale white, almost translucent, with a shock of red hair and a pleasing plumpness that suggested a hearty laugh and that she'd be a good person to be drunk with. Her eyes were almond shaped around Kohl black and her nose was pierced. She had small pieces of colored cotton tying random areas of her hair into tufts.

Two things were immediately evident, too. Neither of the kids were cops, and they had, before being disturbed by Cyndi and Nathan's approach, been huddled over laptop computer screens on which lines of code raced.

They both looked terrified upon seeing Cyndi and Nate, and both had their hands raised. The boy had his eyes closed and was wincing as well, as if he was expecting to get shot through the head at any moment.

Nathan motioned for the girl to get out of the Interceptor and she complied, closing the laptop and putting it under her arm, making it difficult for her to keep both arms raised.

"It's okay, hands down," Nathan indicated, and as if to drive the point home that he didn't want to be seen as a threat, he put the AR-15 safety back on and copied Cyndi's form by putting the rifle over his shoulder. The four of them moved to the front of the Interceptor, which was also pretty shot up. Nine bullet holes in the hood had made the engine eventually drop its lunch and stop moving.

"Where are the cops?" Cyndi asked. "You're obviously not cops."

"Hardly," said the girl—who, now they knew they weren't going to be shot, was allowing a streak of arrogance and annoyance to seep through. "And you're not the authorities, either, so what gives you the right to point guns at us in the first place? Were we a threat to you?"

The boy touched her arm and gave it a placating squeeze. "Donie, cool it… look, they've got transport." His eyes indicated the head of the spur, where the Land Cruiser and Dodge Airstream combo could just be seen.

"Look," he continued, his green eyes nervously flicking from Cyndi to Nathan and back again, looking for a lead on who he needed to address as the leader. Like any good kid who didn't see traditional gender roles as anything but fluid, he said to Cyndi, "We need a ride out of here. Can you help?"

"Depends," said Cyndi. "What can you offer us in return?"

It turned out that the kids, who were called Donie and Dave, had quite a lot to offer inside the dead Interceptor. There were two shotguns, plenty of ammo, a nifty pair of P1050 Steiner Police tactical binoculars which Nathan knew Tony would really dig, a fire extinguisher—which would always come in handy—and two medical kits, as well as two police plate-carriers, which would be useful for wearing to carry spare mags for the rifles when checking out places en route. In a rifle bag, there was a well-used but serviceable Rock River LAR-15, fitted with an Aimpoint pro optic site and a bunch of spare magazines. Cyndi seemed particularly happy with that. There were also two metal bulky flight cases, which didn't look at all police-issue, and Dave commented, "We'll show you what's inside when we get back to your transport, and it will, I promise, blow your mind."

One thing Donie and Dave didn't offer, however, were surnames or any information about how they'd come to be driving a shot-up Police Interceptor, other than Donie saying grudgingly, "It was my dad's."

Nathan's question about where her dad was now remained soundly ignored by both of them.

Dave's indie-band t-shirt and Levis combo under his parka was a little more traditional than Donie's alt-to-the-max gear of bullet belt and mini-denim skirt over dragon-printed leggings. Adding more color, huge suede boots erupting with yellow fur were orange leopard-spotted with what looked like homemade dyes. Beneath Donie's parka, which was the same police-issue wear as Dave's, she wore a crimson Basque tied over a black t-shirt that rolled up in a polo neck below her chubby chin.

When they climbed into the Airstream to get acquainted with the others and take off their parkas, Nathan could see Syd checking out Donie's fashion credibility before she'd even had a chance to speak to them.

Dave and Donie had dragged the two metal flight cases on wheels, through the snow and back to the trailer. They'd hauled them out of the back of the Interceptor and not wanted Cyndi or Nathan to help them at all. They already had had the cases fitted with straps for easy purchase. As they'd moved back along the spur, they'd reminded Nathan of roadies getting ready for a gig.

As to what the flight cases contained, Nathan had no clue.

Once Freeson had been helped by Lucy back to the Airstream and introductions had been made, Dave and Donie held court outside the Airstream to show off what was in the flight cases.

"We have three collapsible wind turbines—set them up, and they'll run 'puters and monitors in a breeze. Very efficient. We have two solar arrays, too, for trickle charging. Put them on the roof of your car, even on an overcast day like this, there's enough sunlight getting through to fully charge a laptop battery in a few hours, and a killer sound system. If you want to open a club, we're your guys." Dave was the salesman of the two. With a hot coffee in his hand, surprisingly supplied by Lucy, he was warming to the task of telling them about their toys. "Scads of lithium-sodium batteries. Run power tools; run a refrigerator. Not that anyone needs one of those these days…"

"Oh, but champagne," Lucy whispered lustily, "needs to be cold, but not frozen. Imagine a few bottles being kept just right!"

"What about communications?" Nathan broke in.

Donie took over—she was the comms expert, it seemed. "We have satellite phones, digital walkie-talkies, and a satellite uplink; cop tech, but we'd just finished hacking into the network when you came pointing guns."

"Hold the sarcasm," Nathan said. "We can be mutually good for each other."

Donie set her chin. "I'll be the judge of that, thank you very much. First of all, where are you heading?"

"Detroit," said Nathan, figuring there was no point in hiding the truth if they were going to build up mutual trust with these kids. Their equipment and computer gear made them a good addition to the party.

Donie and Dave had been whispering heatedly in each other's ears. Donie looked up. "We heard Detroit was a waste."

"Can you get onto the web with the satellite uplink?"

"Does a bear poop in the woods?" Donie answered.

"Get a connection, and I'll introduce you to our contact in Detroit. He might change your mind."

Donie and Dave went back to whispering and Nathan stomped around in the cold, wishing they'd hurry it up.

Eventually, Donie looked up and said, "Okay, we'll help you out with stuff—charging, computers and the like. In exchange, we come with you to Detroit, and you provide the transport, food, and shelter."

Nathan smiled. "Sounds like a basis for an agreement. Can you set the communication link up now?"

Dave shook his head. "When we have line of sight and a break in the cloud cover, yes. But not right now. Later today, maybe. We've got a downloaded searchable database of ten-meter ground maps of the whole of the U.S. It's like an always on SatNav, however fritzed the communications to the grid are, which means we're always on when it comes to route planning."

That, Nathan thought, was something which they *could* use. Now that they were off the highways, Freeson's maps weren't of a small enough scale, or up to date enough, to give accurate information for travel.

"Okay, I think we can deal. You want to travel with us, yes?" Nathan asked.

"For now," Donie said.

"For sure," Dave said over top of her.

"Then you need to get me online. Tonight."

But before Dave could answer, Nathan heard the growl of a Ski-Doo.

13

Nathan helped heave the flight cases into the Airstream as Syd and Cyndi took up defensive positions, using the Land Cruiser and Dodge as cover.

What they'd heard had been the growl of a single engine, and it was clearly some distance away, but Nathan needed to be sure it wasn't heading towards them.

When the cases were packed back up, and Tony, Lucy, Freeson, and the two new arrivals were hunkered down inside the trailer, Nathan took an AR-15 and called Cyndi forward with a hissed command to join him. The sound of the Ski-Doo was coming from the south, which suggested, since Nathan's party had been travelling west, that they weren't on their trail —but that they were near enough to stumble on them accidentally.

They walked through the snow-filled ditch on the opposite side of the road of the spur, up to where there was a patch of raised ground, topped by trees, giving them a view over the fields beyond.

They reached the rise and crouched down in the line of trees. The land sloped away for half a mile, to where the highway they'd been traveling on the day before was visible. There on the road, almost directly parallel to their vantage point, was a dark colored sedan moving along the highway as best it could in the conditions.

With horror, Nathan watched as the yellow Ski-Doo, probably the same model as the one he'd disabled outside the mall back in Glens Falls, caught up with it. He saw the muzzle flashes before he heard the cracks of the bullets being fired and hitting home.

The sedan slewed into a wide skid and crashed off the highway into a ditch. The Ski-Doo slowed and halted beside it. Three more shots rang out, and the Ski-Doo's engine died.

There were two riders. Nonchalantly, they unhooked their legs from the Ski-Doo, opened the sedan door, and fired two more shots into the sedan's interior. Muzzle flashes seared themselves on Nathan's eyes, the dull thud of the impacts on the metal inside of the chassis being dampened by the distance, but still chillingly unmistakable.

The identity of the raiders as Seven-Ones was confirmed when two limp corpses were pulled from the car. Each raider dropped to his knees and began to work on the faces of the dead.

It was a procedure that didn't take long.

After they'd finished with the bodies, the raiders looted what they could from the car, putting what they found in their packs and then skidding away on the Ski-Doo as if this had been a routine stop to pick up cokes and burgers from a gas station.

Nathan felt sick to his stomach. Firstly, because he hadn't been able to help the stricken victims, but also because he couldn't help imagining the faces of the victims in his mind's eye as those of Cyndi and Tony.

Back at the Airstream, they held a quick council to decide what the best course of action would be. If they stayed where they were for the night, then they risked discovery because the Seven-Ones were in the area. But, as the gang could travel cross-country on their Ski-Doos, the Seven-Ones, although not hunting them specifically, might also just find them by accident.

"But if we move now," said Lucy, "they might hear us. You said the highway was half a mile away. These old buses make more noise than a thousand coffee grinders in a cemetery."

"If we stay, we're sitting ducks," said Cyndi. "At least if

we move and we're lucky, we might find somewhere before dark. Somewhere with a barn where we can hide the trucks and the trailer for a bit. Give us some breathing space until they move out of the area."

"We don't know that they are moving out of the area," Freeson noted. His eyes looked clear and his speech seemed less groggy. Although his forehead was still a mess, he wasn't showing signs of concussion. For that, at least, Nathan felt grateful.

"We know a place," Dave offered.

"Shut up!" Donie commanded.

"It's okay. The Seven-Ones haven't found it yet!"

"And there's no need to lead them there."

"If we're all dead, it doesn't matter if they find this place or not," Nathan pointed out.

And to that, Donie had no comeback.

"There's a set of cabins, up in the woods, about five miles from here. Hunting lodges, that sort of deal," Dave said. "We holed up there a week ago. They're not on any maps because they're new, and unless you know the tracks up to them, you're never gonna find them. It's rough country, but the Dodge and Cruiser will make it easy. You'll have to be careful with the trailer."

Donie's face was thunderous, her eyes bulging as the information tumbled from Dave's mouth. "That's it. Tell the world."

Nathan ignored her. "How long to get there?"

"Two hours, tops."

"Could you get us there at night?"

Dave considered, and then answered, "Yes. I think so. I have the route on the map database."

Nathan looked at his watch. Two-thirty. "Then we leave in three hours."

Dave and Syd went back to the Interceptor to retrieve the guns and equipment they hadn't been able to carry in one trip.

Donie sat grumpily in the Airstream, refusing to answer questions from Lucy, Freeson, or anyone else.

Nathan and Cyndi patrolled the perimeter of their makeshift camp, listening for the distant sound of Ski-Doos and periodically going up to the treeline to look down along the stretch of highway. It hurt Nathan's sensibilities not to go down there and care for the dead, but the situation was too hot right now to do the right thing by the murder victims. He did drop his eyes and stand silent for a minute in the best analog of respecting a fellow fallen human he could muster. Nathan didn't know if there was a God or if people had souls that could be released by heinous death, but it didn't hurt him to at least offer up some silence to whatever might fill the void in their honor.

Whatever God was up there, if indeed there was one, the

deity was surely testing all humanity right now, and if even a little bit of peace could be transmitted to those recently departed people, it was worth Nathan's time doing it.

"This Big Winter makes strange bedfellows of all of us, doesn't it?" Cyndi had appeared at his side. He didn't know how long she'd been watching him, and for a moment he felt foolish about doing what he'd done for the dead.

"Me, you, Tony, Free, and then Syd the wild child, Lucy, one of the richest women on the planet, and two geeks we've known for five minutes who have two trunks of tech and a stolen police car full of bullet holes."

"And the dog."

"And the dog," she acknowledged. "But face it, Nate; the dog is the least strange of the lot of them. At least the dog's behavior is predictable. The rest, I'm not so sure."

"Do you think we can trust them?"

"All of them?"

"Well, Lucy I wouldn't trust as far as I could throw a Buick full of bricks—and the jury is still out on Syd, but Dave and Donie…" Nate trailed off, and then asked, "What do you make of them?"

Cyndi considered the question for a moment, and then asked in return, "What can we make of anyone right now? Who knows how any of us will react in any given situation, and this is absolutely not a *usual* situation. If you'd told me a year ago that we'd be on the run from a group of forehead-carving scumbags, trying to get to Detroit so I can have a baby, I'd have been on the telephone to the nearest psychiatrist and pouring Rohypnol into your coffee…"

"Well, I'm glad you have it already worked out how to deal with me if my brain breaks down."

"It's what prepping is all about, baby. Think the unthinkable, and then plan for it."

Nathan had been living the unthinkable for a while now, but was glad that Cyndi had done something about it. If it had all been left up to him, his head would still be stuck in the sand, thinking summer would come and business would pick up...

He'd let go of almost everything he'd thought of as certain, but he certainly wasn't letting go of Cyndi.

The track up to the hunting lodges was worse than Dave had indicated. Maneuvering it in the dark added an extra layer of terror that Nathan could have done without.

There had been no more Ski-Doos, and they'd left the head of the spur without incident although they'd had to back up on themselves again, as the start of the route up to the lodge had been two miles back in the direction they'd already come from.

Cyndi had felt antsy about wasting more fuel but getting

out of the way of the Seven-Ones and their murderous intents made sense for a couple of days, at least.

In the Land Cruiser, in touch with Nathan via Dave's digital walkie-talkies, Cyndi drove with Dave while Donie sat with Nathan in the Dodge. She'd flat-out refused to get into the back with the dog and others. This had caused the atmosphere in the cab to fall below the already freezing one outside. Nathan saw Syd visibly biting her lip to keep from giving Donie a roasting. Nathan kept looking back into the cab while he could at Syd's stony face, her eyes drilling into the back of Donie's head. Nathan had hoped he'd be able to get some more helpful information about the Seven-Ones from Syd, but she'd clammed up again, and from the looks of things, he thought she maybe wouldn't open up again until Donie and Dave were either gone or traveling permanently in another vehicle, out of her sight.

The track was rutted badly from previous vehicles coming and going, but because of the overhanging pines and the rise of the hills on both side, it had escaped more a cursory layer of snow, which the Dodge's tires carved through with a sure-footedness that belied the vehicle's weight.

They heard occasional little crashes from the Airstream as it bounced along behind them, but everything that could be tied down had been. And when they'd look in later, they'd see that they had only lost a few bits of easily replaceable crockery and some glasses.

The hunting lodge, when they reached it at full dark, just on the evening side of 9 p.m., was a welcome sight. Three low, one-story pine buildings, their outside faces painted black. The roofs were pitched gently and there was more snow on them than had made it down onto the track. As the Land Cruiser and Dodge's headlights scythed across the front of the buildings, the crenelated gables, wood fronts, and snow-caked roofs made it look less like a hunting lodge than a Swedish Christmas scene.

The middle cabin was the largest, and Cyndi decided that they would all bed down in there. Yes, that would be less private, but it would also allow everyone to be kept an eye on, and simultaneously conserve warmth and energy.

There was no working electricity inside the cabin, which had a main living area of paneled wood and Indian design rugs, as well as plenty of sofa throws. The center of the living space was a stone hearth which, when lit, would allow everyone to sit in a circle around it. There was even a rotisserie for hunters to roast their gutted catches over the fire. It was the sort of place Nathan's dad would have loved to have visited, but he'd never had the kind of money to afford a stay somewhere like this. This was a rich person's playground, and Lucy, once the place was illuminated and the fire lit, fit right in.

"Oh, we should stay—we really should. We've got guns, we can hunt, and we can keep the fire lit. Have you seen the beds? They're to die for. Literally. To. Die. For. We shouldn't just stay for a few days until the bad people have moved out of the area; we should stay here forever!"

Nathan saw no point in arguing with her, as Lucy's selfishness was a force of nature. She'd even begun asking if Freeson could drive into the nearest town in the morning to locate some champagne and caviar. When he declined, she suggested, "Maybe we could go out and shoot a deer. There are deer in these woods, aren't there, David? Please say there are deer."

Dave shrugged. "I don't know. I'm not a hunter."

"Oh, you must let me teach you, my dear. You can be the dear who gets the deer."

Lucy was the only one who laughed, and it made sense when Nathan discovered later that she'd been filling a discrete flask in her purse from his whiskey in the Airstream when she'd been in there on her own.

Now, though, Nathan didn't see the point in making a scene, because Lucy was the kind of person who would shrug off the disappointment of others as the concerns of lesser mortals. She was on a roll, and it was best to let her get on with it.

Syd prepared to go outside with Saber, perhaps to let the dog have a run and stretch her legs, but maybe just to get away from Lucy and Donie, who Nathan could see were both winding Syd up tighter than a clock spring.

"Can I go, too, Mom?" Tony asked as Syd put her coat on, called Saber, and headed for the door, going out like the cold she let in when going through the door.

"No, you can help me prepare food."

"Awww, Mom," said Tony, Cyndi, Nathan, and Freeson all at once, and with that moment of collective levity, the atmosphere in the cabin lightened.

"How are you doing, bud?" Freeson asked Nathan.

"I should be asking you the same thing."

It was the first time he'd been alone with Freeson since he'd pulled him and the Land Cruiser out of the hole. Lucy had been stuck to Freeson like a limpet. Not that Freeson had seemed to mind any. Now, Lucy was away choosing beds like Goldilocks on amphetamines. Her voice drifted into the living area on a gust of delight as she found one that was "Just right!"

Freeson grinned at Nathan, then shrugged in a *what's a guy supposed to do?* manner at Lucy's antics. "I'm getting there. Head looks like an alien baby and I've got a headache that sounds as if Metallica's moved into my skull, but I'm on the mend, compadre."

"Glad to hear it. Cyndi and I could use a break from the driving."

"I hear you, man, I'm getting stir-crazy getting driven. I'll be more careful crossing bridges in the future."

Nathan grinned, secretly happy that his friend wasn't

buying into Lucy's near drunken rants about staying in the lodge forever.

While the others had been unpacking, cooking, and sorting where they were going to sleep, Dave had been setting up the satellite uplink outside, and he came in just as Free finished assuring Nate that he'd be driving sooner than later.

Before they'd heard the Ski-Doos that morning, Nathan had been about to tell Dave that the price for getting to travel with them would be access to the internet whenever he needed it with the uplink to the cop tech laptop. The boy had agreed readily when they'd finally gotten to talk about getting in touch with Stryker again, but Donie had just sucked her teeth with displeasure. She might be the comms expert of the pair, but she was leaving it to Dave to build the bridges.

Dave was falling over himself to help, though, which made him the polar opposite of Donie, and Nathan planned to use that attitude to his advantage.

Sitting up on a table in the open-plan kitchen area of the lodge building, Dave's cop laptop was chunky, with metal corners like those on the flight cases. It was utilitarian in design, with a smaller than average LCD screen that made it look like the workhorse it was meant to be. The keys on the pad were white and red, giving it a Fisher-Price indestructible feel that made Nathan appreciate it as an old-world thing, even though he knew it was a new and pokily powerful piece of kit.

It took some time for Dave to get the uplink connected, and

he had to go outside in the cold to reposition the base station, hoping the clouds of ash and dust obscuring the stars in the night sky would thin out enough for him to get a connection. After an hour, however, the laptop told them it was connected to the satellite, and it handshook and downlinked to the police service VPN in a matter of seconds. Once in the internet area of the police system, Dave turned the laptop around to Nathan.

There was no webcam, so he didn't bother with Skype, sending Stryker an instant message and hoping that, as it was the end of the day, he'd be near his computer.

He was. Almost instantly.

NATHAN: Don't you ever go outside?

STRYKER: I've been out all day. Doing man's work. What have you been doing? Driving and sightseeing?

NATHAN: I wish. It might take us longer to get to you than advertised.

STRYKER: You always were the slowest driver in school. I remember Daisy Henning complaining that you were too busy watching the stop signs to even look at her!

NATHAN: This is serious, Stryker.

STRYKER: Okay, okay. What's up?

NATHAN: We're holed up in a hunting lodge, somewhere in Coulthard State Park.

STRYKER: Vacation. I knew it!

NATHAN: Shut up. We can't travel on the highway. Too dangerous right now. There are gangs out there, holding up evacuees, killing them and stealing their stuff.

STRYKER: No kidding?

NATHAN: None. We're in a dicey situation right now, but we're gonna have to take our time, travel when we can, and keep our heads down when we can't. We're still coming and we still want that house.

STRYKER: You got it. If I say it happens, then it happens.

NATHAN: That's not what Daisy's sister Lacey told me LOL.

STRYKER: Hardy har har. Just get your ass here so I can whup it.

NATHAN: In your dreams. Have you heard anything about this gang? We've been told they're called the Seven-Ones on account of the way they carve their initials into the heads of the people they kill.

There was a long pause before Stryker replied.

STRYKER: Man. I'm sorry. You didn't need me giving you a hard time. No, I never heard of them, but we've been hearing some pretty scary stories from New York and Boston. Food riots. Inter-city battles. The police have evacuated south like everyone else. We haven't had any guidance from the government for five days. Washington's dead and no one knows where the president is. It's anarchy in the other cities. Windsor is burning. We figured out in the country it would be OK.

NATHAN: Nothing's okay, Stryker. Nothing. You having riots in Detroit?

STRYKER: Don't worry. It's cool here. Someone stubs a toe, it's news. We got food and shelter, and we're warm. Look.

Three photographs appeared in the window with musical pings. They showed broad city plazas that had been glassed in, people walking around in shirtsleeves. Banks of hydroponic gardens and a swimming pool, azure blue, under glass. The windows looked out over a dense snowfield—the people in the pool warm, playful, and happy.

NATHAN: What Cyndi and Tony wouldn't give to be there now!

STRYKER: Not you?

NATHAN: Family First.

STRYKER: Amen.

The chat window went dark. The pictures had been saved to the desktop, but Stryker was gone.

"Sorry, we lost the uplink," Dave said. "Ash."

He went back outside to noodle with the base station, but the link couldn't be made again, however hard Dave tried. "We'll have another try in the morning," he said, about to close the lid of the laptop when Nathan stilled his hand for a moment.

He stared at the pictures, not able to reconcile the serene, warm, happy people in the pool with the horror that was going on outside the city.

Tony brought Nathan a bowl of stew, balancing it carefully on a tray with a glass of Coke. His eyes were steady on the bowl, making sure not to spill any, but when he saw what was on the screen of the laptop, the tray wavered and Nathan had to reach out to steady it. "Wow! A swimming pool! Is there a swimming pool where we're going, Daddy?"

Nathan put the tray down on the table next to the laptop and ruffled Tony's hair. "The way Stryker was talking, we'll all have a swimming pool."

Tony's face like up like a supernova. And then he thought, and turned to Syd, who'd just come in. "Hey. Can Saber swim?"

Nathan lifted his boy before she could answer and laid him flat on his arms. "Swim, Tony! Swim like a dolphin!"

Tony twirled his arms and Nathan ran him through the fire and lantern-lit ground rooms as fast as he could. They darted around furniture and pretend-splashed past the laughing adults. Tony wailed with joy, did an excellent breaststroke, and made splashing noises with his mouth.

Even Syd smiled, and some of the tension even seemed to dissipate from Donie.

"This is just the pool, Tony!" Nathan announced. "Are you ready for the ocean?"

Tony pushed his arms and kicked his legs even harder. Nathan ran towards the door, and Freeson, who was by it, helpfully pushed it open so that Nathan could sidestep through, out onto the porch below the smearily moonlit sky.

The dust in the heavens had turned the fat new moon blue across its face. As if the Man in the Moon had caught a cold. But Nathan didn't mind. He was high on his son, and high on the idea of Detroit now that he'd seen pictures. Real pictures of where they would be living in just a few short weeks.

He was so intent on the memory of the photographs, and his brilliantly swimming boy, laughing and splashing and giggling in the cold, that when the bullet came from the woods and slammed him in the temple, Nathan was still smiling as he hit the snow.

14

It was the pain that woke Nathan, not the cold. Digging into his skull like someone was twisting a screwdriver through the flesh and scraping it along the bone. He tried to open his eyes, but his right eyelid was stuck, and what he could see through his left eye was a lot of blurry wood—lit not by lanterns, but by a dull, blue, morning light seeping in from somewhere.

One side of his body felt freezing cold, and both damp and stiff. The other side of his body was chilly but seemed workable. He lifted his right hand to his face and felt the sticky presence of a drying liquid that had welded his eye shut. Above the eye was a crumbly mass of material crusted around the area being assaulted by the proverbial screwdriver.

The wound seemed to be a wide furrow, its bleeding edges

starting to form into scabs around the center where all the pain was pulpy and soft. Gingerly, he pressed down. The bone beneath seemed closer to his fingers under the flesh than he would have liked, and the bolt of pain that coursed across his head like hot lightning made him wince, but his skull was intact, at least.

"He's awake."

A voice he recognized, but not one of the voices he wanted to hear. *Donie.* She swam into the view of his left eye and, through the film of tears in his vision, resolved into a concerned face covered in mud. Her red hair was streaked with it, and her Basque top/t-shirt combo had gone ragged with tears.

"Any movement?" Donie asked someone Nathan could hear walking around on the wooden floor, but he couldn't see who it was.

"No, they're long gone."

Dave. That was Dave.

The pain in Nathan's head dug in deeper and he gasped. These were not the voices he needed. He wanted to hear Cyndi. Tony. Even Freeson. Someone familiar. Someone he trusted. He tried to get up on one elbow.

A hand pressed down on his chest and he didn't have the strength to resist. "Stay still. You've been shot."

Shot?

Nathan reached up to his head again, and Donie tugged his wrist away. "Don't touch. I'm going to clean it and put something on it. You've been laying out there in the snow for an hour. Anything could have gotten on your hands or in the wound. Unless you piss antibiotics, we're going to have the Devil's own job of preventing an infection."

Nathan let his hand drop and closed his eyes while Donie wiped at his face with a cloth that had been dipped in warm water.

"Where are the others?" he croaked as Donie worked.

"We don't know."

The digging screwdriver moved to Nathan's heart and twisted there for some time.

Family First.

"I need to find my family."

"And we need to find our stuff. So let me fix your head, and then we'll work out how we're going to do both those things. Okay?"

No. It wasn't okay. It was never going to be okay until Tony and Cyndi were back in his arms.

Family First.

When Donie had finished cleaning the wound, both she and Dave helped him up off the floor and onto the sofa. Dave had thrown too much wet wood on the fire, and so the room was smoky, the wood popping and cracking noisily. The morning light coming through the windows illuminated the smoke more than anything, filling the room with a milky incoherence that matched the fog in Nathan's brain. He was having all sorts of trouble processing what had happened, but he felt so groggy and fatigued that he had difficulty forming words.

The cold side of his body, the one that he assumed was the half that had lain in the snow for an hour, was warming now that he'd gotten in out of the cold, but he still wanted to change into dry clothes—he just didn't have the strength to take off even a sock.

Donie had rummaged in her mud-smeared pack and pulled out a wound pad, which she took from its peel-away plastic sheath, stuck to Nathan's head, and adhered there with tape. As she worked, Dave told Nathan what had happened.

"It was the Seven-Ones. They shot you and left you for dead. Donie and me were in the back bedroom unpacking when we heard the commotion and the shots. We went out the back window and dove into the bushes; we crawled under cover."

Nathan swallowed. "My family."

"Yeah. Sorry. But I had to save my family, too."

That cut Nathan, but he couldn't fault it.

"There was a lot of screaming and shouting, but no more shots. When we heard them driving the trucks and the trailer away, we came back. Found you half-buried in the snow. Guess they figured shooting you in the head was the end of it. You have a thick skull, Nathan. Either that or you're the luck-iest sonovabitch ever. The bullet just grazed you. Tore a hole in your skin, and it probably needs stitches, but that's not something we're equipped to do. And considering it should have killed you…"

Nathan thought of the Reynolds nurses. Miles away, heading south, with their medical skills and their medical equipment. Heading to the warmth of the south, away from the cold.

"They took everyone?" he asked.

"Yeah."

The screwdriver had finished its digging and left a hollow in Nathan that felt a mile wide and ten miles deep. He reached out and grabbed the edge of the sofa to stop his body collapsing into itself.

And then Saber licked his hand.

The dog had been sitting next to the sofa. Nathan hadn't even noticed. The huge Malamute got up and walked around so that she could put her head in Nathan's lap and get some fussing. She was limping on her front left paw, causing her head to bob and her shoulders to rock. There was a muddy mark on her flank's fur, too. The mark could have been the shape of a boot. Saber slid her head along his knees and pressed her nose into Nathan's belly.

They'd both lost their family.

Nathan used the last reserves of his strength to scritch at the dog's ears before sleep rolled over him like a cloud on a summer's day.

"We can't. Look at the sky!"

"I don't care!"

"Nathan, you won't last an hour out there. You've got no transport and the weather is closing in!"

"I can't just wait here while they get further away!"

"They'll get as far as they want if you're dead!"

The porch was being whipped by the wind as snow blew off the surrounding trees and the glowering clouds overhead promised more of the same. Nathan was too weak still to shake Dave's hand from his shoulder, and Donie stood in front of him, her hands stationed on his chest and stopping him from walking off the porch to trudge off into the encroaching storm.

"We can't just do nothing!" he wailed, his heart cracking and his stomach churning. "I want my boy! I want my wife!"

Donie grabbed hold of the material of his jacket. "If there's a blizzard coming, they're going to have to hunker down, too. They won't be able to travel. They won't get any further, and we *will* be able to find them. Killing yourself now helps no one except the Seven-Ones!"

That stopped Nathan pushing forward, the clarity of Donie's argument finally crashing through him like a wave of logic. If there was a blizzard coming, then yes, the Seven-Ones would have to stop and batten down the hatches. They wouldn't be able to pull the Airstream through that kind of weather. They were as stuck as Nathan.

He relaxed and let the two kids guide him back inside the hunting lodge.

The fire was working better now, but other than melted snow for water, they had no food or other supplies.

Dave and Donie had both copped shotguns, plus two boxes of shells they'd managed to get out of the back of the lodge when the Seven-Ones had attacked. But that was it as far as weapons were concerned.

Apart from the usual cutlery you'd find in any kitchen drawer, they had nothing other than four steak knives and a marble rolling pin to use in any offensive capacity.

Beyond weapons, Donie and Dave had two high-energy survival bars in their packs, as well as a small amount of first aid materials. They also had laptops, walkie-talkies, and the satellite base station. But nothing left to charge any of it.

Nathan had the clothes he stood in.

In the hours Nathan had slept, before waking up and immediately throwing himself at the door, Saber had been licking at her paw and was now able to put some weight on it.

It boiled Nathan's sensibilities that these assholes would hurt a dog like that, but then, if they'd not think twice about shooting people dead and carving their initials into their fore-heads, he had to accept that hurting an animal would be considered small potatoes.

The awful of image of Tony dead in the snow, with 71 carved into his pale skin, vomited up from Nathan's imagination in all its Technicolor abhorrence. Nathan screwed up his eyes and tried to make it go away, but all he succeeded in doing was replacing Tony with Cyndi.

The storm came in hard from the north, snow flurries obscuring the view from the windows, bringing visibility down to three or four yards even before night fell and the storm dumped its belly of ice and snow into the clearing and the surrounding trees. The lodge rattled in the intense wind and, at times, Nathan thought one of the walls might crack down the middle and open them up to the maw of the storm. The two lanterns swayed on their ceiling hooks as the building rocked in the brunt of the gale, casting crazy shadows. It made Nathan think of being lost in a boat on a storm-ravaged sea. The sickness of anxiety he felt about his lost family mirroring that vast ocean out there, all of it waiting for unwilling mariners. And that was exactly what Nathan felt he was now. Adrift and far from harbor—either in Detroit or Glens Falls.

Man, how he wished he'd fought harder to stay home, to convince Cyndi that they'd be able to survive in their own town and in their own valley, with their truck and their son and their hopes.

And now, Nathan was too tired even to sleep. The exhaustion weighed him down to the sofa, but fear kept clawing at his eyes to stay open. In truth, he was afraid to shut them, as they then became the screen on which his imagination projected constant horror movies of his family cut down, cut open, and carved like meat for the psychotic amusement of the Seven-Ones.

Nathan needed something to distract himself from the horror of it. Normally, if he felt out of sorts, he'd have gone to work on the Airstream or another project. Two years ago, as the extent of the world's ills had become known to people, he'd started a project on the Dodge to convert the engine so that it could run on any kind of fuel oil. From diesel right down the line to the oil used in industrial fryers in canteens. The sudden shift of the Earth's axis, and then the tectonic catastrophes on the west coast of the United States, had become apparent, and made Nathan turn his background anxieties about the state of the world into an exercise in pure distraction, ostriching his fears deep into the sand of hobby mechanics.

Cyndi's instincts had been to redouble her efforts to make sure they had enough supplies. She'd wanted them prepped to survive *anything*. Nathan's instinct had been to put his head into an engine and make it do something it wasn't supposed to.

Thinking back on it, on how differently they'd reacted, Nathan's mind settled on the razor edge of his failure as a husband and as a father. What had he done to protect them, other than to disassociate himself from the trouble while Cyndi had made sure they had food, supplies, and weapons?

And Nathan *really* needed something to distract his mind now.

Dave and Donie weren't sleeping, either, but they were sitting at the table, both working on their laptops. Both typing furiously and intent on whatever they were doing. Were they really only eight years younger than Nathan? What a gulf those years represented—a gulf in life experience and maturity. Nathan had the years on them, but it had been Donie who'd had all the maturity to stop him from going after the Seven-Ones alone, into the teeth of the storm. They'd had the presence of mind to get out and hide when they knew the odds were too great, because sometimes it's better to live to fight another day than to become a dead hero.

Nathan wasn't used to getting life lessons from twenty year olds, but here he was, learning that his failures had put his family in danger, and that he didn't have the skills and smarts to rescue them on his own.

It was a salutary lesson. Now, when there wasn't an engine to absorb his attention, Nathan had been forced into some cold, hard self-reflection through a mirror he held up to himself unwillingly. Nathan didn't like what he saw there.

Distraction.

Nathan pushed the blanket from his legs and got up, stretching. Dave and Donie might as well not have noticed he was there, so intent were they on their screens.

"What are you doing?" he asked.

Donie stopped typing and looked up with some annoyance. "Playing *White Hats*."

"I don't know what that is. Is it like a PlayStation game?"

Donie rolled her eyes. "Go back to sleep… old man."

Dave answered, "It's a game hackers play. We set up security systems on our 'puters and one tries to hack the other. It's like capture the flag, except it's in machine code."

Donie's fiery ire spat at Dave from her molten eyes. "Concentrate on the game!"

Dave pushed his laptop lid down with a slam. "You're winning anyway. You always win."

"That's because you're too distracted."

"Well, I'm glad you two feel okay enough to play a game. Isn't there something more important you could be doing?"

Donie closed her laptop down, too. "A) you're not in charge of us, and, b) we already have done something more important."

"What?"

"Yeah, we did," Dave said. "We've found where the Seven-Ones are holed up with our stuff, and your family."

15

"Why didn't you tell me sooner?" Nathan demanded.

Donie rolled her eyes and Dave pointed to the swinging lanterns casting their crazy pirate ship shadows around the room.

Nathan simmered.

Maybe if his daddy had told him to *Think First*, none of this would be happening and he wouldn't look like a tantrumming toddler in front of a Goth hacker and her boyfriend who was almost still too young to shave.

Donie met his eyes. "We couldn't get the uplink working, so we don't know how long the storm is going to last, so if you want to help your family and help us, you should force yourself to get some rest," Donie said sharply. "If we're going to go after those assholes and not screw this up completely, we all need to be ready. You've got a hole in the side of your head the size of a golf divot. Why don't you just sit the hell down and wait for the storm to blow over? That's what we're doing."

Nathan stood there staring at them, wanting to ask a million questions, but knew Donie was in no mood to cut him any slack.

"She gets cranky when she doesn't eat," Dave said simply.

"I do not!" Donie screamed, thumping the table so hard that the laptop jumped half an inch off the table.

Dave looked at Nathan. "See? Cranky."

Donie screeched her frustration, kicked the chair she'd been sitting in back, and then stormed off to the bedroom. "I'm only going so I don't kill you, you *jerk*!"

She slammed the door hard behind her.

"She loves me really," Dave said with a smile.

"No, I do not!" the bedroom door yelled.

Nathan retuned to the sofa, shaking his head.

Nathan's stomach ached. He couldn't tell if it was from hunger or from anxiety, and truth be told, it was probably a combination of both.

He still hadn't really been able to sleep, so as the storm raged outside the lodge, Dave showed him on the digital cop maps where he figured the Seven-Ones would have to have gone to shelter from the worst of the blizzard. He'd even worked out how long they'd had to get there before the storm hit. For the first time since he'd awoken from being shot, Nathan felt that at least they had a credible idea about where the gang had taken his family.

There were three possible places within five miles of the lodge where the Seven-Ones might have gone to. The furthest was just how far Dave figured they could have traveled before they'd have had to park and camp in the Airstream on the road.

Two other possibilities included, first, a farmstead three miles from the lodge that had a barn, two rows of battery chicken farm buildings, and a ranch house, while the second and the nearest rested at the head of a freshwater reservoir; a large pumping and filtration station that would provide great cover if the Seven-Ones had known where to find it.

"What makes you think they did?" Nathan asked Dave.

"Logic, Nathan. Logic. They have local knowledge, or they have the same cop maps we do. This lodge isn't on any of the civilian maps. Too new. So, one of them must have thought to check for us here because he knew it, or they've been systematically checking everywhere, ticking off buildings as they go. Whatever the reason, dude, you and your stuff are special to them. This wasn't just about a supply grab."

Nathan's throbbing head made his thinking even more muzzy. "Explain."

"Why didn't they just kill everyone?"

The thought hit Nathan like a train at a level crossing. Yes. The attack they'd seen from the ridge above the highway had been a straight kill-and-steal. This had been something altogether different. "Why would they want hostages?"

"Exactly," Dave said quietly. "Why *would* they?"

Nathan flashed back to the conversation he'd overheard between Syd and Tony about her lighting out if the gang got anywhere near her. Maybe they *were* looking for Syd. Maybe she was the focus of their hunt, and they'd scored the rest of Nathan's family and friends as a bonus.

"Why didn't they just stay here if they knew the storm was coming?"

"I guess they've got somewhere they want to be, so it was better to set off and get a few hours down the trail before the storm stopped their progress. They got out of here fast. Seems like they were on a clock."

As soon as the storm broke, they would head out.

Dave had retired to a bedroom after that exchange, and Nathan didn't know whether to be horrified or embarrassed as he heard him and Donie making love vigorously and noisily behind the door. Whether they'd become engaged in a hate-screw or make-up sex, Nathan couldn't be sure, but it was loud enough to be either, even with the storm still rattling the lodge. In the end, he covered his face with a blanket and buried the uninjured side of his head under a pillow.

In the morning, Donie pulled the blanket from Nathan's face and put half of a high-energy nutrition bar in his hand.

"That's breakfast and lunch, and probably dinner, so make the most of it."

The storm lasted a couple more hours while Nathan pensively stared out the window, willing it to stop. When the blizzard was finally done, the square of clearing outside the lodges looked to be covered in whipped cream, with the trees surrounding it bearded like ancient men crowding around a post office on pension day.

The day was bright and razor cold and the blizzard had obliterated any chance they might have had of following the Seven-Ones by tire tracks alone, and even Saber, whose limp had all but disappeared, didn't seem to know which direction they might have gone in, but they suited up and left the lodge. They walked in silence down the trail to the road and struck out east towards the pumping station.

The reservoir was frozen over, and a thick blanket of snow lay across the ice. They hung back in the trees, having approached the area through the woods rather than via the service road, worried about meeting the Seven-Ones leaving their bolt hole in the process if they had. Even without binoculars, looking across the ice-stilled body of water, they could see the pumping station hadn't been used to shelter the gang from the storm.

There were no buildings large enough to hide the trucks and the Airstream, and Donie came back from checking the service road to tell them that there were no tire tracks leading away from the pump station to suggest the gang had already left in the two hours of hard walking it had taken the three of them to get there.

"The farm then," Nathan announced, pushing off without waiting for Dave or Donie to answer.

They let him walk ten yards before shouting to him that he was walking in the wrong direction.

Donie caught up, flipped open the clamshell case on her phablet, and showed Nathan the map. "I get you're in a hurry, Nate, but we lead. Okay?"

Nathan nodded, cursing himself silently. How many lessons were these kids going to teach him before the day was out?

Think first.

Yeah, Daddy. Thanks for that.

Two hours of exhausting, stiff-legged, cross-country, snow walking later, they broke over the ridge above the farmstead. What the map hadn't told them, however, was that it had been raided and burned out some time ago. One of the barns still sat undamaged, but the main ranch-style house had been gutted. The chicken sheds, which had been unharmed on the satellite images of the cop maps, had been razed entirely to the ground.

No activity could be seen around the farm and Nathan saw no point in looking further. "Let's go," he said.

"I need a rest somewhere warm-ish," Donie replied. "We've been yomping for nearly five hours. I'm wasted."

Without another word, she struck out over the five hundred yards of open country from the ridge to the farmstead. She'd left two dozen footprint dots on the perfect white of the field before Dave followed. Nathan, knowing that he'd never be able to find the gang without his young companions, reluctantly followed.

And in the end he was glad he had.

The double-doored entrance to the large clapboard barn was open, and Donie made for it directly, her trajectory firmly set. She clearly wanted out of the wind, and to sit down somewhere that wasn't "covered in snow"—as she called back while Dave and Nathan struggled to catch up. She may have been carrying a few extra pounds, but when Donie set her mind to it, she wasn't easily deterred from any path.

Out of the cutting breeze, the barn, although old and rickety, was basically sound. Why it hadn't been torched in the raid was anyone's guess. Perhaps it hadn't been the gang who had raided and torched it at all. There were enough abandoned properties where fire might start spontaneously for a number of reasons if the storms had brought down electrical cables, and a fire from the house wouldn't have reached the old barn, Nathan knew.

And seeing the house already burned out from a distance might have had a similar effect on scavengers as it had on Nathan. No point in going there because it was already wrecked. And, certainly, what they found in the barn showed them something that looters wouldn't have left behind.

It was the rich aroma of diesel and engine oil that drew

Nathan to the tarp-covered tractor before he'd even registered what might lie beneath the strained green fabric.

While Donie sat on a deep bed of hay that was still on the dry side of becoming animal feed or silage, and Dave set up a base station to see if he could get a satellite uplink, Nathan uncovered a miracle.

The green John Deere 5020 tractor was fifty years old if it was a day. It had all the hallmarks of being someone's weekend project, as it didn't look like it had been a working farm machine for many years. There was no other farm machinery nearby—no plows or threshers, or seed drills—all but cementing the impression of it has a hobby vehicle for whoever had lived in the ranch house.

Maybe the guy who'd fixed it up was the same kind of ostrich as Nathan, he considered, and then he shook the thought from his head and got on with checking over the tractor.

The engine was clean, the fuel tank showed itself to be three-quarters full, and the tires, both front and back, seemed well pressured and sound. Nathan climbed up into the glass cab. It was a one-person vehicle with just a bucket seat, a steering wheel, and green-painted operating levers topped with black plastic spheres.

"This tractor is immaculate," Nathan called down to Dave and Donie.

Neither of them seemed that interested.

"Guys! We can use this!"

"Go ahead. Plow a field. Have fun." Donie's sarcasm bit hard, but Nathan wasn't deterred.

"There's enough diesel to go a hundred miles. More."

Dave looked up from the laptop where he'd been failing to get an uplink, suddenly interested.

Donie was still laid out in the hay with her eyes closed. "And? It's a tractor. It's noisy as hell. They'll hear us coming from two counties away."

"Maybe, but we know now they didn't spend the night here, so they're on the road. They'll be moving now, and my Dodge sounds just as loud as this tractor. Then there's their Ski-Doos. We'll move faster over the snow because of the tires and they won't hear us coming while they're moving. I can't imagine they're going to stop moving if they don't have to. They're in a hurry, remember? That's what we're guessing? And they're going to have to stick to roads. With this beauty, we can cut corners and go across country. Once we pick up their trail, we can use the maps to overtake them. Maybe plan an ambush."

And to back up his idea, Nathan took two wires from inside the steering column and twisted them together. The hotwired tractor started on the first try, its rumble shaking the barn so that streams of old dust fell from the wooden rafters. "We don't even need a key!"

With only the driving seat for occupants, it was so cramped in the glass-sided cab that Dave and Donie had to affix their packs onto the rear of the John Deere tractor, tying them on as tight as they could and making sure all the zips were secure. Saber was happy to trot alongside and sometimes ahead. Her leg was fine now. Occasionally, she would dive off into the woods to either side of the road, and she came back with bloody jaws and a succession of broken squirrels in her mouth. At least one of them was getting fed.

Donie and Dave crouched behind and to the side of Nathan as he drove. The only possessions they'd brought into the cab were their laptops and the shotguns. The glass cab gave them good all-around vision and would afford them lots of warning if anyone tried to sneak up on them from behind.

Nathan's head wound was stiff and felt hot to the touch around the pad, though he could deal with the pain well enough now that he had other things to focus on, and felt they were actually getting somewhere with the tractor. He knew the wound pad would have to be changed soon, however, as it was soaked through with exudate—if the fissure below wasn't cleaned regularly, he'd be in a whole heap of trouble.

The John Deere ate up the miles easily, and Nathan estimated they were averaging ten miles an hour over the virgin snow. Saber kept up a steady trot nearby, and while Nathan knew nothing about the breed, he guessed all working Arctic dogs had travel like this as their bread and butter. That said, he would slow the tractor occasionally so that Saber could catch up. She'd bark happily and jump up when she reached them, and then fall back into step as Nathan pushed forward.

The morning wore onto afternoon, and Nathan knew that they only had a couple of hours to pick up the Seven-Ones' trail. He'd been recognizing the country for some miles now, too—they'd traversed it in the other direction only a few days before on their way towards Detroit. That glittering haven of enclosed plazas and swimming pools had never felt more distant that it did now. Without his family, there would be no sanctuary for Nathan there. If his family was gone, then he didn't know what he would do... other than to keep looking for them, to find out their fate one way or another.

"Look!" The signal had come from Dave, pointing past Nathan's ear. He'd been so lost in his reverie that the uniformity of the road had become something he'd processed on automatic pilot, and he hadn't noticed what Dave and Donie had already seen up ahead.

It was Freeson's Land Cruiser.

And it was now a burned-out wreck.

16

Walking to the Land Cruiser was the longest walk Nathan had ever taken in his life.

Even jumping down from the cab of the tractor had been near impossible. He'd almost had to tell his legs to move before they would, he'd been so frozen by the fear of what he might find within the burned-out wreck.

The stink of the dead truck was thick in his nostrils before he could see inside, the stench of burned rubber, charred plastic, seat foam, and hot metal having become a concoction that clogged his throat and stung his eyes.

Or were his eyes pouring preemptive tears?

Nathan didn't know.

Dave and Donie hung back as Saber caught up. The gravity of what they were witnessing had even been picked up on by the dog. She sat by the steaming tractor, her ears pricked up, attentive, but she didn't venture forward as Nathan moved on his mechanical legs, fear gripping him with a steely stranglehold.

All the windows on the truck had burst as a result of the flames which had engulfed it. Chunks of glass glittered on the ground where the intense heat generated by the car's end had melted all the snow and ice back to nothing but a wide circle of blackened earth. The back section of the Cruiser, where Freeson had stored the diesel cans, was empty. The vehicle had been thoroughly looted before being torched.

Nathan edged forward a little more, needing to bend his head to see through the charred metal skeletons of the seats, both front and back, all the way up to the melted dash.

The car was empty.

Whatever Nathan had imagined he'd find there—some dead horror of charred skin and split red, limbs tortured into impossible shapes—it wasn't within the Cruiser.

The relief rushed through him, bursting the dam of fear in a gushing of released terror, his bones scoured clean and his heart released. "Thank God," he whispered to himself, not knowing if there was anyone or anything to hear him.

And then, looking through the Toyota to the heat-uncovered patch of ground beyond it, he saw the body.

Nathan's knees collapsed beneath him.

It was only the nearness of the Toyota, and his instinctive move to throw out his hand to steady himself, that stopped Nathan from crashing to the ground in a heap of pain.

Dave jumped from the tractor and ran to Nathan. Relief was evident in his voice when he spoke. "Man, I thought you'd been hit by sniper."

Nathan shook his head, trying to point at the burned carcass on the other side of the Cruiser, but he was just unable to get his muscle memory together enough before he vomited caustic bile from an empty stomach over the door of the Toyota.

Dave saw the body. "Is that…?"

"I don't know," Nathan managed to say between breaths. He wiped the remains of the foul-tasting liquid from his lips.

Dave waved Donie down from the tractor and went around the Cruiser. Nathan forced his back to straighten, and then he followed.

The smell of roasted meat was enough to turn the most enthusiastic carnivore vegan. The body was adult, and charred black, but streaked yellow-pink where the flesh and fat had roasted through. White bone poked out at both elbows, and what clothes there had been were just black tatters of material. The skull at the back of the head had been scraped clear of hair and split down to the bone. Nathan hadn't seen a burned-up person before, and the corpse's face—seen as Dave bent, reached across it, and turned it over stiff as a surfboard—was a study in agony.

Nathan forced himself to stare at the face, with its cooked eyes and rictus grin pulled back severely from the teeth. And it was only then he could be sure it wasn't Cyndi, Lucy, or Freeson.

The face, although scorched and burned, wasn't so charred as the rest of the body. Perhaps the person had managed to pull himself from the burning car and push his face down into the snow before the end. The rest of the body had been left to burn, but the face at least still had some remnants of humanity about it—the skin around the chin suggesting a thick beard had been burned away, with a silver nose ring on top of that and tattoos of sparrows on both sides of the neck.

Nathan sagged in his flesh, feeling like he was being loosened from himself. Whoever the person was, his end hadn't been easy. Nathan could be sure of that. But at least until he found evidence to the contrary, his family were still notionally alive.

Dave let the body fall back onto the ground with a smart crack. It was already frozen through. "Been here a while. Enough for the frost to settle. Hard to tell, but I'd say at least five hours, maybe more."

Nathan wondered how Dave could be so matter-of-fact, and the look he gave him must have unlocked a little shame in the young man's eyes. He shrugged and answered, "Life goes on, dude. If we're gonna catch up with them, we can't afford to be sentimental."

Nathan nodded. "Yeah. I just… I just thought the worst."

Dave clapped Nathan's shoulder like a teacher comforting a slow pupil in class. "Yeah, man. I get that."

Donie, who had gone into the trees, was returning. She had a red plastic gasoline container in her hand, and she put it on the roof of the Land Cruiser, where it sat incongruously intact among all the destruction.

"Found it in the trees. Empty." Donie added, "Guess we can rule out the truck catching fire by accident."

Dave had gone forward to where the snow hadn't been melted by the heat and was studying the tire tracks that remained.

"There's the Dodge and the trailer, two Ski-Doos, and another truck. Going east." He looked back at the charred Land Cruiser. "Guess they had another truck waiting here and decided to leave the Cruiser once they'd transferred the supplies." Dave pointed at the body, commenting, "Maybe Chuckles here wanted to keep the Cruiser for himself. The boss man objected. There was a fight. Chuckles and the Cruiser get barbequed and the caravan continued on."

"Nice people to do business with, if they'd kill one of their own so cheaply," Donie said.

Nathan was still riding a wave of nausea and disgust at what he'd seen. "You two sound like you come across this sort of thing every day."

"We've seen our share," Dave said.

"It doesn't get any easier," Donie finished.

And that was a statement that Nathan could get on board with without any trouble. None of this was getting easier.

Not even close.

The terrain became even more recognizable as they moved on.

The tracks led them back onto the highway, and within an hour, they had passed Lucy's burned-out limo.

The echo of the sight against the burned-out Land Cruiser wasn't lost on Nathan. Each vehicle, burned for very different reasons, but with the same outcome.

"You torched that one?" Dave asked incredulously as they passed the wreck, and Nathan explained how they'd met Lucy.

"She's a piece of work, that one," Donie said, and Nathan felt the ironic burn of her non-self-aware and judgmental attitude rising like lava within him.

He didn't feel like he had the headspace to use up on an argument with Donie, though. It wasn't his place to tell her how much of an asshole she sounded to be. In any case, would it make any difference? Dave, he had warmed to, but he still felt a chill distance between him and Donie. It was a bridge that he didn't know if he'd ever be able to cross… maybe if things had been different and they hadn't been on the edge of desolation, she might have been a whole different person, but he couldn't know.

Then again, maybe Nathan would have been, too. He just didn't know. All he did know was that he didn't like himself very much right now. He wasn't impressed with himself at all, and wondered how his daddy would have dealt with the situation.

Family First.

Okay, sure, but where did that leave him?

Nathan hated that he was wallowing a little in his own self-pity. He needed to shake it loose and get his ducks in a row. Saving his wife and his son was not going to allow him to just go back to being the old Nathan. Old Nathan had to break, slough his skin, and come out bigger, stronger, and harder.

And if he didn't do that, everything would be lost.

"Well, that's just great."

The tracks they'd been following, which Dave seemed to have a real skill at doing—he called it his only "real-world skill" as opposed to his "virtual skills as a White Hat Hacker" (*Whatever that was*, Nathan had thought)—had led them to the highway off-ramp leading to *Marty's Trucker Love.*

Nathan wouldn't risk taking the tractor down the ramp and pulling into the parking lot before reconnoitering the area first.

The three of them tramped down the snowy slope,

through the young pines and the thick brush, looking out over the windswept parking lot maybe sixty yards to the truck stop. The scene was pretty much as it had been before, with the two big rigs and the tanker. Parked closer to the diner, though, was Nathan's Dodge, still yoked to the Airstream, with two Ski-Doos and a chunky black, late model Ford F-350.

As Nathan scanned from the diner to the gas station, a movement by the pumps caught his eye, and what he saw there made the breath still in his throat like a solid mass.

Freeson had been tied between the two pumps, his arms outstretched as if he'd been crucified. His head lolled to one side. His knees were bent, and his feet were naked and folded up beneath him. There wasn't enough give in what had been used to tether him to the pumps to allow his knees to fall fully to the concrete, and it was his rolling head, moving near deliriously from side to side across his chest, which had caught Nathan's attention.

His best friend, hog-tied outside in the freezing cold. No anorak, no gloves, no hat, no shoes.

If he'd been there more than a couple of hours, he wouldn't be far from frostbite or a fatal case of hypothermia.

"Free..."

Dave and Donie stared forward at Freeson as his head moved.

"We gotta get him down," Nathan breathed out as much to himself as to the others.

"No. Wait," Donie hissed, and with that she pointed back to the diner.

Three men were coming out from the glass-fronted building. They were dressed in gaudy, brightly-colored ski jackets. And they had balaclavas rolled up over their faces, sitting on their heads like beanie hats.

Nathan labeled them automatically as he took them in. Mustache was rangy, and sharp-faced, like a rat walking on his hind legs, a bushy frontiersman's handlebar drooping from his top lip. Redhead had a thick rope of hair tied behind his skull in a ponytail. He was fatter than Mustache and walked with his head and eyes down, like he was in a permanent state of submission to the others.

The third was the tallest, and as they walked towards Freeson's crucified form, he pulled off his balaclava to scratch at his massive, bald head. The skin of it ran with tattoos, the content of which Nathan couldn't define from this distance, but the near fully covered expanse of exposed skin reminded Nathan of a hardened gang member from a death-row documentary on *National Geographic*. Bald walked with a swagger that marked him out, if not within the whole group then certainly within this trio, as the top dog.

Mustache reached Freeson first and, without any preamble, punched the stricken mechanic in the face, snapping his head back and sending up a spray of blood from his nose.

The deadened acoustics of the snow-laden surroundings carried the men's laughter across to the brush where Nathan and the others hid. Dave and Donie both had their shotguns in hand, but if they fired from this range, the spread of shot would pepper everyone—including Freeson.

"My turn!" roared Redhead with a throaty laugh, and he kicked Freeson in the guts.

It seemed the gang members had come out just to beat up Freeson. They weren't asking him for information, and they weren't trying to gain tactical knowledge of where he might know of supplies hiding. They just wanted to hurt him and make his last moments as painful and terror-filled as they could.

Nathan felt torn, watching it all unfold. Yes, they could burst from the brush and, with some element of surprise, get close enough to the torture scene to open fire from a more advantageous range—but if they did that, then what about Cyndi, Tony, Syd, and Lucy? There was no way they were unguarded in the diner.

In saving Freeson, Nathan might condemn his family to their deaths.

Nathan's head wound throbbed with the jagged thoughts leaping up from the brain beneath. He'd taken little notice of the wound since they'd acquired the tractor, and as he thought about what they should do, he felt a trickle of liquid running down his face. He touched his cheek, and his trembling fingers came away smeared with the pus and blood that had seeped out from under the wound pad. Whatever happened, Nathan's bullet tear was infected, and he didn't have a lot of time before he was going to need some serious antibiotics therapy if he wanted to avoid a system-wide infection. An infection that might lead, untreated, to septicemia or worse.

Nathan looked questioningly from Donie to Dave. Their faces and shrugging shoulders told him they were feeling the weight of the same dilemma. There were no easy solutions to this, and things were coming to a head in more ways than one. The cruel laughter needling across the parking lot was reaching some kind of a crescendo even as they tried to formulate a plan.

Nathan forced himself to look back at Freeson and the trio. Freeson was being punched in the guts by Mustache, and the mechanic vomited noisily down his front, his arms straining at his bonds.

Seeing the mess, Redhead pulled a pistol from a shoulder holster inside his ski jacket and pointed it at Freeson's face.

"How about some target practice?"

17

N athan was halfway to his feet before Donie yanked him back into the brush. "You can't! You know you can't," she hissed into his ear.

"You gotta let them do what they want, or your family is dead," Dave spat into Nathan's other ear. "You understand? Dead!"

Nathan knew they were right, and realized he had to let Freeson go if there was any chance of getting his family back. Nathan let the tension dissipate from his muscles and stopped struggling against the kids' hands.

"I'm sorry, Free," he said quietly, and then he closed his eyes, waiting for the shooting to start.

But the gun didn't fire, and all Nathan heard from behind his closed eyes was a harsh slap across bare skin. This was followed by a girlish yelp of pain and a commanding voice that shouted, "It's a gas station, you redheaded moron! What the heck are you thinking?"

"Sorry… sorry, yeah, Owen. Sorry."

"You better be, you nitwit. I burned Robbie to a crisp for backchat. You wanna go the same way? 'Cause, you fat piece of crap, I got plenty more gas to roast you in your own juices. Are we clear?"

"Yes, Owen. Sorry, Owen. I just wasn't thinking."

"Well, now's the time to start!"

Nathan's eyes had come fully open now, and the scene around Freeson appeared as intense in vision as it had in sound. Owen—the bald and tattooed monster—had apparently slapped Redhead hard on the cheek. He was still rubbing at the spot furiously. His gun had fallen to the concrete.

As Nathan looked at the gun, though, something caught his eye, glinting from way beyond it. The Airstream's doors were open; boxes and cartons had been removed from it and littered the ground in front of it. But also, waiting to be opened or rolled away, there were Donie and Dave's flight cases. And from where Owen, Mustache, and Redhead were surrounding Freeson, their line of sight didn't allow them to see the flight cases. Anyone might be able to get up to them and…

A plan started to formulate in the fuzzy reaches of Nathan's brain. As Owen, Mustache, and Redhead beat up on Freeson a little more, he told Donie and Dave the skeleton bones of it—he'd need to put flesh on the plan's bones with some more information, but he had the start of something.

If he could put it into action before Freeson was punched to death, they might be able to save the mechanic, too.

Nathan ran fast and low towards the rear of the diner in the encroaching night. A chain link fence enclosed a small compound filled with snow-covered engine parts, body panels, dead catering refrigerators, and an upended stove. Gas-rings the size of a ship's portholes across its face.

The gate on the compound's fence wasn't locked, but it was on a squeaky latch. Nathan tried hard to operate it without transmitting his presence to anyone who might be in the back of the building.

The snow in the compound was undisturbed, and that at least told Nathan the gang hadn't been interested in the piled-up junk there. Nathan wished he could cover the ground without leaving footprints, but that was a non-starter, no matter the fact that if anyone did come out, they would see immediately that he'd been casing the diner.

There was a blank-faced green door set into the wall, and Nathan could just make out its color as the darkness completed its arrival. The sky was ashen, but free of clouds, and the last streaks of sunlight were spreading orange flares on the underside of the ash layer.

It was coming up on full dark now, and if Nathan's plan was going to come to fruition, the confusion it caused would be well exacerbated by the dark. But first he had to get inside the building.

The door had no handle on the outside—just a hole in which a key could be inserted and the door pulled open when the mechanism caught. Nathan prayed that, like the chain link gate, security wasn't a top priority for Betty. She had more than enough to worry about with making sure Marty stayed happy and healthy.

Nathan leaned the shotgun against the wall and pulled a small tool pack from inside his coat. The wallet-sized fold of leather always sat in his inside pocket in case of fiddly work needing to done out on the road, and it could come in handy now. He selected a small flathead screwdriver and inserted it into the keyhole, hoping against hope that he'd be right about Betty and her priorities.

The screwdriver wedged its way into the hole, and it gave Nathan just enough purchase to be able to move the door.

The door came open a sliver on a breath of warm air from the heated guts of the diner.

Nathan's memory of the internal geography of the diner told him that unless someone was at the back of the building, past the store cupboard and the four free-standing stainless steel refrigerators, nobody out front would be able to see this door opening.

Nathan pulled the door a sliver further and peered inside.

The lights were off in the kitchen, but there was enough illumination coming in from the restaurant to give him a view of the space beyond the door. The breeze outside the building was cold, and he could feel it moving past his ear into the kitchen. He would need to get in now if the gang members inside weren't going to be alerted by an attendant drop in temperature.

From what he could see, no one was near the door, and so he opened it just enough to get him, the shotgun, and his bulky anorak inside. He slid into the diner's warmth and gently shut the door behind himself.

Harsh voices were coming from the diner beyond the counter. There was laughter, as well, and indistinct words, and Nathan was surprised to hear that the majority of the voices were female.

Dropping into a crouch, Nathan snicked the door fully shut and moved across the tan tiled floor, settling against the cool metal of one of the stainless steel refrigerators. The chill steel felt good against the side of his head with the wound, drawing the heat of infection momentarily away. But as he pressed into the metal, he also felt another trickle of liquid pop from beneath the pad and run along his cheekbone.

Nathan moved forward. A woman with a broad Bronx accent was saying, "You're a skinny kid. That'll be good for us. You'll be able to get into places we can't. You don't wanna be like that asshole, Syd. She screwed Danny good, but you're not like that are you, boy? You're not like that skinny Goth."

Nathan's heart skipped several beats as he heard Tony answer, "I just wanna be with my mom and dad. Let me be with my mom!"

"Your mom and Miss Hoiti-Toiti are gonna be fine, kid," Bronx said. "Your dad and any other guys we meet, not so much. And the Goth? When we get her back to Danny in New York, she's gonna wish even her grandmother hadn't been born, not just her."

There was another round of harsh laughter.

"I... don't... don't... understand."

"Sydney's been a bad, bad girl. That's why we came after her. Your mom and the stuck-up bitch? Well, Owen and Danny have plans for them."

"Plans?"

"Yeah. You see your momma's fat belly, kid?"

"The baby?"

"Outstanding. Owen's gonna make her make some more."

Another staccato round of laughter twisted Nathan's guts up as tight as a cross-threaded bolt.

"Ladies make babies, kid. Men, they're just trouble. You join up with us and we'll take care of you better than any daddy will. Or you'll end up like Mr. Punchbag over there at the gas pumps, and you don't want that, do you?"

Tony's only reply was a hacking cough and the wheeze that could be the start of an asthma attack.

"Leave him alone, you bitch!"

Cyndi's voice.

The only reply Nathan heard was the whip crack of a slap, a crash of furniture, and a yelp of pain from Cyndi.

"You gonna leave me to talk to your boy," Bronx said, "or I can slit his throat now. Which one will it be?"

Tony's coughing had stopped, and although his voice was feathery with fear, he managed to say, "If you leave my mom alone, I'll listen... but you gotta stop hitting her... please."

Although hot agony burned through him at the fact that he couldn't do anything to help them, at least Nathan could work out why the Seven-Ones had taken his family and the others rather than killing them on the spot. Women they could breed, a kid who they could train, and then Freeson, to use as an example and leverage to get the women to do what they wanted them to do. The unbelievably fast and complete break-down of social norms and morality writ large in this one loca-tion. Nathan churned and ground his teeth.

No longer would he be the reluctant and indecisive man of engines and other displacement activities. Nathan was all that stood between his family and their doom.

"Hello."

The shock of the nearby voice hit Nathan so hard, the shotgun almost slipped from his fingers and clattered to the floor. He snapped his head around.

It was Marty. He was shuffling forward with his hand outstretched in greeting, his 11th Airborne cap turned around in the style of a fifteen-year-old. His belt had been loosened and his trousers were hanging gangsta-style from his ample hips, and Nathan saw with a glance down that the laces had been removed from his white sneakers. Perhaps saddest of all, a chain made from yellow toilet paper had been hung around his neck in the rapper way. The Seven-Ones had clearly been playing with the old man, humiliating him in front of his wife and the others. Nathan could imagine the cruel laughter of the scumbag gang members defiling the old man because of his mental state and trusting nature.

Nathan couldn't risk Marty saying anything more, so he raised his finger to his lips and took the old man's hand. Using the refrigerator as cover, he stood up and whispered to him, "Marty, please, please be quiet—can you do that for me?"

Marty nodded with serious eyes and then winked. "I like games," he said quietly.

"Hey, old man!" Bronx shouted from the other side of the counter.

"His name is Marty," Betty said.

"Whatever. Old man. You got the bourbon?"

Nathan looked down at Marty's other hand. There it was, gripping the neck of a bottle.

"If you don't come here with that bourbon now, I'm gonna kick your missus' teeth out of her head."

Nathan winced as he heard Betty's muffled yelp of indignation.

Bronx went on, "And as these teeth are all her own, I guess that's gonna hurt a whole lot more than I was expectin'."

Nathan moved behind Marty and gently maneuvered the truckstop owner to the edge of the refrigerator, and then he whispered, "Go give them the bourbon, Marty. We're going to get you out of here real soon."

"But I don't want to go!" Marty said, a note of panic in his voice.

Nathan waited for the rush of Seven-Ones to come head-long into the kitchen, but when Bronx spoke again, it was clear she thought the panic in his voice to be an emotion she'd drawn out of Marty through the threats she'd made to Betty's teeth.

"I don't care what you want to do, you smelly old fart. Get that drink over hear or that'll be all she wrote!"

Marty looked back at Nathan, tears balancing on the lids of his eyes. He held up the bourbon bottle towards the counter, but the confusion danced across his face. Looking at Nathan, offering the bottle.

"Screw it, if I have to come and get it, I'm going to punch your face inside out!"

There was a long moment of silence, and then Nathan heard the door to the side of the counter open, and then the door into the kitchen. Footsteps moved towards the back of the kitchen, and Nathan could do nothing but raise his shotgun and wait.

18

Nathan watched the color drain from Cyndi's face like liquid rushing from a broken spigot in a barrel. He'd heard the rush of breath escaping his wife's mouth and nostrils as she'd reached Marty and saw her husband standing there, pointing the shotgun at her. Seeing it was her, he lowered the business end of the shotgun as Cyndi's eyes bulged like a bull-frog's throat pouch. Luckily, Cyndi had the presence of mind to catch herself before the words backing up in her brain could catch up with her mouth.

"I… got the bourbon…" Marty said, his eyes flicking between Cyndi, Nathan, and the space beyond the counter.

Marty began raising his free hand to point at Nathan, and it seemed that luck was draining from the tableaux like the color from Cyndi's cheeks, but his wife was suddenly on fire. She caught Marty's wrist before he could finish his point, and said, "Don't worry, Marty, we'll shut the store room door in a little while. Let's get back to Betty."

"Okay," Marty said with the trusting voice of a child. "Let's go back to Betty. Betty! I got the bottle."

Nathan hadn't breathed for nearly a minute, so that his lungs ached and his head swam. Cyndi hadn't dared a look back at him. Watching her go without grabbing her and dragging her out of the back of the diner had taken a supreme effort, but he kept himself still.

The matter in hand, the part of the plan he needed to enact before he could put the rest of it into action, came back to the forefront of his thinking. It wasn't enough to hear the voices. He had to find out where everyone was...

Nathan moved back three steps, to where there was a thin gap between two refrigerators. He kept low enough to get a look across the far counter, out across the three rows of red vinyl booths. Bronx was a tall blonde-haired woman with a severe face and razor thin lips. She was watching as Cyndi led Marty back towards the kitchen door.

She had them covered with a crossbow.

The sight of the weapon dried what little spit had been left in Nathan's mouth. Behind Bronx were two other hard-faced women. A short, bubble-afroed black woman in a pink anorak worn below a jutting chin with a pursed mouth like a cat's butt. She held the muzzle of an AR-15 like a ski pole, its butt against the floor. Behind Assmouth was a beanpole-thin woman who looked consumptive and ill. As if to underline that assessment, she coughed hard enough to put Tony to shame. She was holding a SIG Sauer loosely in the hand she'd brought up to her mouth to inadequately cover the cough.

Looking out of the window at the front of the diner, keeping watch, was a man whose thick mat of hair on the back of his head was the only feature Nathan could see. He had an AK-47 slung across his shoulders, and he was waving through the glass to Owen, who was walking back alone from his Free-son-as-a-punching-bag session.

Nathan's sensibilities keened at the idea of Freeson being left in the hands of Mustache and Redhead. He could only hope the fact that they were still with him meant he was still alive. Still, Nathan knew, from the state of Freeson before he'd made his wide run to the back of the diner, that the mechanic didn't have much time. The extra half an hour since he'd seen him might have finished him off already.

Mustache and Redhead might just be burying him in the snow, it suddenly occurred to him.

Focus. Where is everybody?

Syd, Betty, and Lucy were in a booth on the opposite side of the diner, furthest from the exit. Syd's eye had a blackening bruise and Betty was gently sobbing. Lucy sat impassively and imperiously—staring into the middle distance with defocused eyes. She didn't even look up as Cyndi came back through the kitchen door with Marty to rejoin them in the booth.

Bronx snatched the bottle from Marty's hand and pushed

him into a seat next to Tony, who had until now been sitting on his own in the next booth down from the women. It was there that Bronx had been working on him to join the Seven-Ones of his own free will rather than force. Tony looked brow-beaten and drained of color. The sight made Nathan's heart ache.

Owen came into the diner, the fists swinging by his side stained with fresh blood, his knuckles red with it. He walked down the aisle and picked up a handful of napkins from a dispenser to clean his caked hands of Freeson's blood.

Bronx had been taking thick slugs from the bottle of bourbon, and in deference to Owen, she stopped short of draining it and passed it to him. Owen took a long gulp and passed it back.

"Fightin' and drinkin' always put me in the mood for sexin'," he announced to the room.

Nathan's hands tightened on the shotgun.

Still, he didn't have enough of an advantage to attack. Assmouth or Bronx would zero in on him before he got a chance to take down either, and he wasn't even sure he had the skill to take any of them down in one shot before Blackhair unhooked his AK-47 or Consumpta felled him with the SIG.

Owen approached the booth where Cyndi, Syd, and Lucy were sitting. Watching, Nathan bit into his lip so hard that he drew blood and felt it spreading across his tongue.

Owen reached out a hand and pulled Lucy to her feet. She didn't resist, and for all his doubts about the woman, Nathan was impressed that she didn't cower or look scared. Her eyes were demons, her knuckles white as the snow outside as they made fists.

"You know why we call ourselves the Seven-Ones, blondie?"

Lucy made a show of thinking hard. "Because seven plus one is your collective IQ?"

Nathan felt the air sucking out of the room. Owen was on the cusp of striking her with his fist, and Nathan noted the supreme effort it took him not to hit Lucy where she stood. "No, sweet cheeks," the tattooed thug said, trying to give the impression her words hadn't vexed him. "For every man, seven women."

Lucy's face grew even more unimpressed. "I knew you incels were crazy, but I didn't realize you were demanding harems now. I must read *Sad Lonely Masturbator Mother's Boy Weekly* more often."

Owen boiled. He clearly wasn't used to being back-chatted in this way. "Maybe you like that kinky, tied-up-in-a-cage crap, but I don't want to have to find the key every time I want you to get me beer."

"The world has frozen over, but hell would have to follow, too, before I urinated in your cup to quench your thirst."

"You can join us the easy way or the hard way, lady."

"Do you have problems staying hard? I understand there are tablets you can take…"

"I admire spirit," Owen drawled, letting his hand lift from Lucy's wrist, brushing her breast slowly, to scratch at his stubbled chin. Suddenly, it was the loudest sound in the universe. That was until Lucy reached down to the table, picked up a plate, and smashed it over the side of Owen's head.

"I hope you like your spirit on the rocks," Lucy said simply as Owen spun away, crashing into an empty booth with shards of china clattering around his feet as he fell.

Every gun in the room pointed at Lucy.

She just raised a questioning eyebrow and waited.

A hand appeared from the booth where Owen had fallen. "Wait," Owen said croakily, lifting himself up, rubbing at the damage to the side of his head with the other. "If we're gonna get the old bird to tell us where the gold is, we're gonna have to keep her alive for... persuasion."

With all raiders' eyes on Lucy, Nathan realized with sudden terror, that in an unthinking reflex action, he'd stepped from behind the refrigerator to defend her. He was out in the open. Fully visible. All it would take was for one of the raiders to turn their head and he would be toast.

The only other pair of eyes in the room not on Lucy were Cyndi's. Cyndi was looking at him with an expression morphing back and forth between horror and elation.

Cyndi's eyes were willing him to step back, and so he did, pressing his face against the cool flat steel he'd been hiding behind, trying to fight the rising beat of his heart.

"Stop! Stop! Stop it! Stop it!"

Marty.

Nathan could hear the wailing sobs of the old man's breath

and could feel the wrenching of twisted emotion in his voice. "Don't! Don't! Momma! Momma!"

Marty's dementia-fueled distress popped the balloon of tension in the room for the scavengers. Suddenly, there was sniggering and laughter.

"He pissed his pants!" The remark had come from Bronx, the cruel delight in her voice palpable.

"Momma! Momma! Make it stop!"

"I'll make it stop for you, grandpa." Owen's voice was accompanied by the steely shuffle of him putting a round in the chamber of his pistol. Nathan screwed up his eyes. He'd never felt so useless in his life, just having to listen to this horror show. He ground the back of his head into the steel of the refrigerator and waited for Owen to put Marty down like a dog.

"Please don't!" Cyndi. Voice wavering, but her intent clear. "If I put the tape player on, it'll calm him down. I promise."

"Momma! Momma! Please, Momma!"

"Can I?" Cyndi pressed.

"Momma! I wet my pants, Momma! I wet my pants!"

Cyndi must have been given permission because, seconds later, she walked past Nathan's hiding place to the cassette player, and within moments, Elvis began singing about Heartbreak Hotel and Marty fell silent.

Nathan watched his wife walk back past him, and as she again didn't dare look at him, he just blew a kiss and sent every positive thought out to her that he could.

I'm coming for you, baby.

Nathan rendezvoused with Donie and Dave back in the brush. They'd been on their own mission to the parked Airstream. They were ruddy-faced and out of breath, but their faces were alight with excitement.

"You can do this?" Nathan asked, still not sure if his plan was going to work or get them all killed.

Donie brushed imaginary dirt from her shoulder. "We got this. You just say the word and all hell will break loose."

Nathan pointed to where Mustache and Redhead were trying to wake Freeson up from his battered stupor by rubbing snow in his face and howling like hyenas. "Okay. When I've dealt with those two, hit it."

"You got it," Dave said, holding up his smart phone. "All I gotta do is hit *send*. Bluetooth is strong with this one."

Nathan waited until Redhead and Mustache had their backs to him working on Freeson, and then, keeping the gas pumps between him and the diner to prevent anyone in there seeing him, he broke cover. He prayed to whatever deity was looking after men running across snowy concrete that he wouldn't slip as he sprinted diagonally across the forecourt.

Nathan shoulder-smashed into Mustache at full pelt. The man crashed into a gas pump as Nathan brained Redhead with the butt of his shotgun. Redhead went down in a crash, his scalp spraying blood.

Nathan smashed the foreheads of both men with the butt of his gun twice more to ensure their unconsciousness, and then, bending, he placed his ear against Freeson's mouth. He was in a bad way, but he was breathing. Nathan had to be grateful for that. He used his knife to cut Freeson down and then propped his friend against the pump, his head lolling.

"What... kept you?" A broken smile through torn lips, purple bruises, and smears of dark blood split Freeson's face. "Thanks for not leaving me, buddy."

Nathan squeezed Freeson's shoulder. "Sorry I couldn't get here sooner, man. Now, just keep your head down. We're not out of this yet."

"Ten... four."

Nathan turned and signaled to Dave, whose dark form he could just make out in the brush.

Thub-Thub-Thub Thub-Thub-Thub Thub-Thub-Thub

The rotor sound of a hovering helicopter rent the air. Blue police flashers turned, illuminating the walls of the diner. Sirens wailed and engines roared into life.

Nathan sprinted for the wrecker, hoping against hope that the lights and noise would keep the scavengers' eyes away from him.

He reached the wrecker, hauled himself into the driving seat, fumbled the keys into the ignition, and had the engine started almost before his ass hit the leather. The engine roared into life, full-throated and glorious, and he stamped on the gas and drove the truck forward, its tires spinning in the snow but gripping just enough to build momentum.

Assmouth and Bronx had panicked and run from the diner with their hands high. The Dodge mowed them down in one easy movement from a direction they hadn't been expecting.

Nathan hauled the wheel of the wrecker then and turned it so that the vehicle was four-square to the diner. Through the well-lit window, he saw that everyone and everything he held dear was on one side of the diner, and the scavengers were on the other. The only person in jeopardy as he smashed the truck through the plate glass was Lucy—but because she was facing the window, with Owen still with his back to it, she'd seen him coming and dived away from the torrent of glass and busted wood to fall onto the floor of a booth.

Instead of raising her SIG, Consumpta raised her arms as if that would ward off five tons of American steel and aluminum. She disappeared out of Nathan's vision, and he didn't know if the sudden bump he felt beneath the vehicle was a collapsing booth or her body.

Blackhair had enough time to unhook his AK-47 and level it at the cab, but Lucy had dived from the path of the careening wrecker and was at his feet. As Blackhair squeezed the trigger, she'd already pulled a SIG from his belt, flicked the safety, and begun pumping bullets into his spine.

Nathan ducked as the AK-47 bullets Blackhair had

managed to loose dinged the bodywork of the wrecker, but they mostly ended up in the ceiling.

Owen moved quickly enough to dive out of the way of the wrecker as it plowed on through the diner, lifting wood and smashing chairs and booths. The wrecker skimmed past him and, for a moment, Nathan couldn't be sure if the truck had ground him into the tiles or not.

Then the wrecker grumbled to a halt and Nathan, grabbing the shotgun, jumped down from the cab and faced a fresh horror.

Owen was holding Tony around his throat and had his pistol to the boy's head, digging it in hard enough to make the boy wince in pain, squeezing tears from his eyes.

"Stay back, or you'll be wearing your boy's brains as cologne!"

No one had been near enough to tackle Owen. Betty was bent over Marty, who was deathly pale, laying back in a booth with his eyes rolling. Cyndi had been pushed against the wall by a sliding bench and was pinioned there, helpless. Syd was unconscious on the floor of the booth, looking like she'd taken a blow to the head and slid to the floor.

Lucy was slowly getting up from beneath Blackhair's fallen body, covered in his blood. She held out the SIG towards Owen, but the useless clicking of her fingers told Nathan that the gun was empty. Her eyes flicked to the AK-47 on the ground.

"Try it, bitch, Just try it," Owen said, grinding the point of his pistol harder into Tony's head.

Tony screamed and cried, "Daddy!"

Nathan's shotgun was loose in his hand, his finger not even close to the trigger, and even if he'd been able to lift the gun and fire at Owen before his son was executed, the spray of pellets from the gun would end his boy along with his intended target anyway.

"For a guy who got shot in the head, you look far more alive than you should be."

"Just let these people go. Let my son go. You can have me. Do what you want with me. Get all the revenge you want. Just let them go." Nathan bent, put his shotgun down, and raised his hands.

"You think the cops and everyone out there gonna let me just walk away from here? You think I was born yesterday?"

"There's no cops, man. No helicopter. Two people I'm with have computers, sound gear, and amplifiers. It was just used to make a distraction while I drove my truck in. You're free to go. I swear. I just wanted my family back."

Owen's face twisted with confusion. "This some wild double bluff, cause if it isn't, you've got balls of steel, brother. Balls. Of. Steel."

Tony started to cough.

"Shut up, kid!"

"He's got asthma. Take your arm from across his throat. If

you hold him tight like that, you'll give him an attack. It might kill him."

"Yeah?"

"Yes."

Nathan watched as the muscles bunched in Owen's arm as he purposefully tightened his grip around Tony's throat. The boy's eyes bulged, his closed throat trying to cough—his dry lips worked, but he couldn't find any words or air; it was only his eyes that communicated his fear and distress to his daddy.

Fear and distress that Nathan could do nothing about.

"Shall we watch him die now, before I shoot you all?"

"No!" Cyndi screamed, still pinned against the wall and thumping her fists down on the piece of wood that held her there.

Nathan tried to keep his voice level against all the rising horror he was feeling welling in his guts. "Please, let my son go."

"Maybe. Hey, Betty. Where's the gold?"

Betty didn't hear Owen. She was concentrating on Marty, whose breath was coming in gulping heaves, his lips trembling, his eyes now fixed frozen ahead as he looked at a different view of the world.

He was dying.

Nathan had been with his daddy in the hospital when he'd breathed his last. It had taken him most of the morning to die, gradually running down after the cancer had filled his lungs with death, like a clock running out of ticks. The doctors had told Nathan there was nothing they could do—the cancer had hastened his end, but his drowning lungs would complete the job. Nathan remembered the gray pallor of his daddy's dying skin; it had been the same pallor that had spread across Marty's face now.

"I said, Betty, where's the gold? Tell me now or the boy chokes."

Before Betty turned, Marty gave a slight moan and his breathing stopped.

It was over.

Betty closed Marty's eyes with tender fingers and then stood up. "I've told you a thousand times already, you jerk, there is no gold. We traded it before you got here. You can kill us all you want, but you won't find any gold!"

Her voice had risen in a crescendo of old agony and fresh grief, and suddenly she bunched her fists and ran screaming at Owen.

The scavenger fired one shot through the top of her skull and she crashed to the floor without a sound, the lights going out in her eyes as her life spread across the floor in a puddle of red and gray.

It had all happened in a moment, giving Nathan no time to react, and now Owen had put the gun back against Tony's head.

"No gold? Oh well. No cops is a bonus. Might as well just kill you all and head out again. I guess the Seven-Ones can rise again in another town. There's always women, and they love a bad guy. Right, bitches?"

At first, Nathan thought the sound of reply was Tony coughing. A harsh asthmatic bark that cut across the shocked silence in the room as if Death himself had snapped his bony fingers.

It took Nathan nearly a second to register the spray of blood that dappled the top of his son's skull and the side of his face. The thud in his heart telling him that Owen had pulled the trigger and Tony was no more.

But it wasn't Tony's blood.

It was Owen's.

Owen's grip relaxed. Tony slithered to the floor, pawing at the wet blood on his face.

Owen sighed out a miserable sound. The wind in an abandoned graveyard, the shoosh of funeral feet carrying a coffin through too long grass.

The bullet had entered through his ear and powered through his skull at an angle, popping out his eye with the pressure, distorting his face into a deathly grimace. It was as if he didn't know whether to stand or fall for whole seconds, so Freeson, leaning ragged and bloody in the doorway with an AR-15 in his hands, put the matter to rest.

Freeson squeezed the trigger again.

This bullet lifted the back off Owen's head, and he was felled. Crashing into the torn wood, destroyed leather, and smashed crockery of the diner.

"They kinda like a good guy with a gun, too," Freeson said, sagging in his own broken skin with pain and exhaustion. He stumbled forward towards Lucy and she held her arms open.

There were perhaps ten seconds of silence, in which Nathan was able to bend down, pick up his son, and clutch him to his chest, before the Molotov cocktails Mustache and Redhead threw into the diner exploded in twin balls of flame.

19

"Get in the truck! Get in the truck!"

Nathan threw Tony into the wrecker's crew cab, then took five steps towards the prone form of Syd. He grabbed her ankle and slid her out from under the table, her head banging and lolling against debris. Freeson had turned to shoot at the scavengers who had thrown the petrol bombs, but they'd already gone off into the night and snow. The flames were filling the front of the diner now, catching already on all the broken wood and plastic, sending up billows of black smoke.

Freeson half-stumbled and half-ran to where Cyndi was trapped against the wall and pulled hard at the bench that was holding her in place. He moved it just enough to get her free as Nathan and Lucy heaved the unconscious Syd into the crew cab.

The flames were licking at the ceiling tiles now, the front half of the diner almost fully alight and the heat coming through in sledgehammer blows. Nathan didn't stop to hug his wife as she came past with Freeson; he just pushed both their asses back up into the cab and dived in behind them.

The engine roared and the cab shook. In the rearview mirrors, the conflagration was total. The entire front half of the diner had caught alight now.

It had taken seconds.

Nathan didn't want to risk going backward through all the debris and flames.

"Hang on!" he screamed, and with that he floored the gas pedal.

The Dodge's engine boomed and raged, its wheels biting into the debris as the truck stormed forward, smashing easily through the counter and into the kitchen.

The fryers and stoves spun out of the way on their still-locked wheels, smashing into steel units and spilling crockery and cutlery like vomit. Cyndi gripped Nathan's arm and buried her face in his shoulder as they crashed forward, taking out the refrigerators that Nathan had hidden behind less than fifteen minutes before.

They rolled on.

It wasn't far across the kitchen, but it could have been miles. The impending impact making it feel like more.

"Brace yourselves!" Nathan roared as the truck crashed through the shelves and steel sinks at the back of the kitchen, flattening the table on which Marty's cassette player had been located, and powering on and hitting the back wall hard.

The diner was a wooden-framed and plasterboard construction, with a low brick pier for foundations. The wrecker took off and burst through the wall, exploding from the electricity and flame-lit interior out into the cold night of the compound.

Nathan gripped the steering wheel tighter than a triggered bear trap and rolled the vehicle forward as the gas lines that had fed the stoves were finally reached by the flames—and the diner exploded.

The rush of debris and hot flame burst past the wrecker on all sides. It was like being in a space shuttle reentering the atmosphere, but it was just a fast rush of flame and it was gone as soon as it appeared.

The wrecker drove on across the back of the compound, turning and swinging around behind the gas station.

Nathan saw figures running across the concrete towards the parked Ski-Doos, and he turned the wheel and pointed the truck right at them.

Before Mustache and Redhead could get the engines started on either machine, Nathan crushed them both beneath the wheels of the wrecker.

"Good for you, Nathan!" Lucy shouted. "Good for you!"

The scavengers had moved the majority of the stores from the Airstream into the diner for inventory, and to check over what they'd liberated in the relative comfort of the building. It meant that the attack with the Molotov cocktails hadn't just been an attempt to hurt and injure the party, but a deliberate act to destroy the stores. A message that said: *If we can't have it, neither can you.*

That Mustache and Redhead had paid with their lives to torch the diner had only one logical conclusion for Nathan. This group of scavengers saw the survival of his group as a direct threat to them. There were only so many resources to go around, so eliminating the opposition became an imperative strategy. Ensuring Nathan's group was robbed of those essential supplies piled pressure upon pressure on their situation, and it would make them desperate, possibly more careless, and in turn vulnerable to attack.

Cyndi streamed silent tears as they searched through the exploded wreck of the diner to find whatever was left that they could salvage, but apart from a few scorched ready meals, a number of tins of ham, and a catering bag of rice, there was nothing. The diner had become a blackened stain next to the highway, and without it as cover or shelter, Nathan felt even more exposed.

Tony sat in the crew cab for most of the morning that followed the violence, hugging Saber with Syd as the sun came up over the frozen landscape, orange beams fingering the snow and illuminating the smoke that was still rising into the sky.

Nathan shielded his eyes and looked to the sky. The column of smoke billowing up from the wreckage would be a convenient locator signal for anyone on the lookout for a place to bring or make mischief.

"We don't know that there aren't more of them on their way here now," he said to Freeson and Lucy as Cyndi insisted on checking the burned shell of the diner again for anything she could save.

Freeson, who was just able to stand up, appeared hollowed and desperately ill from his beating and night of exposure to the elements. Lucy had her arm around his waist as if she were offering more than just the support of a warm body. She also looked as though she was clinging onto him as much as he was holding onto her. Freeson's voice sounded croaky and his lips split to new blood if he talked too much, but he agreed, "Yeah. We need to get as far away from here as we can."

"They left the fuel in the Airstream, but we're so low on food that we're going to have to ration if we don't find anything soon." Cyndi's face remained covered in soot from the fire, her hair a mess of sweat and blood. Not her blood, at least. She'd also caught a spray of material from Owen's head as the second bullet had hit home.

They all needed a shower and to rest for a month, but there was no chance of that. Not right now.

Donie and Dave were happy that their flight cases had been left intact in the Airstream, as Owen and his scavengers had prioritized food over anything else. From what Nathan had seen of them before he'd driven the truck into the diner, most of them had had the hungry, rangy look of people who regularly went a long time between meals.

The two Mack trucks were cosmetically intact but had already been cannibalized for parts sometime in the last few months. The scavengers' black Ford F-350 was still in good shape, though, showing few signs of damage from the fire, except for a few bubbles of paint lifted by the heat and spreading like a rash down one side.

As they got ready to head out, Lucy offered to drive it while Freeson rested with her. Nathan hooked up the Airstream to the Dodge, and he, Cyndi, Dave, and Donie joined the kids in the crew cab with the dog.

And then, without an ounce of restful sleep between them, they drove up the snowy ramp and back onto the highway.

The wind howled around the Airstream and the blizzard rattled its hide. A storm had closed in six hours from the diner. They were traveling back roads again now and had gotten off the highway as soon as they could, but there'd been no way they could avoid the storm.

Nathan had parked the group in the parking lot next to a

small lake where, in better, warmer times, people had come to sail, relax, and barbeque.

As the wind brought the first burst of snow out of the darkening sky, Nathan couldn't think of any scene more opposite of that summer picture in his head than the one that greeted them now.

"Ahhhh! Come on!"

Cyndi was doing the best she could with the frostbite in the soles of Freeson's feet.

The scavengers had left him barefoot on the frozen forecourt of the gas station for many hours, and the flesh had set solid. In the party's rush to get away from the diner, they hadn't had the time to do even the most cursory bit of first aid on the mechanic. The beating he'd taken wouldn't damage him long-term, but his frozen feet were another matter.

Cyndi had warmed some water on the Airstream's stove and put Freeson's feet into it. His toes were near black, though, where six hours of neglect as they'd hightailed it away from the diner had left only a paltry blood supply to reach them. Cyndi put salt and lavender oil into the water. "Not to thaw them, that's already happened, but to clean them and try to stop any infection."

"It hurts! Damn, it hurts!"

"It will. Now shut up and put your feet back in the bowl."

Cyndi had also attended as best she could to the wound on the side of Nathan's head from the bullet graze. "It's infected," she told him, turning her attention to her husband and popping some antibiotics from a pack she'd found in the looted medicine chest. They had ten pills left. "You'll need them all, Nate."

"Give them to Free. Or save them for you and Tony."

"Let's see if I can stop his feet taking bad first. Your head has to be a priority."

Nathan nodded, but although his head wound was still leaking pus and felt hot to the touch, moving squelchily beneath his fingers, he still felt Freeson's feet looked worse than his head felt.

"It's okay, buddy," Freeson said before pulling the cork from a bottle of single malt with his teeth. "I got my own kind of painkillers."

Donie and Dave were still high on their light and sound show, more than pleased with themselves. Nathan didn't tackle them on the fact that they'd left Freeson to pick himself up and come to the diner to end Owen. Still, it grated on him. Perhaps if they'd not been backslapping so much, maybe Betty would still be alive. It wasn't that he resented their silly grins and their high-fiving every time one of them mentioned how well the sound system had worked out, but their moods didn't match the rest of those who were holed up in the Airstream while the storm raged on outside.

When Cyndi had finished with Nathan's head and Freeson's feet, she and Lucy prepared a meager meal of rice and ham.

"No. Don't do that!"

Syd's hand stopped halfway to Saber's salivating mouth and sparkly-eyed gaze. In her fingers was a chunk of ham that had been rolled in rice and gravy. "She's got to eat, Cyndi."

"Not our food. She can go hunt after the storm. Now, come on. You took quite a blow to the head, and we need to make sure you're not concussed and that you're getting some protein in you."

"I'm not hungry anyway," Syd said with maximum defiance, and threw the meat to the dog. Saber swallowed it so fast it didn't touch the sides of her mouth.

"Syd!"

The mood had suddenly become toxic. Cyndi was ready to explode, and Syd was all belligerence and attitude, setting her chin and looking around for something else to feed to the dog.

Syd's changed mood made sense to Nathan, though. To have been kidnapped by the Seven-Ones, potentially taken back to be conscripted for a rape-harem after all she'd been through... Nathan felt sure she wouldn't be able to articulate it yet, but the experience might just have proven to her that joining up with Nathan and the others made sense.

"Okay, okay." Nathan got to his feet and stomped over to Syd, caught between concern for the teen and a need to back up his wife. He softened his voice, but inside he was wound up tighter than an airlock door on a space shuttle. "Look, Syd, we've all got to get along here, okay? Cyndi is doing the best she can with the little we have left. We're still three hundred miles from Detroit. We don't know where the next food is coming from. The dog will hunt—I've seen her do it. Saber will be okay. When the storm breaks, you and me will go hunting, okay? See what we can find. But you're not doing anyone any favors right now, resisting the needs of the party."

"You're not my dad!"

And that unspun the wheel. *Boom.*

"I wouldn't want to be!" Nathan yelled.

He hadn't realized how frayed his own temper was right now, and that response had just bludgeoned his lips open and crawled out. Nathan had fallen into the bear pit, too, and after everything he'd been through in the last couple of days, Nathan was ready to tear the bear several new assholes.

The argument raged like the storm outside until Syd got up, stormed the length of the Airstream, and locked herself into the toilet for an hour.

When she came out, her face was streaked with tears and, yet again, the hard-nosed bitch had turned into the sensitive child. She didn't say anything, but she went straight to Cyndi, wrapped her arms around her, and squeezed for all she was worth.

"It's okay," said Cyndi. "It's all okay."

Nathan looked around the Airstream. At Lucy huddled under a blanket with Freeson, sipping from her hipflask, at Dave and Donie, their faces serious and drained of their joy over the sound system working out, and at Tony sitting with his hand on Saber, stroking silently—then, finally, to Cyndi hugging the errant teen, whispering in her ear that everything would be okay.

Right then, Nathan couldn't in all honestly agree with her that it would be, so he said nothing.

The storm lasted fourteen hours.

When Nathan finally emerged, blinking into the gray mid-morning light, it was on a breath of fetid air and human body odor that Lucy had complained she could chew on, to the extent that she wished they hadn't ended up in the "Black Hole of Calcutta."

Nathan didn't know what the "Black Hole of Calcutta" was, but by the way Dave had side-eyed the rich woman, it didn't look like her choice of words had made her anymore friends. They all needed space and air. Saber dived through the door behind him and headed off into the woods to forage.

In the six hours of travel before the storm, they'd put a good distance between them and the diner, but Nathan still felt exposed by the lake. The fresh snow had added another two feet of powder to the already frozen lakeside, and as Nathan headed down the slope of land to where he figured the water began, his feet scooted from under him on a patch of ice. He slid onto his ass and plowed through the cold snow to bark his knee against the concrete side of a park trash can.

It was only when he heard Syd laughing behind him that

he realized she'd followed him out. She shooshed down through the snow and offered him a hand. Although the girl was slight, she was strong enough to help him up.

"Did I look like I needed a girl to help me up?" he asked, feigning hurt.

"Doesn't every man?" she answered, digging through the snow with her gloved hands and locating the surface of the ice on the lake.

Nathan and Syd broke the crust with their heels and then filled water cans to lug back up towards the Airstream.

"Are you okay?" he asked as they hauled the water.

Syd shrugged. "I thought... I can't go back to them. To Danny. To the Seven-Ones. I don't want to live like that..."

Nathan didn't want to overstep the moment by trying for a hug, so he just paused to put the water down for a moment, held out his hand, and waited till she stopped and took it. Something of that connective truce achieved, they completed the walk back to the Airstream.

Cyndi was in full-on ration mode. The coffee she made was weak and gritty, and the breakfast was sweetened rice fried on the stove.

"Until we find another source of food, it's going to be meat every other day if we can't catch it," she announced.

The glum faces receiving this pronouncement accepted Cyndi's assessment, but their eyes told a whole other story. Things had been upended so thoroughly in such a short amount of time. In one engagement, they'd gone from having more than enough food to get them through, right on to a feeling of desperation and poverty.

And after two hours of fruitless hunting around the lakeshore and the surrounding woodland, Nathan and Syd hadn't managed to shoot anything. Not even a bird.

Saber came back with a half-eaten rat, but nobody felt like sharing. It was as if all the animals in the area had followed the fleeing humans south.

"Dave, can you get a signal on the base station?" Nathan asked.

In response, Dave dipped into the flight case and pulled out the equipment he needed. Half an hour later, he came back shaking his head. "Nada. I can't even geo-locate us."

"We can't be too far from the nearest town. Do you think you can find out where we are on the map?"

Dave shrugged. "We left in a hurry. I've sorta got an idea, but I don't know how accurate I can be."

"We should avoid towns," Donie cut in, jumping down from the Airstream with her face set.

Nathan shook his head at her, resigned to the difficulty ahead. "We need food, supplies, and medicine. We need antibiotics."

"You think there's anything left down there that the people leaving or the scavengers haven't already taken? We go down into a town, we're an easy target for an ambush. If I was a scavenger, that's what I'd do. Wait for the good stuff to come to me. Why waste energy if people are just driving by ready to be picked off?"

Things felt too desperate to avoid looking for supplies, but Nathan couldn't, at the moment, refute her logic. Not that he was in a position to. A throbbing bitch of a headache had come on since he'd fallen over near the lake, and it had worsened during the failed hunt. He felt like he might be coming down with a cold or, worse, flu—the back of his throat felt raspy and dry.

"Whatever. We'll look out for isolated homesteads then as we go, but we're going to have to check them all. Okay?"

"Okay," Donie and Dave said in tandem.

"Do the best you can to find out where we are on your cop maps and plan a route that will take us by the most farms. We might get lucky again like we did with the tractor."

They set off an hour later, with Lucy, Freeson, Dave, and Donie leading in the F-350, and Cyndi announcing she would drive the Dodge, having taken pity on Nathan's ashen face and shivery shoulders.

Cyndi put a hand on Nathan's forehead before she put the Dodge into gear.

"You're sweating. Hot, too."

"I'm freezing."

"Take more antibiotics. Two instead of one. And get in the crew cab. I'll be fine driving."

Nathan didn't have the strength to argue. He climbed over both seats into the rear of the cab, dropping into the cargo space at the back. Wedged in, he lay down and aimed for sleep, hoping that Cyndi didn't notice he'd not taken any of the antibiotics at all.

Tony and Cyndi were his priority, and if they needed the capsules before they found extra, Nathan wouldn't be able to live with himself, knowing he'd used them up when they needed them. The pills would be saved for them.

And that was that.

Nathan awoke with a start. His head felt thick with fever and he was shivering like he'd been left out in the snow. Voices were raised outside, though, and there was an argument going on somewhere not far out of earshot.

His head still thrummed with a headache, though, and he didn't know if he wanted to throw up, or whether his world was going to fall out of the other end of his body.

The crew cab was empty of anyone but him. Not even Tony or Saber were there. He lifted his head off of Lucy's fur coat and tried, fuzzily, to concentrate on the voices.

"We haven't been near anywhere! Show me the map!"

That had been Cyndi's voice, and she added, "Where are we?"

"There. I think," Dave said, sounding unsure.

"The snow's taken all the road signs down—it's not his fault!" Donie, her voice risen several notches in pitch.

"This road isn't getting us anywhere except more lost. We need to find our way back to the highway." Cyndi again. The tone of voice wasn't one for taking any crap, either. Nathan knew it of old. Cyndi's stubbornness was her superpower.

"Can we just decide? I'm as cold as a snowman's dick." Lucy. Even in his haze of fever, Nathan couldn't help smiling. That was one of Freeson's choice phrases that had rubbed off on Lucy, and she seemed to be happily assimilating his broader turns of phrase.

Nathan tried to sit up, but it felt like there was a weight on his shoulders, too massive to shift. Then a swirl of darkness rushed up towards him, and he could do nothing but sink towards it.

When he woke again, the truck was moving. It seemed to be making a good speed, too, the comforting rumbles of the engine moving up through his spine. Somebody was mopping his forehead with a rag. He opened his eyes. Syd hovered above him, her face a mask of concern. He tried to smile, to put her mind at rest, but with some panic he realized that his mouth wasn't working.

Nathan tried to lift his hand.

It felt tingly and swollen, as if it had been pumped full of helium and was floating up to the edge of space. In fact, Nathan felt like his whole body was floating free of the floor of the crew cab, and up towards the ceiling, bumping around inside the truck like a balloon…

Next time he woke, he was as cold as ice. He'd been

wrapped in a blanket, though. The engine was still running and the blowers were still on, but the truck wasn't moving. No one was with him in the crew cab. He tried to call out, but the fever was ruining his ability to talk. He could only be glad that his floating body had come back down to earth.

The windows were dark, he saw. It was night again.

Had he slept all day? More than that? He had no way of knowing how much time he'd lost to the fever.

He couldn't hear voices, either. A sudden panic gripped his chest. Were Cyndi and Tony okay? Where were they?

He sat up, shucking the sweat-damp blanket from his body, and the rush of cold that hit him then turned his heart into ice.

Family First.

Family FIRST.

A wave of blackness rolled over him again.

20

"Webishtew?"

Huh?

"Mr. Tolley? Webishtew? Ah… long time since I speak English."

Nathan's eyes flickered and his face creased in continued confusion at the voice. It was soft, male, accented European, and completely wrong.

"Ah. Yes. You do not understand. You, Mr. Tolley… *you* are an *English.* And *webishtew…* it means, I think, 'how are you?'"

Nathan sat up sharply and opened his eyes. Where he'd expected to see the inside of the Dodge's crew cab, instead he saw a room that was fully constructed from wood, suffused with a golden light coming from one window that had frost bunched in its corners. Through the glass, a rolling plain of snowy fields ran all the way up to a low hill where the skeletons of trees moved in a stiff breeze. The golden light wasn't really coming fully from the window but was, in reality, the light being reflected off all the wood in the room. Nathan could even smell resins and wood shavings, as if the room had been freshly cut and constructed just that morning.

"I heard you calling in your sleep. I came to see if, by God's grace, you had woken from your fever, and found that, by glory, you have."

Nathan lay on a bed under a rough hemp blanket and, next to him, sitting on a well-made, if obviously home-constructed chair, there rested a full-bearded man in plain clothes. He had a care-worn but pleasant face and was holding out a hand for Nathan to shake.

"You are feeling better, yes?"

Nathan took the proffered hand and shook it. The grip came across as firm and confident, the man's skin being calloused and rough. This was a man who worked with his hands, and Nathan felt an immediate affinity with him.

"Where am I? Who are you?"

"My name is Jacob Anderson. You are in my home, Mr. Tolley."

"How...?"

"You have many questions, but you must rest more. You have been very ill. Near to death, I think. Naomi, my wife, will bring you soup in a short while."

Jacob got up and clutched a broad-brimmed black hat, which had been resting on his lap, to his chest. "Praise be to God that you are awake, Mr. Tolley. I will take the good news to your wife and son immediately."

"Where are they?"

"In the hands of God. As are we all. Now rest, Mr. Tolley. There is water there next to the bed, and the blankets are warm. Naomi will light the stove when she brings the soup. Please. Everything is in hand."

Jacob was a tall man, the top of his head reaching up not far from the pine boards running across the ceiling. It was difficult to judge his age, but Nathan guessed he wasn't far from his own. Jacob's boots were heavy, and they plodded him to the door in a rustle of thick overcoat and black linen pants.

Nathan reached out a hand, and although he felt kitten-weak, he tried to move a leg off the bed. "Wait…"

Jacob turned. "Yes, English?"

"My wife. Boy. How… are they? Are they okay?"

Jacob clomped back, lifting Nathan's leg by the ankle, sliding it back under the blanket and saying, "They are well, and they are safe. You are less well, but just as safe. Please stay in the bed, and rest. All things, by God's grace, will be revealed to you presently. But please remain in this bed."

"But…"

Jacob patted the blanket. "Rest now."

With one smile and a small wave of the hand, Jacob was gone. Nathan lay his head back on the pillow, feeling for the first time the chill of the unheated room against his cheek. He felt shivery and drained of all energy, as if he was still travelling in the hinterlands of a fever. The blankets were as Jacob had said, warm, and so Nathan pulled the covers closer to him.

He had no memory of coming to this place, or of Jacob or whoever Naomi would turn out to be. All he could remember was the floating, tingling, and the arguing, and then... nothing.

Nathan tentatively felt at the wound in his head. The skin was firm and dry, the scab there hard and crusty, but there was no heat. The infection had gone and the wound was healing.

When his fingers came away, he caught the whiff of something sweet and vegetable—as if the crust on his scalp had not just been the residue of healing but had been this mixed with some other medicament.

As his hand came down, Nathan next felt the thick growth of beard that covered his cheek. A good three weeks or more of growth there. That shocked him. Could he really have been out of it for that long?

There was another matter to attend to, though; his bladder was straining in his groin, and he'd need to take care of that sooner than later. Being under a blanket and in a strange room in an unknown house might make that a more difficult operation that it needed to be, so he tried to push it from the front of his mind to the back.

Jacob Anderson was Amish. That much was clear. The beard without the mustache, the peppering of Godliness through his speech, and the European Dutch-German accent told him as much. Nathan had never met an Amish man before —or spent any time in Amish country—but Cyndi had.

Her family had originally been from Michigan, and before moving first to Albany and then to Glens Falls, she'd grown up on the outskirts of Walnut Creek Holmes County, Ohio, near one of the largest Amish communities in the region. Her dad had traded furniture with them for plows and meat. As a dedicated hunter and woodsman, Cyndi's dad, Connor, had appreciated the Amish way of life, with their traditional values and their skills—many of which he'd taken the time to learn, and then pass onto his daughter. It made sense to Nathan that, if he'd been incapacitated, and Freeson's feet had been shot, that Cyndi would have made the decision to seek out a place and people she felt safe and at home with, thus giving Nathan the time to work though his fever.

Seeing the reason in her choice, his love and admiration for his wife couldn't have been fuller in that moment.

However, no matter how much he might need rest, Nathan couldn't wait to get up any longer, not with the pressing matter of his bladder—he had to find a john.

He pulled back the covers, swung his legs out of the bed, and put his bare feet on the cold floor. He was dressed only in a long white night shirt, and he didn't feel the constrictions of underwear. There were no shoes he could see to slip onto his feet, so he'd have to go looking barefoot.

As he stood, he could feel the weakness in his muscles,

and by the looks of his arms and his legs, he guessed he'd lost thirty pounds.

Still, he felt okay standing, and moved to the nearby window.

Snow was the prevalent image. Drifts and swirls surrounded the five wooden houses and three barns in near proximity, all of which marked this out as a small community rather than an isolated farm. In fact, this room, and one of the houses fifty yards away, had the feel of being brand-new. Beyond the barns, Nathan could see the spars and exposed rafters of another house in mid-construction.

This was a community that was expanding.

A couple of dark figures in black hats, mustache-less beards, and long overcoats were walking between the houses. A woman in a white head covering—a kapp, Nathan remembered them being called from conversations with Cyndi—was leading a goat into one of the barns.

The community wasn't exactly bustling with movement, but it was a community.

Bladder.

Turning from the window, Nathan saw the china pot under the bed. It was a white, wide bowl with a handle, and its use was obvious.

To his straining bladder, it looked exactly like salvation.

Nathan reached down, slid the empty bowl out from beneath the bed, rearranged his night shirt, and began the blessed relief of filling the basin.

It was only when he heard the small screech, the soup bowl dropping to the floor, and footsteps running away down the hall that, in his blissful, eye-closed relief, he realized he hadn't noticed Naomi come into the room to bring him his food.

The next three weeks passed in something of a blur.

Nathan's idea that Cyndi had led the group to this settlement had been correct. When they'd gotten over the phase of hugging, kissing, and expressing general relief that Nathan's body wasn't another one they'd have to send off in a Viking funeral, Cyndi had explained what had happened.

"We got here with just enough fuel to spare. We had no medicines, no food, nothing. And we were finding nothing en route. Everything's been looted already and everyone, *everyone*, Nathan, has left the east, either going straight south or, we're guessing, heading for Detroit. The cities and towns were burning. We couldn't even get close. The weather was hard, but we carried on. Syd and Tony fed you water while I drove."

Tears appeared in her eyes at remembering the journey he'd been comatose throughout. "I thought you were going to die. And then you slipped into the coma. I don't know what kept you alive, honey. I just don't know. Dave got a fix from the satellite and I saw exactly where we were. We were no more than twenty miles from here. Fuel was down to fumes, so we lit out. Made it here, and Naomi and Jacob remembered me and my dad and they took us in. They took us in without a word of complaint, Nate. They've fed us, looked after us, and Naomi fixed your head. We'll never be able to repay them."

And standing up half naked, whizzing in a bowl as Naomi came into the room, probably wasn't the best place to start, Nathan thought.

There had been much more hugging after Cyndi had finished filling him in, and having her back in his arms was the best relief of all.

Tony was thriving, and the Andersons had five children from ages two to seven. The couple hosting them—tall and thin Jacob and his Naomi, dark-haired, plump, and open-faced —had been busy. And meanwhile, Tony had simply enjoyed playing with their kids in the family room in front of a well-stocked fire.

The community itself was made up of four families, the Andersons, Troyers, Yoders, and Schwartzes, with more planning to move in as evidenced by the Graber family, who'd recently traveled here from their own isolated farm in order to build a new family home in the killing weather. These Grabers were hardy and strong. They could work two hours straight in the cold before coming in for warm drinks and food, their fingers and noses blue from the cold but their spirits high. There was much laughter in the evening as the families got together to eat and talk, praising God for His abundance and beneficence.

Freeson's frostbite had healed after a fashion, as well. He'd lost two of the smaller toes on each foot, and had patches of raw skin on his heels, but Cyndi's work had given them a fighting chance. Naomi had treated them with the same poultice and drink. Both medicines appeared to be made from the same ingredients—honey, lemon, pepper, and horseradish. It was much better for use as an ointment than as a drink, Freeson had told him, making a face. But as with Nathan's head, it had worked wonders on Free's feet. Now he could walk well enough and was getting better by the day.

For everyone else, however, their time in this community was a different story. Lucy wouldn't cover her head or her cleavage as a mark of respect to the Amish—"I am not a nun!" Nathan had heard her shout to a Troyer who'd remarked on her immodest dress.

For their part, Dave and Donie were antsy and fractious. Nathan couldn't put his finger on why, and they didn't really want to talk much beyond calling the Andersons' settlement a "technophobic hole."

Syd, however, seemed to be getting the worst of the experience. Every day, she found a way to fall out with Naomi or any of the other demure, head-covered, morally judgmental women in the settlement. Part of the deal for living with the Andersons was that those who *could* work *would* work. Perhaps this setup was too much like a watered-down version of the Seven-Ones for her to cope with, Nathan found himself wondering. Women in subservient roles to men. A devout, kind people, but lacking any modern sensibilities. And, simply, Syd refused to help with house chores.

"I don't cook," she'd say.

"Well then, Miss Syd, you can clean."

"Ms."

"Ms.?"

"Yes, Ms."

"This is an English word? What does it mean?"

"It means I don't have to clean, cover up my head, or live like a CAVE WOMAN!"

"Mercy!"

Cyndi had been doing her best to pour oil on the troubled waters, but Syd's stubbornness wasn't evolving. While Nathan's strength returned, she spent the days sullenly sitting by a window, staring out into the wild winter with Saber at her feet looking mean.

As the third week of his recovery came to an end, Nathan knew that a choice would have to be made as soon as possible.

Stay, or go?

"It's not where I want to give birth, if that's what you're asking..." Cyndi said baldly to Nathan as they'd lain in bed and Nathan had sought counsel.

"Free's happy. Well, whatever passes for happy in Free's world. Tony's settled."

Cyndi gave him a whole bunch of side-eye. "I know, and

that's great. But he's the only one who has. But he'd settle on a razor blade if we asked him to. He's that kind of kid."

"Ain't that the truth."

Cyndi draped an arm across Nathan, and he could feel the swell of her belly pressing into his side. "I like it here. I *do*. I like Jacob and Naomi. It reminds me of my dad and growing up around here, but I can't let nostalgia get in the way of good medical care."

However comfortable he might feel there, and however settled his son had become in such a short span of time, Cyndi was still pregnant. No matter how good the Amish might be at popping out children by the half-dozen, the lure of Stryker's Detroit, with its promise of hospitals, education, homes, and work meant that staying here with the Andersons wasn't so viable a state of affairs, regardless of how kind the Amish families had been to his family. Especially when over half of Nathan's extended friends and family literally hated every second of living here with the Amish. Things would come to a head and poison this well sooner rather than later, he knew. They should get out before the Andersons' settlement became a place to which they could never return.

So it was no surprise that the sense of relief was palpable, on all sides, when Nathan communicated as much at the dinner table one night, three weeks after he'd woken up. "Mr. Anderson, I don't know how to thank you for the hospitality you've shown to my family and my friends, but in a couple of days, we're going to have to move on. It's only a hundred and fifty miles to Detroit from here, and we've got a good chance of making it there if we set out soon and press hard. The weather doesn't look like it's going to be changing any time soon, and we need to be in Detroit before it gets worse."

Syd almost running from the window to throw her arms around Nathan told him everything he needed to know about his decision.

21

Leaving the Andersons' settlement wasn't as easy as Nathan might have hoped. For a start, they were all out of gas, and an Amish community wasn't going to have a gas station on hand. Secondly, walking the one hundred and fifty miles to Detroit through the depth of the Earth's tilted winter wasn't a prospect any of them relished—especially Freeson, whose frostbitten feet, now ninety percent healed, were still painful to walk on.

"Nathan, we have everything here," he'd argued when the possibility of walking had come up.

"We don't have a hospital, Free, and in a few months, Cyndi is going to need one big-time."

Freeson had looked down at his own feet. Seemingly more out of concern for his frostbite injuries than shame over asking

Nathan to choose here over Detroit. In the end, Freeson had nodded and, scratching his head, said, "I guess we've come this far, so I suppose we should see it through. Hardly worth leaving Glens Falls if we don't."

They'd shaken hands on it, and Freeson had gone up to his room to help Lucy pack their things.

Alone again, Nathan stared into the fire in the Andersons' family room. Had it been worth it? He knew that he'd had to be persuaded to leave all that he'd known and had worked for, but along the way, he'd been pushed into making decisions that even a few short weeks ago he would have balked at, or hid his head in the snow to avoid making. If nothing else, Nathan thought, he *felt* like a better man. The night before, laying in his bed in the resin-scented room with Cyndi, she'd taken his hand and placed it on the swell of her five-and-a-half-month pregnant belly.

"Did you feel that?"

Nathan had shaken his head, thinking that perhaps his hands were too calloused and work-worn from a thousand engines to feel the growing life within. Cyndi had stopped breathing and relaxed, so that he could almost feel her willing the person within her to transmit something, anything, to his or her father.

Nathan had waited, willing it, too.

When the movement had come, in the gentlest of ripples beneath Cyndi's skin, the smile across both their faces could have outshone the sun on a summer's day.

The new baby Cyndi was carrying, the promise of the future that might not have arrived if they'd stayed in Glens Falls in the deepening winter, and the collapse of all the safety nets that modern society could provide—all of it meant that Nathan could feel proud that he'd gotten them this far.

Cyndi had moved the hand from her belly to her cheek, kissing his palm and looking into his eyes with something like total love. She'd offered, "I know this hasn't been easy, baby. And it's still not over, but thank you. Thank you for everything. For coming to rescue us, for putting your life on the line."

"I couldn't have done anything else."

She had nodded, and then thumped him in the arm.

"Owww! What was *that* for?"

"If I tell you to take antibiotics, you take the damn antibiotics!"

And then they'd collapsed in laughter on the bed.

"Mr. Tolley?"

Nathan spun out of the memory and looked up from the fire. Jacob was approaching him from across the family room.

Jacob's children were rolling around on the spotlessly clean wooden floors with Tony, wrestling and laughing. Nathan had never imagined there would be warmth and fun and vital life like this in an Amish house, but he guessed kids were kids the world over. *It's only when we impose our ideals on them that they change.* He only hoped that Tony would never feel the need to take on his father's baggage.

"Yes, Jacob, we're packing up now. We'll wait until the morning if that's fine with you, and set off at first light?"

"That is, of course, fine, Mr. Tolley. I wonder if perhaps I might speak with you as the head of your household."

"Sure," Nathan said, smiling at the title he'd been given which, in so many respects, belonged to Cyndi and not to him.

In the three weeks he'd been there and awake, Nathan had grown to respect the calm, gentle demeanor of this Amish man and his people. Of course, they had some crazy throwback ideas about God, technology, and the role of women, but Jacob was a man at ease with himself, someone who didn't need to impose his will on others. A natural leader who people wanted to follow. The community of families he was building here was testament to that.

Nathan had wondered more than once whether, if the cities were failing, this kind of new village living would be a way of facing the future with a shot at survival. The Amish skills with animal husbandry were second to none. They had constructed barns for their goats and pigs, had a ton of feed stockpiled, and were going out on a daily basis to forage for glass panels to construct greenhouses. If the weather didn't change, greenhouses would be places needed to supplement their food stocks in the future through grown produce. In many respects, the Amish were the best equipped people in the land to stay put and fight the winter.

"I overheard Mrs. Tolley say that you have a stock of seeds?" Jacob asked now.

Nathan nodded. "Yeah, it was one of the things the scavengers weren't interested in. Left them in the Airstream. We're taking them to Detroit. Hydroponics is the future."

"Greenhouses are as far into the future as we will be going, I think, by the grace of God."

"You're going to do fine here, Jacob."

"I hope that we will. But I have been thinking about your predicament. You have no fuel for your vehicles, and we can't spare any of our horses, but I might be able to propose a trade."

"A trade?"

"Yes, Mr. Tolley. Would you come with me, please?"

There were three pulling mules, bred from donkey and dray. In better times, they'd been hefty enough to pull carriages and plows, but no one was going to be plowing the iron-cold earth around the Amish settlement this year. Their bony shoulders showed that perhaps they weren't getting all the feed they needed, but they were young, strong, and still sturdy.

"You can have them, in exchange for seed," Jacob said simply, thumbing his suspenders and nodding sagely.

"We'd ride them?"

Jacob threw back his head and laughed. "No, not to ride! To pull your caravan. They are strong. It will be easy for them. It will give you a place to rest if the weather comes in. A vehicle to carry your supplies of water and grain. The land between here and Detroit, although covered in snow, will have hay enough deep down for you to thaw and feed them. It's not enough, perhaps, but it will suffice."

Nathan looked at the beasts. Could it work?

"We have harness and tack, and I'm sure someone of your skill and ingenuity could find a way to hitch them to your caravan."

And so they would stay a few more days until the logistics of hauling the Airstream could be worked out.

Cyndi and the others took out everything from the Airstream that was surplus to requirements—keeping only the bare minimum of equipment, the stove and the propane canister to run it, and mattresses to sleep upon. Everything else, the cupboards and storage units, and anything except the bare minimum of crockery and cutlery, even the toilet, were taken out so that they could reduce the weight of the thing and make it possible for the animals to bear it.

"We're pulling a trailer, not trying to get a balloon over the Alps!" Lucy had complained as Freeson unbolted the toilet from the floor of the Airstream. "I'm not doing my business in the snow! I'm going to hold it all the way to Detroit!"

Supplies were meager. Rice, some grains, and tins of ham they'd saved from the fire at Marty's. Naomi offered up a generous package of pork jerky, wrapped in hessian and tied up with twine. Jacob gave them two gallons of his blackberry cider. Cyndi reckoned that, if they rationed well, and maybe picked up some things on the way—if they were lucky—they should have enough for the trip. Just.

Nathan and Freeson got on with converting the shafts and hitching bars from one of the Amish's retired buggies into a jury-rigged contraption that would allow them to attach the three mules abreast in a driving block to pull the Airstream.

They worked in one of the barns, but it was still bitter cold, and they could only stay out for a couple of hours before needing to come in and warm up in the family room.

When Nathan finally hitched the mules' breast collars to the buggy shafts he'd cold-riveted to the Airstream's aluminum sides two mornings later, and walked them forward, the obedient animals complied, and the Airstream rolled.

Two members of the party would walk out, leading the mules, while the rest would stay inside the Airstream. Freeson's feet were still in no real shape to trudge through snow, so the leading duties would be shared between the others. Nathan's attempt to have Cyndi stay inside the Airstream as well was met with a curt reply. "It's not an illness, Nate. For a million years, we've dropped sprogs in the field and gone back to work in the afternoon. I can lead the mules."

Jacob's expression was a picture to behold as Nathan was put in his place by his wife. But Jacob's supreme politeness didn't allow him to comment—he just side-eyed Naomi, who Nathan was sure winked back with a tiny grin.

Jacob coughed and put his thumbs in his suspenders, indicating to Nathan greenhouses really were as far into the future as he was willing to go… for now.

The Amish gave them thick overcoats that would fit over their anoraks and wide-brimmed hats so that, as they got ready to move out, Nathan and Cyndi looked indistinguishable from the Amish they were leaving behind as they prepared to take the first stint at leading.

"Good luck, Nathan. By the grace of God, you will be in Detroit within the month." Jacob shook Nathan's hand and Naomi hugged Cyndi.

The sky was gray, the wind a cold scythe, and the road hard to follow through the deep covering of snow, but even with the daunting journey ahead, it felt good to be on the move again.

As the Amish settlement diminished into the distance and Saber trotted alongside—seemingly happy to be on the move again herself—Nathan wondered how long this all too rare slice of optimism would last. It wasn't hard to imagine that incredibly hard times still lay ahead.

Later, when they were starving, near dead from exhaustion and on the verge of just laying down in the snow and giving up, Nathan would look back on this moment and think it had been the worst decision he'd made in his life.

22

N athan fell to his knees, the snow reaching up to his groin with cold snowmelt water seeping into the material of his jeans. When the mules pulling the Airstream had crested the rise in the flurrying flakes of the oncoming storm, and he'd seen what they faced now, Nathan had felt his heart collapse.

The bridge was out.

The far end of the rusty, iron lattice roadway had collapsed into the river, turned thirty degrees on its plane. Even if they might have used the slope of the felled bridge to get to the other side of the river, there was no way the mules would get up the other side.

The sides of the river cut on this bank were too steep to get the Airstream down to the frozen river, and there were ten miles—*two* days of hard walking—behind them, all of which would have to be traversed again in order to get back to the road connecting this backroad to a tributary highway near Doland Creek, that would inch them nearer to Detroit.

The river here was only fifty yards or so across, but the far bank might as well have been on Mars, so far was it from their ability to cross it.

Nathan's guts were hollow, and had been since the food had run out five days before, but this kick in the belly made the grinding pain of hunger even worse. The sores on his lips spoke of malnutrition and neglect, and his beard was straggly and crisp with ice, but this pain felt like a last straw.

The mules were exhausted, hardy though they were, and fed better than the humans in the party since tree bark and dead vegetation were easy enough to harvest for them from beneath the wintry covering on the roadside.

The last storm they'd been dealt had kept them battened down for three days and made it impossible to hunt, even when the food, rationed heroically by Cyndi, had run out at last. Their final meal of cold rice—the stove long since having run out of propane—hadn't filled a single belly.

Every city, town, or farm they'd passed along the way in the last six weeks had either been burned-out or desolate. They'd found nothing to eat. Where in early summer they might have expected to find fruit or tubers in the ground or on bushes, anything along those lines had been denied to them by this seemingly endless winter. And the hunting had not been good, either. Every day, Nathan, Freeson, Syd, and Lucy would go out in pairs to see what they could trap or shoot… and they had shot nothing. They set snares overnight, which were still empty loops in the morning. If jackrabbits and rodents were around, they were still hibernating, and they certainly weren't breeding.

Even Saber was eating whatever she found instead of bringing it home to share, and what she did retrieve wasn't enough for even her, judging by her reduced heft and nightly whimpering.

"What will we do?" Cyndi asked, squatting down next to Nathan as the mules moved their feet to stop them from freezing, her voice as strained as Nathan's heartstrings. She was cradling her seven-month swelling with hands and arms that, when out of their coverings, were as thin as sticks. The baby inside her was still moving, but it was taking everything and anything Cyndi put into her body before such sustenance had a chance to pass any energy on to Cyndi. Her eyes were surrounded by black circles, and her lips and nostrils were a mess of red, crusty-topped sores.

The others jumped down from the Airstream to see what was causing the holdup. They approached slowly, no ability to do anything else, like gray wraiths in the flurries.

"I have no idea," was all that Nathan could find to say.

The intensity of the snowfall increased steadily, flakes settling on the brim of Nathan's Amish hat and on his shoulders. Soon, he would be a snowman staring into a white abyss, and right now he didn't care.

Take me. I got nothing.

Freeson limped up to stand beside Nathan, his knees still down in the powder. "What are we supposed to do with that?"

Nathan just shook his head.

Freeson put his hand underneath Nathan's arm and pulled on him. "Come on, fella, and get out of the snow. Cyndi needs your balls to make more kids; you freeze them off and she's gonna be asking me to deputize."

Under any other circumstance, Nathan would have found Freeson's crudeness funny or shocking, but he felt so empty, so wasted, that there were no words in his throat to be spoken, and no energy to change his expression away from one of blank misery. Hunger wasn't just a physical thing, he'd found in the last week or so. However much it crippled the body, its hollow agony also wrapped an iron band around Nathan's mind and squeezed away any last drops of faith in his ability to get his family to Detroit, pushing them out to disappear into the murderous winter.

Family First.

Oh, kiss *off*, Dad.

They were done. This was the end.

Eventually, Cyndi and Freeson got Nathan back into the

Airstream and out of his wet clothes. He hadn't resisted as they'd pulled him to his feet and walked him gently back inside. The situation in the trailer did little to raise Nathan's mood, though, such was the pall of resignation and defeat that hung there like a black cloud.

Tony hadn't moved from the bed for some hours, laying still, his eyes closed and his belly rumbling loud enough for everyone to hear. Lucy was sobbing, curled up on the mattress she shared with Freeson at night, her knees drawn up and her shoulders spasming with every sob.

Donie and Dave sat silently together, occasionally fingering their battery-dead tech. They'd had to leave much of their gear back with the Amish on the promise that, when they could, they'd be able to go back and collect it. They'd kept the base station, the walkie-talkies, and some solar trickle chargers, but the last storm had ripped those from the roof of the Airstream and cast them away into the night.

Only Syd was alert and ready to move around.

"Saber, come on, girl!" she said, and with that she opened the door, letting in a flurry of snow. The dog leapt up from where she had been lying next to Tony, transmitting her warmth to the boy.

"You can't go out," Cyndi said to the teenager. "The storm will hit soon."

"I'm not going far. Saber will get me back. I'm going to see what I can get us for dinner." She picked up an AR-15 and a pistol from where they'd been stowed in a rack beside the door and jumped down into the snow.

Nathan heard all this with his head between his knees, a blanket around his shoulders, the dark welling up from his belly and fogging his brain. He couldn't clear the doom from his thinking. The collapsed bridge had finally forced him to give up trying.

Six weeks of hard traveling, moving five miles a day when they could and weren't pinned down by storms, had taken its toll on everyone. Nathan had kept spirits high when he could, motivating and cajoling the others. Aping Jacob Anderson's calmness, bearing, and self-belief... trying to spread it among the others, driven by the optimism he'd felt as they'd left the settlement that first day. At first, it had worked, and Nathan had suddenly been the leader the group needed. Cyndi's skillsets were overburdened by her being the 'go-to' persona of the group in terms of survival decisions. Nathan had felt he could take on that mantle fully after all they'd been through, leaving the cooking and the details to her, and for a couple of weeks it had gone well.

But every dead house and empty town and burning city they'd passed had been another puncture in the skin of his resolve. The storms that lashed down on them, sometimes entirely without warning, meant that they couldn't travel as far as they wanted. They just couldn't pass up a house or farm to stable the mules if they felt a storm was imminent. This meant that, some days, they traveled only a pittance of miles before losing their nerve and camping for the duration of a storm.

Donie and Dave did what they could with the maps and satellites, but without an engine running to charge their tech, navigation was soon lost to them when the trickle chargers had been lost to the squall. The ash-filled sky made navigating by starlight impossible, and during the day, the sun was so weak in the sky you hardly knew it was there.

Whatever had turned the Earth off its axis and caused the poles to shift had not stopped. It was as if the harshness of the east coast was following them cross-country, so that it wouldn't be long before the whole of America was crushed beneath the white weight of the catastrophe.

Dwindling food, too much time spent in the cold, and the exertion of walking the mules had chipped away at Nathan's health. Although Naomi's attentions at the settlement had helped him back to a semblance of normality, the shock to his system caused by the fever and coma had taken a heavy toll on his stamina. One hour out leading the mules and he felt near collapse. The fact that he often stayed out two hours was his undoing each time. He would almost have to crawl back into the Airstream on his hands and knees. And there he'd lay, chest heaving, trying to regain enough strength to go back out and walk with the animals to relieve Cyndi as quickly as he could, and well before he was fully recovered. This situation had soon made any progress towards Detroit a near miracle.

When the propane had been exhausted, they'd had to chop

wood to make fires, but days of hard walking, low food, bad hunting, and the withering effects of the cold made even the act of chopping wood for a fire a near impossible chore.

Tempers were frayed at all ends, for all of the group. Conversations were short, and devoid of humor or care. Just the bare bones of conversations were had, no one having the energy for anything more. Navigation was blind because the necessity of staying off highways and expressways to keep away from marauding gangs meant exclusively traveling on backroads. And these backroads were poorly signposted and, sometimes, like today, paths to dead ends—with the emphasis on the *dead*...

Some days, Nathan and the others had to choose between making a camp, chopping enough wood for a fire, and getting exhausted and staying there two nights, or just making camp, chopping no wood, getting no warmth, and then moving on the next day with enough energy to go even five miles.

The math of survival was colder than the landscape around them.

"Nathan! Wake up. Nathan!"

A hand shook his shoulder. Nathan didn't remember falling asleep with his head resting on his knees, but now Cyndi's voice rang urgent in his ear, drilling shrilly through his sleep.

The wind was still howling outside, rattling the side panels, and he could hear Saber yelping and barking. With a supreme effort he didn't want to make, Nathan lifted his head and opened his eyes. A dull light came through the windows, illuminating the scene in the Airstream. The air was thick with the odor of communal living and it seemed to move in eddies of condensation around him, as if the whole world was resting behind a steamed-up lens. Breath was coming in clouds from everyone beneath their blankets except for Cyndi, who knelt by Nathan, shaking him.

"It's Syd, for Pete's sake, Nathan, wake up!"

Nathan rubbed at his eyes. "What is it?"

"Saber's back, but Syd isn't."

For the first time, Nathan could see that the Airstream door was being held open a crack against the wind by Dave. Through the gap, he could see Saber. She was leaping up at the Airstream, barking and yelping, flurries of flakes circling around her. She got down, spread her front paws wide, and barked again.

"Suddenly, I'm in a Lassie movie." Lucy rolled over, covering her ears. "Where's Timmy, Lassie? Has he fallen down a well?" she snipped.

Nathan didn't want to do this. He didn't *care*. Channeling Lucy, and feeling okay about it, he turned his face away from the door and tried to shut out the yelping of the damn dog.

And that's when Cyndi attacked him.

Her fists rained down on his head, spittle streaking from

her mouth, her incoherent words taking ten or fifteen seconds to make some sense.

"Damn you, Nathan, damn you! We are not going to leave that girl to die in the snow. We are not going to leave her! Get up! Get *up!*"

The blows lessened, Cyndi's sobbing increased, and her body slumped to the floor of the trailer where she lay holding her ever-swelling stomach and crying like she was dredging up her tears from the very wells of hell.

Nathan stared without seeing, and then, suddenly, it registered what he was looking at.

Like a switch being flicked, the light came back on in Nathan's head.

Damn the hunger. Damn the cold.

As his heart pumped a new fire into his chest, Nathan knew that this wasn't him—this broken, depressed, hungry wretch was not Nathan Tolley. This wasn't the man his daddy had raised, this wasn't the husband that Cyndi had married, this wasn't the father Tony needed, and, most of all, this wasn't the man who would leave a child to die in the cold.

Nathan hauled himself to his feet, climbed back into his damp pants, picked out a shotgun from the rack, and leapt out into the wind.

The storm had almost blown itself out.

It had only lasted a couple of hours, but in that time it had dumped a fresh load of snow across the road and piled it up against the Airstream's side. Someone, probably Freeson, had unhitched the mules and tied them up in the trees, covered in blankets and out of the worst of the wind and snow.

Saber barked excitedly, turning around Nathan's legs and then trying to jump up to lick his face. He rubbed her ears and patted her back, and said, "Okay, Lassie, do your thing. Where is she?"

Saber double-barked and then turned, haring off into the trees. Nathan followed as fast as he could, but when Saber got too far ahead, he would call her to stand fast until he caught up.

How could he have gotten so close to giving up? The level of self-loathing was a rising tide within him as he stalked after the dog. He couldn't let the cold, the hunger, and the depression it brought with it get the better of him again. He had never been this low before, ready to let his family and his friends slip through his fingers. It wouldn't happen again.

"Syd! Syd!"

The wind whipped his words away and flung them into the trees, and Saber barked, too, kicking up sprays of powder with her back paws as she stood and howled.

Within minutes, when Nathan looked back, he couldn't see the mules, the Airstream, or the road. But he should be able to follow his footprints back in the snow if the wind, which was still dropping as the storm rolled away, didn't wipe them clean in the meantime.

"N...t...n!"

Nathan spun, unsure of the direction that the voice had come from. Saber was off as it came again, and this time there was no calling her back. Saber left a fresh trail for him to follow and he made good progress through the silent trees.

"Syd! Syd! Can you hear me?"

"Nathan!"

It was faint, but the voice drew Nathan on, Saber's bark pulling him like a chain-fall. He saw the bloody snow and the F-150 Raptor SVT in the Green Livery of the Michigan Great Lakes Park Ranger service long before he saw the dead body of a 16-pointer elk that pinned Syd to the ground.

"Syd?"

"Thank God. Nathan. Help me. Please!"

Syd was beneath the elk, and so large was the dead bull that all that was protruding from beneath it was Syd's head. It took Nathan ten minutes of hauling to get the dead weight off the girl.

She was lying in a depression from which all the snow had melted from the combined heat of their bodies. Like the snow around them, Syd was smeared in blood, but thankfully none of it was her own.

When she was out from under the dead animal and had checked herself for injuries, finding nothing but a few small cuts and bruises, she told Nathan what had happened.

"I found the Ranger truck half-buried in snow. And I was checking it out when I saw the elk. Biggest thing I ever saw. I tried to shoot it with the AR, but I slipped and missed. The bullet musta ricocheted and spooked it. It ran straight at me! I fired and got its shoulder, but it carried on. I guess it was just running blindly. I shot it in the head, but it was still moving and slammed into me. Then, *bang*, I was underneath it, couldn't move, and it was bleeding all over me."

Her words came in an excited rush as she continued, "I've been here three hours, I reckon, and I am cold and I am wet and I've never been so glad to see anyone in my life!"

She stepped tighter into Nathan and hugged him like she had at Jacob's house. Nathan just looked down at the elk in shock and commented, "This is going to feed us for a month."

"It doesn't need to. Not now."

Nathan looked at the girl, feeling the confusion leaking out of his face.

"Easier if I show you," she said.

And so Syd took Nathan's hand, and led him away from the truck and up through the treeline to come out with a view straight over paradise.

23

"Nate! You made it! You actually made it!"

Stryker, the collar of his hideous Hawaiian shirt sticking up from the neck of his parka, ran down the steps outside the grand limestone edifice of the huge Masonic Temple. The enormous gothic façade was the perfect vision to complement the billion icicles that hung murderously from its ledges and finials. If Bela Lugosi had followed Stryker out of the building, Nathan wouldn't have been at all surprised. The sixteen-story slab of history, turreted and formal, thrust its bulk up into the sky, daring the weather to attack first. The top of the building, where once had been the clean, straight lines of civic architecture, was now festooned with over a dozen wind turbines on jury-rigged steel gantries.

Detroit's grand Masonic Temple looked like it was half

city structure and half a monstrous Howard Hawks' prop engine sea-plane, about to take off and power up into the ashen sky.

"It's okay, you don't have to bare your breast or roll up your pant leg to get in. Everyone is welcome here. Everyone!" Stryker threw out his hands and pirouetted on his heels. "Let's get you guys inside, into the warmth!"

Downtown Detroit had been a mess of half-cleared snow, wrecked cars, and a million broken windows. The streets were mainly empty except for a few city cops who'd checked on them periodically as they'd rolled through. Nathan had driven the Raptor with Cyndi up front, and Tony, Syd, and Saber in the vehicle's crew cab. The four others had ridden in the Airstream. The journey over the last ten miles by the shore of Lake Erie, and along the banks of the Detroit River into the city, had taken the best part of a day. But in contrast to the last six weeks, it felt faster than ice skimming across an oil slick. The mules had been reliably steadfast, but also totally more *stead* than *fast*.

The weather had held off for the last few miles and the run along the expressway across the compacted snow had been the smoothest they'd experienced in months.

After Syd had taken Nathan away from the Raptor and dead elk, up through the treeline, and pointed across the frozen expanse of Lake Erie, Nathan had been able to see the skyscrapers and bulk of their final destination.

Detroit. Shining in a golden vision below the sun-pinked, ash-filled sky like a mirage.

"I was coming back to tell you, but I got elked," Syd said with the matter-of-fact simplicity of someone to whom that kind of thing happened every day.

They'd been perhaps only a couple of days away from Stryker and his promised new life. They'd had a fresh vehicle, elk meat to butcher, and a renewed sense of urgency that Nathan had felt shivering through him like lightning in Victor Frankenstein's laboratory.

Live, my beauty! Live!

Even together, Syd and Nathan hadn't had the strength to get the elk's enormous body onto the back of the ranger's Raptor. But once he'd lit a small fire under the block to thaw the engine and get the truck in a position to start—the tank had been nearly four-fifths full according to the gauge—the rugged vehicle had started on the fourth attempt. Nathan had used strong nylon ropes he'd found in the crew cab to tie the elk around the antlers and drag it behind the Raptor, down a track in the pines and back to the road where the bridge was out—and right to the waiting Airstream.

It was the nearest feeling to Christmas Nathan had experienced since… well, Christmas.

Freeson and Cyndi had butchered the elk, which had traveled well across the ice, losing only a few points from its antlers, and that evening they'd eaten like kings.

"I once ate elk venison in Paris," Lucy said as the meat

roasted over an open flame and the party stood around the fire in the approaching night, their mouths salivating, their eyes glittering. "I didn't like it that much. Can't you go back and find a deer?"

For a moment, Nathan had thought Lucy was being serious, and he'd been forming a rebuke when she'd flat-out winked at him and chucked the beard under his chin with her fingers. It had been the first really human moment he'd seen from her since she'd stood up to Owen in the diner. She had a sense of humor after all, so perhaps she and Freeson would work out.

The next morning, Dave had managed to charge and get the base station working from the power point in the Raptor's dash, and with that, they'd gotten an exact fix on their location and contacted Stryker by Skype.

Stryker had said he'd arrange with the city authorities to give them access to the downtown area of Detroit. And he'd been good to his word.

For perhaps the last time.

The outskirts of the city were burning or burned-out in much the same way as the other cities they'd skirted on their journey to Detroit. Vast blocks of buildings were blackened, roofless stumps sticking out of deep, virgin snow.

They'd nearly reached the downtown area before they'd met the city barricades. The wide, ice-covered expressway was completely blocked by lines of yellow school buses placed end to end. Snow drifted up almost to their roofs where city cops with shotguns, and one machine gun post, waited to challenge anyone who approached.

Stryker's assurances that they would be let into the city had been honored, but as they'd rolled on and continued to witness empty streets, dead windows in the faces of shattered buildings, and a general lack of evidence that the city was anything like the pictures Stryker had sent them over email, Nathan had begun to feel a nagging worry return to his gut—a background thing for the moment, but there, and unsettling.

"Doesn't look like paradise," Syd had said from behind him, putting voice to the niggle of anxiety Nathan had been getting from the deserted streets.

There were small pockets of evidence to show the city had been trying to prep for a future of cataclysmic weather events. But nothing like Nathan had imagined from Stryker's over-heated descriptions. Some public spaces that had once been parks and garden areas were covered in improvised plastic cloches, man-tall and misty with condensation. Nathan had also seen some shadows moving behind the transparent plastic, perhaps tending plants, but not the full evidence of an enclosed city they'd been expecting.

Each small area of city farm had sported three or four spinning, domestic-use wind turbines up on telegraph poles. "I guess they're using wind power to generate the extra heat they need inside the cloches... but the plastic will freeze and crack in the cold and under the weight of snow. They must be fixing them constantly. What happens when they run out of plastic sheeting? Why aren't they using glass?" Cyndi's practical prepper instincts had begun kicking in with her running commentary as they'd rolled through downtown. As they'd headed for Stryker's home in the old Masonic Temple just beyond the Detroit business district, the near total lack of what they had been told to expect had done nothing to assuage Nathan's unease.

Once the hugging and the backslapping greetings were over, Stryker led the party through the doors and into the opulence of the marble entranceway of the Masonic Temple, and soon that unease Nathan had been feeling turned into an unscratchable itch.

The once magnificent spaces of the temple were moving towards ruin. As their party climbed the stairs, the spaces above them showed up as being damp and gloomy. Their breath hung in the air like mist in autumn trees. The carpets were sodden and the place smelled of neglect and decay—like an old church that hadn't had its roof fixed in decades.

The walls on the stairwells were slick with water, too. Holes had been punctured in ceilings so that electrical wires could be fed through.

"No point heating the stairs, guys!" Stryker said, picking up Nathan's concerned looks to Cyndi.

A ripple of *'Is this it? Really?'* was moving through the

party, though, from Nathan, through the kids, and back past Dave and Donie to Freeson and Lucy. Nathan saw Lucy feeling a wall as they moved up past the ninth floor, apparently checking the plaster that came away under her fingernail. Lucy shook her head. "Shocking," she muttered.

Even Saber was picking up the mood, loping behind them along the stairs, eyes unsure, her ears back and flat against her head.

At the tenth-floor lobby, Stryker had to push his shoulder against a mahogany door that was warping in the damp in order to allow them all to get into the corridor beyond. At least here there was a feeling of warmth billowing from the space beyond the lobby.

"See?" Stryker asked brightly. "Once you see the whole place, you'll get a better idea of how well we're doing. We have five rooms up here for you guys. Plenty to go around."

"Rooms?" Nathan stopped, a wave of suspicion rolling up his spine and bursting in his head. "You said we'd get a place of our own."

Stryker smiled widely and clapped Nathan on the shoulder. "Sure you will, buddy. Sure you will, but this is just for settling in. Worry not. Have I ever let you down before?"

I never gave you the chance before, Nathan thought uncharitably, but he said nothing.

"Sorry about the elevators," Stryker said as he moved away down the corridor past a series of wooden doors that had names on them—*The Michaels. Randy's Place. Fullerton.*

Mrs. Kowalski... and half a dozen more. "You'll love the neighbors. All good people. All of them. We'll have a get-together tonight after you've settled in."

"How many people live here, Stry?"

"I'm not a *census* guy, Nate." Stryker laughed and made a joke of counting on his fingers until he shook off the joke and commented, "Coupl'a hundred, I guess. Haven't met them all. We get a daily influx, as well, from downtown and some outlier communities. The main auditorium here in the temple is also the city government chamber. They got a proper parliament going, dude. All the plans. All the ideas. This is a city of ideas, man. It's built on them!"

Stryker stopped outside a set of mahogany double doors, and then turned like he was a three-ring circus ringmaster about to announce the main act.

"Nathan, Cyndi, Tony, and everyone, welcome to the rest of your lives!"

And then came the explosion, blasting the doors apart, filling the corridor with dense black smoke—it crashed through them in a rage of hot breath and red fire.

24

There was an age of black silence, where empires of fear and grief rose and fell in the unhappiness of inevitable history. The years spinning darkly around his head to the buzz of flies rising from a rotting carcass.

Then history moved on, and Nathan was back in the room.

Nathan felt like he'd been dropped into a pressurized diving bell and someone was pushing their thumbs hard into his eyes, while an elephant or similar beast pressed its full weight down on his guts. His nose and mouth were covered in a gritty film of warm soot and the stench of a broken latrine forced its way into his nostrils.

When his ears began to work again, Nathan could hear coughing, spluttering, and groaning all around him. But his eyes were refusing to work, and that immediate frustration brought his hand up to try to clear his vision. The fingers came away smeared with wet earth as if his face had been pushed into a muddy puddle. As he cleared his eyes, gloomy light in the corridor came in a rush through his eyelids, and Tony's sobs, harsh and hacking in the close proximity, began to turn into the wheeze of an asthma attack.

Nathan spun his head, but all that he could see were tears. He rubbed at his eyes again and, when he lowered his fists, he saw that the doors which Stryker had been about to open were hanging on their hinges at crazy angles.

Part of the ceiling had collapsed above them. There were sprays of fresh dirt surrounding them, as if someone had dumped the contents of a freshly dug grave on them, and these lay below wisps of smoke rising from laths of smoldering wood. Through the broken doors, Nathan saw a wrecked apartment of overturned tables, busted chairs, and plastic troughs full of vegetation upended and destroyed. Rubber and plastic pipes spewed water across the floor and a small fire had erupted from an overturned Yukon stove that was about to catch light to a pile of firewood.

Nathan wanted to get to his boy, but the fire had to be a priority on the tenth floor of a building with which he wasn't familiar. Cyndi was sitting up from the pile of limbs and coughing heads, pulling leaves and dirt out of her hair and shaking her head.

"See to Tony," he said, getting up, and Cyndi nodded, still a little disorientated as she reached for their son.

Nathan's feet were unsteady, and his knees felt like candy left in the summer sun, but he stumbled forward, through the shattered doors and into the apartment beyond. The fire was small, and all he had to do was pick up one of the free-trickling hydroponic pipes from the floor and douse the guttering flames. The blown over steel box of the Yukon stove hissed and spat as the water doused the growing blaze into acrid smoke.

Back in the corridor, when Nathan reached it, Cyndi had gotten Tony's inhaler from her bag and was helping the boy relax his constricting throat.

Saber sat licking at Syd's face, trying to clear it of mud. Lucy was being pulled from beneath a section of plasterboard by Freeson, and Dave and Donie weren't checking themselves for injuries, but peering hard at the screens of their tech for damage.

Stryker turned out to be the only one who'd been hurt by the blast coming from his apartment, and it was his pride that smarted more than the cuts and bumps from the blown open mahogany doors which had pole-axed the back of his head.

"Don't move, Stry; let me check you out." Nathan bent to look at the blood welling from two deep cuts in Stryker's blond hair. The wounds were long, but not deep. Given that Nathan knew head wounds bled like bitches, and often looked worse than they actually were, he didn't find them too worrisome.

Stryker pushed Nathan's hands away. "I'm fine, man. No need to fuss yourself…"

Stryker tried to get up then, but his heel slipped from underneath him in the wet mud and his head crashed back onto the floor, knocking himself completely unconscious this time.

Nathan surveyed the corridor—his friends, his family, and finally Stryker, prostate, covered in mud and crap, a puddle of blood leaking from the back of his head and his stupid shirt ruffling in the cold breeze from all the windows the explosion had blown out in his destroyed apartment.

Welcome to the rest of your lives?

"I don't think so," Nathan said to no one and everyone.

25

Stryker had been trying to make methane gas from human, animal, and vegetable waste. His cheap and ancient Chinese-made, 1000-watt inverter for converting the DC current from the Masonic Temple's roof-based wind farm batteries into AC had blown a switch on the circuit board. That electrical fire had fritzed out a burst of flame from the casing, which had blown open the plastic tank of methane. A tank that had been far too near any electrical equipment to be safe—*especially* given the ancient Chinese inverter. The resultant detonation had torn apart the apartment on a gust of flame and billowing brisance.

The blast had wrecked all of Stryker's rudimentary hydroponic frames, too, twisting and snapping the plastic trays, and torching the vast majority of his crop of vegetables, grains, and fruits.

As the shell-shocked and aching party had helped the still dazed Stryker try to clear up the mess, Freeson and Nathan had done their best with the broken windows, stapling plastic sheeting to the frames, which then bulged in from the wind outside the tenth floor like the fat bellies of sails on a pirate ship.

Stryker had a spare inverter, but the wires coming from the roof batteries weren't transmitting any current. "Dammit," he said. "Happens sometimes. Just have to go up and fix it."

Stryker's overcompensating sense of blind optimism took over. He began filling a rucksack with tools.

"You're going up to the roof?" Nathan asked incredulously. "You've just been blown up, man. It can wait."

Everyone was pooped. They were sitting on Stryker's singed furniture, looking like refugees from a war zone. Tony lay sleeping on Cyndi's lap, Saber sprawled over Syd's. Lucy, who hadn't said a word since they'd gotten out of the corridor, had her head on Freeson's shoulder. The tech twins were trying to see if they could get any signal from the base station, but as Dave had said, "We're on the wrong side of the building for line of sight, and there's no cell signal."

Not being able to get a connection to the internet seemed to have upset him more than being caught in an explosion.

Stryker pulled the zip closed on his rucksack.

"We need power or we're just gonna have to huddle

together for warmth and eat raw vegetables, and no one wants to see that happen. Need to run a new line."

Stryker picked up a roll of wire and walked towards the doors, which were still hanging on their hinges. His steps were unsteady and, for a moment, Nathan had the very real image of Stryker becoming unbalanced on the roof, falling past the plastic-covered window frames in the apartment and hurtling to his death. Vivid as could be, the scene popped right into the center of his imagination.

Dammit.

However angry he was with Stryker right now—and there would be a reckoning, for sure—he wasn't going to let his friend go up to the roof alone in this state.

Family *and friends* first.

The afternoon was falling towards twilight.

The roof wind farm above the sixteenth floor of the Masonic Temple could be accessed from one of the two turrets above the façade. The bitterness of the cutting wind and the thrumming of the two dozen turbines were the dominant sensations once they were out in the open.

Windsor, Detroit's Siamese twin across the Detroit River in Canada, was even now, in the failing light, alight with fires. It was a broken cityscape of destroyed, burned-out buildings and vast tracks of snow.

The river, like the Great Lakes at either end of it, was the frozen passage between them. Cargo vessels had been locked into the ice, some raised tail high in the crush of ice, their rusting hulls red and ochre in the darkening light. Nathan could see the lights of a few cars moving down on the waterfront, but nothing else seemed to be moving in Windsor until a gust of flame blew out of a window in a tall building, and the boom of its detonation rolled across the ice to Detroit.

"Guess I'm not the only one trying to make methane." Stryker shrugged as they tramped through the snow on the roof.

Detroit looked less burned out than Windsor, but as their journey in earlier that day had shown them, it was not immune to what had ravaged so many cities they'd seen. Electric lights glowed in many windows across the snowy scene, casting up blue-yellow reflections of the surface of winter. A police siren warped and whooped in on the wind as Nathan and Stryker made their way across the roof to the turbine feeding the batteries meant to provide power to Stryker's level, six floors below.

Nathan had been to Detroit just once before. He'd driven there with his daddy to pick up a 1995 Ford F-150 with a custom FlareSide SuperCab. They'd been hired by his daddy's friend to bring it back to Glens Falls. They'd gone in the Dodge and Nathan had driven it back while his old man drove the Ford. The city then had been dirty and noisy, sure, but it had been alive. Alive with the smells of good food, music blaring from shop fronts, bars sending out gales of laughter, and others blasting out savage hip-hop or barroom rawk. Now the city below them was like a Shadow Detroit. One cast by the light of a dying sun onto barren land. The city, with its burning twin, was a bruise on the earth.

Deep and painful to look at.

They got to the turbine and, instead of getting his tools from his bag, Stryker faced Nathan, putting down the wire and the rucksack. He sighed, and then spoke. "There's nothing wrong with the wire. Sorry, man."

Nathan's confusion coursed ahead of his sudden anger. Nonplussed, he stared at his friend, feeling the vertigo of the huge dome of sky and long drop below him. "Then why have you brought me up here on this fool's errand, Stry? I'm freezing my nuts off…"

Stryker looked at his feet and said something that was whipped away in the wind.

Nathan moved closer. "What?"

Stryker looked up. "I might have been… less than truthful. I'm sorry."

Nathan bunched his fists, but didn't punch Stryker—he'd save that for later, once the explanation landed. "We've already seen the city, Stry, and it's nothing like you told us, nothing like the pictures. I came up here to stop you falling off the roof by accident, but now that you've brought it up, if you don't give me a damn good explanation *right* now, I'll throw you off, myself. Now get to it."

Stryker pushed his hands into his pockets, struggling to make eye contact. When he did, his eyes were watery and his gaze was weak. "We got the ambition, dude. The place is burning with it. Some of the conversions have been made. There are covered-in areas, and we've got the wind farms up and running. Power, we got coming out of our ears."

"Hospital?" Nathan's only thought now was the safety of Cyndi, his unborn child, and Tony.

"Sure, yeah… it might not be the best, but it's still operating. There are doctors and there are nurses, but…"

"There's always a *but*, isn't there?" Nathan nails were digging into his palms. If it hadn't been for the gloves, he'd have drawn blood for sure.

"Supplies and drugs are difficult to get… we've been pretty much abandoned by the federal government now… So, we're not getting information, and there have been raids."

Images of Ski-Doos, burning diners, and carved out foreheads leapt to the front of Nathan's mind. "Raids…?"

"Yeah… look…"

"Raids, as in scavengers? Gangs? We met some of them out on the road." Had he lifted his family from the frying pan only to drop them into the fire? Or, rather, from the refrigerator only to lock them into the freezer?

"No… not gangs. This is… official…"

All the times Nathan had thought Cyndi was being all *Paranoid Conspiracy Prepper* with her insistence that they not rely on the future governments to look after the population, and here it was turning out to be legit advice. "The government? Stealing your hospital supplies? What craziness is infecting this place, Stry? We trusted you! We believed you!"

Stryker held up his hands. "They're calling themselves the government. They could be anyone. Anyone with a tank can be the government these days."

"They've got *tanks*?"

Stryker shook his head, "No, you doofus. That's just a figure of speech, but you know what I mean. Official looking guys show up, wave around official looking ID, and waltz off with what they want. That's why the cops set up the road-blocks. We got wise to it now."

Nathan had to hold onto the gantry to stop his still shaky legs from collapsing beneath him. He couldn't believe what he was hearing, but at the same time, he was kicking himself for letting himself be persuaded into this position. He should have seen it coming. Relying on Stryker was like relying on a politician not to tell lies when his lips moved.

Nathan felt himself being swallowed up in the incredulity of the situation. All this way, all this hurt. For this?

"Why?! Why did you lie to me?" he demanded, his head hot with rage.

"Not technically lying."

"Technically? *Technically?*" And that's when Nathan grabbed Stryker by the front of his jacket. He thumped Stryker back against the turbine gantry. "Come on, you jerk, why did you make me bring my family here? Technically, I'm not going to throw you off the roof. Think of it as a flying lesson."

Stryker's mouth moved quickly, getting his words out in a rush. "We need men like you, Nate. I'm terrible at this stuff. Yeah, sure, I try my best, but look how I screwed up today. I almost blew us up. We need men like you, but more than that…"

Nathan relaxed his grip on Stryker just enough to stop the neck of the anorak from choking him.

The pictures sparked in Nathan's brain again. Tony coughing, his lips blue, the last of the asthma meds keeping him alive until they could find another stock. Cyndi, his hand on her belly, feeling the kick of the uncertain future. The burning cities, Owen's scavengers, and the Reynolds with their tales of *the extinction event*.

A world toppling off its axis, spinning down like a child's top to a cold death and taking everyone on Earth with it.

"More than what?" He was shaking Stryker now, and if his eyes had been marbles, they would have rattled around his skull like roulette balls. "Tell me! Tell me!"

Stryker's eyes stopped spinning and they fixed Nathan with a stare so chilling that it cut through him deeper and colder than the wind coming off the frozen lake, carrying its cargo of burning and the smell of desolation.

"More than you… we need… *Cyndi*."

And that's what finally drove Nathan to hit him.

END OF FREEZING POINT

AFTER THE SHIFT BOOK ONE

Freezing Point, September 13 2018

Killing Frost, November 8 2018

Black Ice, January 10 2019

PS: If you love apocalyptic fiction then keep reading for exclusive extracts from **Killing Frost** and **Dark Retreat.**

ABOUT GRACE HAMILTON

**Loved this book? Share it with a friend,
www.GraceHamiltonBooks.com/books**

**To be notified of the next book release please sign up for
Grace's mailing list at www.GraceHamiltonBooks.com.**

Grace Hamilton is the prepper pen-name for a bad-ass, survivalist momma-bear of four kids, and wife to a wonderful husband. After being stuck in a mountain cabin for six days following a flash flood, she decided she never wanted to feel so powerless or have to send her kids to bed hungry again. Now she lives the prepper lifestyle and knows that if SHTF or TEOTWAWKI happens, she'll be ready to help protect and provide for her family.

Combine this survivalist mentality with a vivid imagination (as well as a slightly unhealthy day dreaming habit) and you get a prepper fiction author. Grace spends her days thinking about the worst possible survival situations that a person could be thrown into, then throwing her characters into these nightmares while trying to figure out "What SHOULD you do in this situation?"

BLURB

Nathan and his family are on the run from a catastrophic polar shift—but the bitter cold is the least of their worries.

Nathan was led to believe that Detroit would be the

proverbial promised land, but when his family arrives they find a city struggling just to survive in the frigid conditions. Nathan's old friend Stryker has made a safe haven in the ancient Masonic Temple, but it soon becomes clear that the comfortable life within its walls is unsustainable. Resources are running out fast, and with a new baby to feed and another son in need of medicine, Nathan and Cyndi face a difficult choice: dig in with the dangerously naïve Stryker, or head west to Wyoming.

As Nathan debates this fateful decision, he learns the horrifying secret behind Stryker's success. In his heart, he knows he's unwilling to pay such a price for his family's safety, but leaving the city is no easy matter when even the walls have eyes. Now, his family, Syd, and their friends will have to use all of their skills to help each other escape and survive whatever comes next, or die trying.

Get your copy of Killing Frost
Available November 8 2018
www.GraceHamiltonBooks.com

EXCERPT

They walked on in silence for a while. The afternoon twilight was thickening towards the first edge of night, and the deserted streets on the journey from Trash Town were deadened by the last deep fall of snow—the quietness pressing hard and uncomfortably against Nathan's ears. Thoughts of how the city of Detroit must have been so different before the Big Winter punched him in the gut.

These streets would have been thronged with cars and people, and their the yelling, music, and conversation—everyone trying to be heard, everyone trying to live their lives and do their do. Now it was like walking through the world's largest cemetery, with gravestones as big a buildings.

Stryker's feet crunched to a halt, snapping Nathan out of his thoughts. "Did you hear that?"

Nathan listened. Nothing but the snow-dead silence of the street greeted him. "No. What did you hear?"

"A click."

Nathan listened again, but there was nothing. "What sort of click?"

"I've had to be around guns more than enough these last few years, Nathan; you get so know the sounds. We're being watched, and I just heard someone take the safety off."

Nathan looked up at the looming, snow-smeared buildings around them, their windows broken and the rooms beyond them dark. The sky was glutted with gray clouds. If they didn't make it back to the Masonic Temple anytime soon, they were going to be out in the snowy wastes of Detroit in full dark. And that didn't bear thinking about.

"You know, I thought my ears were good, but you, sir, have taken it to the next level."

Nathan and Stryker spun around. In the windows of the building they'd passed only moments before, three faces were hovering in the grey gloom, their clothes dark and their faces covered in ski-masks. They were all holding weapons. A shot-gun, a pistol, and a semi-automatic rifle.

"I guess it's the snow that does it, makes the silence more intense, and me just clicking off the safety on my pistol here was too loud under the circumstances."

The voice was harsh and female. It came from the middle figure. "I mean, I was going to shout to you anyways... I was just, as you might say, making preparations in case you two decided to be heroes. So, gentlemen. What's in the crate?" The woman moved her hand with the gun up in a harsh flick. "And would you please, for safety's sake, and my sensibilities, please raise your hands. I wouldn't want to shoot you in the face for nothing."

The woman, after telling one of the figures in the widow, the one with the semi-automatic, to "Cover them," ducked inside and moments later emerged from a door at the top of some snow-covered steps. Behind her, another ski-masked, dark-suited man—by the way he walked—followed her gingerly down the steps.

"Is this a robbery?" Nathan asked as the woman reached the bottom of the steps and planted her feet firmly in the snow, raising her pistol as she did so.

"Well, that depends if you got anything worth stealing. But in reality I hope not. Instead of stealing from you, I think I'd rather make a deal—how does that sound?"

Nathan couldn't have gotten at his gun even if he'd wanted to since it was zipped inside his jacket. And the man in the ski mask was levelling his shotgun at Stryker's waist.

"Your weapons, please," the woman said, "and slowly please; my fingers are cold and they tend to shiver. We don't want that shivering turning into a shooting, do we?"

Stryker and Nathan carefully handed their guns over. The woman relaxed a little. The ski-masked man didn't.

"We know you," the woman said to Stryker. "You're one of those who live in the Masonic Temple."

"Yeah? What of it?" Stryker replied, his voice holding remarkably strong under the circumstances.

"I just want you to know that we know where you live."

"So?"

"So that we can find you and kill you, if you don't do exactly what we say."

The words hung frozen in the air like icicles. "What deal do you want to make?" Nathan asked.

The woman lowered her pistol, but her friend with the shotgun leveled his up. "A sensible man. I like sensible men. What's in the crate?"

"None of your business," Stryker spat.

Nathan turned to Stryker and made a face. "Let's at least hear them out."

The ski-masked woman nodded. "What he said, Stry."

"Don't make the situation worse. While we're talking, we're breathing," Nathan added.

Stryker's skin was reddening and the fingers of his gloved hands spasmed. He seemed far from convinced that this was an acceptable trade-off. "I know exactly what you people are. I've been in this city long enough to recognize vermin when I see them!"

"Rude," the woman commented, her voice dripping with sarcasm, but Nathan thought he could detect a smile in the stretched fabric of the ski mask.

Stryker's eyes burned into Nathan. "They're parasites, Nate, pure and simple. If we give into them now, then they'll keep coming back for more."

"Give in? What are you taking about?"

The woman raised her hand. "If I might contribute?"

Stryker near boiled over, but Nathan nodded even as he realized how stupid he looked, giving her permission to speak while his hands were raised and there was a shotgun pointing at his chest.

"You can put your hands down."

Nathan and Stryker complied.

"That's better," the woman said. "Now, shall we all go inside? There's no fire, but it *is* out of the wind."

The man covered them and the woman led the way towards the tenement, up the steps, through warped green wooden doors, and into a grimly damp entrance hall. The building had been built in the early 20th century, and in that time it might have looked opulent and stately, with checker-board tiled floor, well-carved moldings, and an intricate plaster rose surrounding the central, dead light in the ceiling.

The place now stank of damp, though, and the tiles were cracked, the paint peeling, with indecipherable graffiti covering the walls. If the tenement hadn't been abandoned, Nathan was sure the resident it would have held now wouldn't have been from the same social group as those it had been built for. It had the feel now of a sunken luxury liner which lay broken at the bottom of the Atlantic.

Get your copy of Killing Frost
Available November 8 2018
www.GraceHamiltonBooks.com

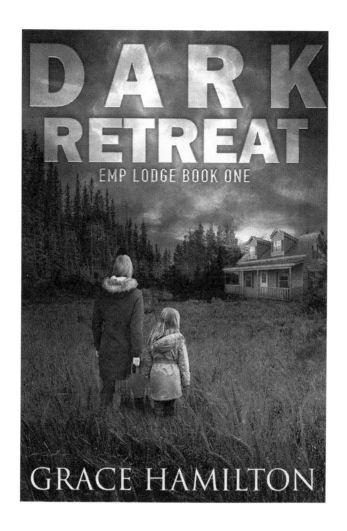

BLURB

Three months after life as she knows it was decimated, Megan Wolford has only one goal: protect her daughter, Caitlin, at any cost. When a mysterious illness strikes Caitlin down, Megan is forced to forage for medical supplies at a remote lodge. The last thing she wants is help from her fellow survivors when so many in her life have let her down—but soon she'll find herself with no other option.

Ex-Navy SEAL Wyatt Morris is doing everything he can to hold his family together after the tragic death of his prepper Dad, so when Megan enters their lands, he is mistrustful at first despite feeling drawn to her. He won't turn away an ill child though—no matter how deadly the world has become. The arrival of another stranger named Kyle soon gives them all a new reason to be suspicious. Wyatt knows he'll have to forge alliances in order to keep his family safe, but trusting the wrong person could be a deadly mistake.

When Megan and Wyatt discover her daughter's illness may be linked to Kyle's arrival, it sets off a race to discover the truth before it's too late to save Caitlin—and the rest of the Morris clan. Can they work together for survival . . . and something more?

Grab your copy of *Dark Retreat* (EMP Lodge Book One) from www.GraceHamiltonBooks.com

EXCERPT

Chapter One

Megan Wolford stumbled over a rock and nearly dropped her daughter before she quickly regained her footing. The sight of a log cabin through the trees had given her a boost of adrenaline and she found she was practically running through the damp forest despite her heavy burden.

She'd fallen several times, bruising her knees and twisting her ankle. Her arms had deep cuts from tree branches that showed no mercy. There wasn't exactly a trail to follow, which meant she was cutting through the heart of the forest and its unforgiving terrain. She was making her own way, as usual, which always seemed to be far harder than it had to be.

"Caitlin, hold on, baby. Hold on," she whispered to the lifeless seven-year-old in her arms.

Megan was doing her best not to panic, but Caitlin had collapsed a couple miles back and she'd been carrying the sleeping child ever since. Carrying her where she didn't know, but now that she saw what appeared to be a hunting lodge of some sort in front of her, she had a destination in mind. She had a goal.

It gave her something to focus on other than the agony that was tearing through her entire body. Another tree branch slapped her in the face, making her wince in pain. Her physical discomfort was nothing compared to the emotional anguish she felt at the thought of losing her daughter. Caitlin was the only thing she'd left in this world. She couldn't lose her.

Her arms were burning and her lungs felt like they would collapse, but nothing would stop her from getting her daughter to what she hoped would be medicine. Without it, Megan knew her only child would die.

She didn't have a clue what had made her so sick, but Caitlin was gravely ill. In the past twenty-four hours, her daughter went from bubbly and energetic to lethargic and weak. Megan had left their most recent camp in the hopes of finding something to help her. They'd walked through one small town yesterday and found nothing. Every single place she checked had been emptied already forcing them to travel for miles.

She was afraid to walk through the city streets overrun with looters. Megan knew it wasn't safe for her and definitely not for Caitlin. It wasn't as if she could leave her daughter alone while she went on a scavenging mission. She had to do it with Caitlin or not all. Common sense told her she didn't have the strength to fight off the hundreds and thousands of other people vying for the same basic supplies. Instead, she'd decided to head out of town in the hopes of finding clinics, stores, and homes in more rural areas that weren't as likely to be quite so dangerous.

Megan took long strides, slightly shifting her daughter, as she kept moving forward. Her sweaty hands were making it difficult for her to hold on to Caitlin. Gripping her hands together under her daughter's backside, Megan pressed on.

She tried to protect her daughter's head as best she could from the branches and sharp twigs that seemed to be jumping out and stabbing the intruders in the forest. Another branch hooked her sleeve, scratching painfully at the skin beneath and she could feel blood trickling down her arm, towards her fingers. She wanted to scream at the trees and order them to stop their assault.

Her back was killing her with the awkward posture of leaning back to keep her daughter secured against her chest. The weight of her pack helped pull her backwards, but also put more strain on her hips. She was grateful to have had an old hiking pack in the closet. The internal frame made it easier for Megan to carry it and allowed her to carry a lot more without much additional strain. She didn't know if she would have been able to carry her daughter and her supplies without it. Right now, she was grateful the pushy salesman had persuaded her to spend the extra money on the pack.

Regardless, everything hurt. She could feel dried blood on her bare arms pulling the fine hairs whenever Caitlin's body rubbed against the cuts, further adding to the misery. Each twist tore open the dried wounds, causing them to start bleeding again.

She'd fallen several times, catching herself with one arm and holding her daughter with the other. She could tell her left knee was swollen. It was stiff and difficult to bend. It didn't matter. Her daughter's life was all that mattered.

"A few more steps," Megan chanted more for her own benefit than her unconscious daughter.

She was thankful the weather had been mild. It was early spring in the northwest, but there were still little piles of snow in the shady areas. Climbing steadily uphill, her overused muscles screamed at her to take a break but she knew if she did, she wouldn't be able to get back up again. The cabin ahead was growing steadily larger as her strides ate up the distance. Because of the harsh winter storms, mountain residents were prepared to outlast storms for weeks at a time, which meant they would have supplies, including medicine.

If it'd been more than the mild seventy degrees that it currently was, Megan wasn't sure she could've walked as far as she did. As it was, she was sweating and the growing fatigue was partly dehydration. Her daughter's feverish body was like carrying a giant lava rock. In addition to finding shelter and medicine, they needed water. The little water she had wouldn't last long; especially if Caitlin woke and needed it.

She'd eaten the last of the food she'd managed to scrounge up at an abandoned home earlier that morning. Megan was now running on empty and knew her collapse would mean her daughter's life. *Push, Megan. Push.*

When she got within three hundred feet of the cabin, she stopped to survey the property, staying partially hidden in the surrounding trees. If someone was here, it could go either way. Unfortunately, the new world was not kind. You didn't simply knock on a stranger's door to beg for food and water.

Not now.

Not after the EMP had plunged the world into the biggest blackout, humankind had ever experienced.

At least those who'd grown up with electricity. Pioneers would do okay in this world, but for those who'd never learned how to work with their hands or hunt for food, this was a form of population control that no one wanted to face. Those who didn't know how to perform some of the most basic skills were suffering.

Megan had seen more dead in the past few weeks than the living. After the first dozen or so, she thought she'd grow immune to the horror of death and could simply move quickly past but the smell reminded her of what it meant to be alive as her gag reflex kicked in.

This new world meant that only the fittest, strongest and most prepared would survive.

Grab your copy of *Dark Retreat* (EMP Lodge Book One) from www.GraceHamiltonBooks.com

WANT MORE?

WWW.GRACEHAMILTONBOOKS.COM

.

Made in the USA
Middletown, DE
15 February 2019